"Can you hear me?"

Julia asked Dutch with desperate urgency.

Nothing. No response.

Her father's henchmen had knocked him out cold. She checked his pupils for abnormalities, and tried to ignore that fact that his eyes were a beautiful shade of blue, a silver-touched sapphire a girl could positively lose herself in.

What she *ought* to do was call a halt to her plans and get the heck out of here before he woke up. All her doubts and fears crowded forward. It was, without question, insane to ask for protection from a man who had reason and skill enough to kill her. This scenario had disaster written all over it.

She sat back on her heels, considering Dutch. She *had* to convince him to help her—without losing her heart to him as she had ten years ago.

This time, she must not fail. Her sister's life depended on it.

Dear Reader,

Make way for spring—and room on your shelf for six must-reads from Silhouette Intimate Moments! Justine Davis bursts onto the scene with another page-turner from her miniseries REDSTONE, INCORPORATED. In *Second-Chance Hero*, a struggling single mother finds herself in danger, having to confront past demons and the man who haunts her waking dreams. Gifted storyteller Ingrid Weaver delights us with *The Angel and the Outlaw*, which begins her miniseries PAYBACK. Here, a rifle-wielding heroine does more than seek revenge—she dazzles a hot-blooded hero into joining her on her mission. Don't miss it!

Can the enemy's daughter seduce a sexy and hardened soldier? Find out in Cindy Dees's latest CHARLIE SQUAD romance, *Her Secret Agent Man*. In Frances Housden's *Stranded with a Stranger*, part of her INTERNATIONAL AFFAIRS miniseries, a determined heroine investigates her sister's murder by tackling Mount Everest and its brutal challenges. Will her charismatic guide be the key to solving this gripping mystery?

You'll get swept away by Margaret Carter's *Embracing Darkness*, about a heart-stopping vampire whose torment is falling for a woman he can't have. Will these two forbidden lovers overcome the limits of mortality—not to mention a cold-blooded killer's treachery—to be together? Newcomer Dianna Love Snell pulls no punches in *Worth Every Risk*, which features a DEA agent who discovers a beautiful stowaway on his plane. She could be trouble...or the woman he's been waiting for.

I'm thrilled to bring you six suspenseful and soul-stirring romances from these talented authors. After you enjoy this month's lineup, be sure to return for another month of unforgettable characters that face life's extraordinary odds. Only in Silhouette Intimate Moments!

Happy reading,

Patience Smith
Associate Senior Editor

Please address questions and book requests to:
Silhouette Reader Service
U.S.: 3010 Walden Ave., P.O. Box 1325, Buffalo, NY 14269
Canadian: P.O. Box 609, Fort Erie, Ont. L2A 5X3

Her Secret Agent Man

CINDY DEES

Silhouette®

INTIMATE MOMENTS™

Published by Silhouette Books

America's Publisher of Contemporary Romance

To Pattie and Stacy for helping make this book
go so smoothly and for keeping me sane
whenever it threatened not to. You're the best.

 SILHOUETTE BOOKS

ISBN 0-373-27423-8

HER SECRET AGENT MAN

Copyright © 2005 by Cynthia Dees

This edition published by arrangement with Harlequin Books S.A.

® and TM are trademarks of Harlequin Books S.A., used under license.
Trademarks indicated with ® are registered in the United States Patent
and Trademark Office, the Canadian Trade Marks Office and in other
countries.

Visit Silhouette Books at www.eHarlequin.com

Printed in U.S.A.

Books by Cindy Dees

Silhouette Intimate Moments

Behind Enemy Lines #1176
Line of Fire #1253
A Gentleman and a Soldier #1307
Her Secret Agent Man #1353

*Charlie Squad

Silhouette Bombshell

Killer Instinct #16
The Medusa Project #31

CINDY DEES

started flying airplanes, sitting in her dad's lap, when she was three, and she was the only kid in the neighborhood who got a pilot's license before she got a driver's license. After college, she fulfilled a lifelong dream and became a U.S. Air Force Pilot. She flew everything from supersonic jets to C-5's, the world's largest cargo airplane. During her career, she got shot at, met her husband, flew in the Gulf War and amassed a lifetime supply of war stories. After she left flying to have a family, she was lucky enough to fulfill another lifelong dream—writing a book. Little did she imagine that it would win the Golden Heart Contest and sell to Silhouette! She's thrilled to be able to share her dream with you. She'd love to hear what you think of her books at www.cindydees.com or P.O. Box 210, Azle, TX 76098.

Chapter 1

Huge snowflakes drifted down around him in a winter-wonderland scene, and the boughs of the pine trees passing beneath his feet sagged under a heavy blanket of white. Neon-garbed skiers whooshed past, laughing, but up here on the ski lift, all was silent. Peaceful. Bucolic. *And his palms positively ached with a need to kill the woman he was here to meet.*

By what right did she call him out of the blue asking for a secret meeting? After all these years? Did she seriously think she could waltz back into his life without repercussions? Her sheer chutzpah was the only reason he'd agreed to meet her at all. And his unprofessional desire to make her pay was the only reason he'd kept this reunion confidential.

Julia Ferrare had to be certifiably insane to have made that late-night call to his private cell phone two days ago. How in the hell did she get the number, anyway? The *only* people who had it were his teammates and command-post controllers on Charlie Squad, the elite and highly classified Air Force Special Forces team he was part of.

This whole meeting stunk to high heaven of a setup. And that's why he'd told her to meet him here at his ski condo time-share far away from his teammates. He leaned back in the lift chair, scowling. Tension coiled tightly across the back of his neck. Fortunately, the resort was relatively empty in spite of the heavy early-season snows. The big weekend rush of skiers wouldn't hit for another couple days. That was good because he didn't exactly deal well with crowds when he was in this frame of mind. Hair-trigger reflexes trained to kill and maim were on high alert in his gut.

The low rumble of a motor became audible, and the overhead cable disappeared into a gear house fifty yards or so ahead. He slipped the wrist straps of his ski poles over his hands. Where *was* she? She said she'd meet him on this mountain today. He'd been down it twice, and there was still no sign of her or the trap she was baiting him into. Fine. He'd ski down the damn hill again.

It would help if he could remember what she looked like.

Reluctantly, he prodded at the black maw that gaped in his memory of that steamy summer ten years ago, but nothing emerged from the void. Whatever'd happened that hot July in the jungle had ceased to matter years ago. The fact remained that his brother, Simon, was dead, and Julia Ferrare was the cause of it. The details were irrelevant. Best to let sleeping dogs lie.

And he'd been happy to do that until a phone call woke him up and a voice from his past asked to see him right away, without involving the other members of Charlie Squad.

As his chair swung over a snow-covered platform, he aligned his skis in its icy ruts and stood up. The chair shoved the back of his knees, sending him down the ramp to the snow. The sleek glide of it beneath his feet sent a reluctant ripple of pleasure through him. He'd always loved skiing. Anticipation filled him. Of speed. Of the sting of snow in his face.

And then he saw her.

Maybe ten yards ahead of him. Stunningly beautiful. Raven-haired with dark, hot eyes. Her cheeks were rosy with cold, but her skin glowed with the warm, golden tones of a tropical beach. He stopped and stared as everything around him blurred and faded to gray. His vision narrowed down to a silvery tunnel, her face shining like a beacon at the other end. Something cracked around his heart, like huge chunks of ice calving from the face of a glacier. He all but heard the sound of it crashing down as a barrier of some sort shattered in his chest.

His gaze locked upon Julia Ferrare. How could he ever have forgotten that spectacular face? He prickled all over. His hands and feet went numb. It felt as if he was disconnecting from his own flesh. It felt damn strange, in fact.

And then darkness raced toward him, a towering wall that broke over him with tsunami force, sweeping him completely away from himself. He couldn't tell if he was flying toward something or away from it. The only sensation that registered was one of drowning panic. And her beautiful face. Always that beautiful face swimming in front of his eyes, beckoning and goading him into the abyss.

Time and space had no meaning in this place. Only the deep, cold blackness embracing him. He drifted, disembodied, in the void. What in the bloody *hell* was happening? The darkness changed, abruptly suffocating him. Tangling itself around him like an unwanted blanket. He battled it back, clawing against its confines, tearing it away with a great heave.

He blinked, disoriented at the white landscape whizzing by at high speed. Where *was* he? He sure as shootin' wasn't at the top of the mountain anymore. An icy ski run fell away before him like a bloody cliff. *The professional downhill run!* Wind clawed at him as if it would rip the flesh from his bones. He must be going close to sixty miles per hour. How in the world had he gotten here? Oh *crraapp...*

He launched into space, flung off the side of the mountain by a huge mogul. He windmilled his arms furiously, fighting with all his strength to stay upright and drag his feet beneath him as he soared down the steep mountainside. He slammed onto the snow once more, his knees smashing into his ribs like twin jackhammers, driving every last ounce of oxygen from his chest.

He gasped for air and by some miracle managed not to fall. The ski run jinked to the right just ahead and he didn't stand a snowball's chance in hell of making the turn. He shot off the run and his ski tips plowed into a deep snowbank. Their abrupt halt sent him airborne, cartwheeling high through the air. Straight toward a wall of orange crash fencing. Headfirst. He didn't even have time to curse as he tucked his shoulder and pulled off a partial midair flip.

He took the fence squarely in the back. And landed sprawled in the snow, what little wind he had knocked clean out of him. He gasped like a fish flopping on a dock. For many long seconds, his lungs refused to cooperate. Finally, he managed to suck in a short breath. And another. Then the pain hit him. Like a train wreck. Jeez, he hurt all over. He knew better than to move after a crash like that. He lay still in the same tangle he'd landed in.

"Can you hear me?" It was a male voice from off to his left. "Are you injured?"

He peered up at a White Cross on a red vinyl vest. Ski patrol. "I hear you. Dunno how messed up I am," he managed to grind out. "Hurts like hell if that counts for anything."

The guy grunted in commiseration. "That was an awesome fall you took. We already called for a medic. He's on his way."

Dutch closed his eyes as the cold from the deep snow he lay half buried in seeped into his body. At least it numbed some of the pain crunching through his bones. What in the hell had just happened to him? With one exception, he'd never blacked out before. And that other time had also been related to the Ferrares. A drinking binge after an ambush had landed him in the hospital and erased a solid month from his memory.

Guys in his line of work who lost consciousness without a damn good reason lost their jobs, oh, instantly. And that would be why he'd never told anyone he had no recollection of the op involving Julia, the op that killed his brother. Thankfully, his teammates respected his silence regarding the mission and never brought it up.

He'd not blacked out in ten years. Why now? Another ski patroller showed up and knelt down, running his hands over Dutch's limbs. The guy's movements were efficient, competent. Dutch went limp and let the medic carefully straighten his arms and legs out of their awkward positions.

The guy rocked back on his heels after poking Dutch's gut and checking his pupils with a little flashlight. "I don't know how you did it, but you seem to have no serious injuries. You must be in killer condition to have hit the fence like that without breaking something."

The guy didn't know the half of it. Dutch, in fact, stayed in good enough condition to kill. And did. Regularly. He planned to do that very thing today as a matter of fact. A movement caught his attention beyond the ring of ski patrollers. A flash of black hair and golden skin.

His heart pounded abruptly. *Her* again. Even garbed in ski overalls and a bulky denim jacket, she had a body that made dirty thoughts run through his mind. He noted the way the thick, dark lashes fringing her eyes flickered apprehensively. The anxious way she bit her lower lip.

She had good cause to be nervous. Rage flooded through him, visceral, white hot. If it was the last thing he did, he was going to make her pay for what happened to his baby brother.

She froze as their gazes locked, as still and frightened as a hunted doe. His vision began to tunnel down again and he ripped his gaze away from her as she staggered backward. How was she robbing him of consciousness like this? A chill chattered down his spine. He'd be kicked out of Charlie Squad so fast it would make his head spin if his boss found out about this inexplicable blackout. Nobody wanted an armed Special Forces soldier floating away to la-la land at a crucial moment in a mission.

The Ferrare woman took a step toward him. Her expression indicated she had something urgent to tell him. She opened her mouth. And then a pair of men moved into his line of vision, skiing horizontally across the hill toward a less challenging slope. Nothing struck him as unusual about them, but panic flared in Julia's eyes. She nodded at him fractionally, a single subtle dip of her chin.

Now, what was that supposed to mean?

She turned, took a couple awkward steps and pushed off quickly down the slope. Fleeing. Good call. Except for all the world it looked as if she was running not from him but from that pair of men. She'd learn the error in her thinking soon enough. His gaze narrowed as he stared at her retreating back.

The wall of darkness roared forward again. He blinked his eyes hard and shook his head to clear it. Pain shot across his shoulders and up his neck. *Ow! Damn, that hurt. Note to self:*

no abrupt head movements. It was a tough-won victory, but he fought back the encroaching blackout by main force of will. In its wake, a single question burned across his brain like a comet in the night sky.

Why did Julia Ferrare want to meet him?

He clambered to his feet, determined to follow her. But the medic detained him, insisting on testing his balance before he'd clear Dutch to ski again. He shook off the guy. Ignoring the queasy sensation rumbling in his gut, he stepped into his ski bindings and pushed back out onto the run. He crested a mogul and stopped sharply. The bottom of the mountain lay in gorgeous panorama at his feet. He searched it for a woman in blue. There. A slender denim outline. Below him on the downhill run, making careful S-curves back and forth across the course to keep her speed down.

Something else caught his eye as he scanned the mountain. A half-dozen skiers arrayed in a large, perfect starburst, all moving in arrow-straight lines, all converging purposefully on something. Or someone. He checked the center of their loose formation. Julia! What were the odds *that* was a chance occurrence? He looked more closely. Two of the skiers looked like the same ones who'd cut across the downhill run and panicked her.

He let rip with a foul curse and plunged off the mogul, gathering speed. Given how afraid she'd been, it was obvious she was in some sort of trouble. He had to get to her before those men did. Talk to her. Find out what she wanted from him. Find out why the sight of her did such weird things to his head. Then, he'd make her pay.

His speed continued to build, and he couldn't spare any more brainpower for questions. All his attention riveted on the deadly slope falling away before him. He didn't even want to think about how much another crash would hurt. The ski lodge came into view, and with it a chilling sight. Julia stood directly in front of the huge log structure, and the ring of men was almost on her.

Dutch crouched in a racer's tuck and flew toward her. Other skiers squawked in protest as he blasted by them. He zoomed past one of her pursuers and caught a brief glimpse of a cap and goggles obscuring the guy's face. Not that he could have gotten much of a look, anyway, at the speed he was traveling.

He aimed his skis straight at her where she bent down to unfasten her bindings. He screeched to a halt, pelting her with snow. She jumped and spun to face him. Her eyes went wide with shock. He hit the quick releases on his boots with the tips of his poles and jumped out of his skis, not bothering to pick them up. He grabbed her arm. "Come on," he growled.

Although he was a big, powerful man, he rarely took advantage of his strength to overpower anyone. But there was no time for explanations. He half lifted her off the ground and dragged her along with him. He bit out the words, "A bunch of guys are closing in on you. They're right behind us. Let's *go.*"

She clumped along awkwardly beside him in her ski boots. "Where to?" she gasped as they raced into the crowded lobby of the lodge.

He looked around fast. They'd never make it out of here before their pursuers arrived. "This way," he ordered tersely.

They darted toward a coatroom beside the main restaurant. He pushed past a startled attendant and pulled Julia into the small room, out of sight of the lobby. He wedged her deep into the packed rows of coats, shielding her body protectively with his own. Awareness of her screamed through him like a banshee. She smelled like cinnamon. Her hair was silky against his cheek; her lithe body hummed with tension. The bulky layers of clothing between them did little to dampen the way his baser instincts roared to life.

She looked up at him, fear raging in her huge eyes. "Now what?" she whispered.

His head swam, and he fought off a sick, drowning feeling. The swirling sensation in his skull intensified. He braced his hands on the hanger rod above her head, his outspread arms caging her against him. The room spun, and a wild cacophony of color assaulted his eyes as the racks of ski jackets twirled like a carousel.

"Are you all right?" she murmured in concern. Her voice was soft and throaty and felt like sex on his skin.

"Yeah. I'll be fine," he mumbled.

"That was a terrible fall you took up on the mountain. Did you hit your head, maybe give yourself a concussion?"

Like she actually cared. He replied dryly, "I've been told on more than one occasion that I have an exceptionally thick skull."

Her eyes sparkled with humor for a moment. Their gazes met. Something zinged between them. Something hot and wild, and more than the physical attraction hanging thick between them. The humor faded from her eyes as they stared at each other.

A female voice from behind spun him around and sent him reaching reflexively for the pistol in the small of his back.

"Hey. What are you doing in here?"

He straightened from the defensive half crouch he'd fallen into and answered dryly, "Hiding, of course. The lady's ex is psycho. He sent goons after us. Any chance you could check the lobby and see if they're gone?"

"Sure," the college-age girl replied. "All clear," she announced.

He peered over the attendant's shoulder into the main lobby. Based on the consternation on the faces of most of the people in the lobby and the directions of their gazes, he surmised that Julia's tails had scattered. A couple went back outside, one headed into the bar, another probably hit the restaurant, and the rest headed down the hallways to his right.

He didn't have to look back to feel Julia peering over his shoulder. Her exotic cinnamon scent swirled around him like an opium haze. "Take off your boots," he ordered. "We've got to move fast and quiet." He took his off as well, and handed over both pairs to the attendant. "I'll come back later to collect those. I'll give you a big tip."

The coed grinned. "No problem. I'm always happy to help out a pair of lovebirds."

He grabbed Julia's hand. What in the hell was that electric sensation that shot up his arm and down his spine? He ignored his reaction as they strolled across the lobby in their socks. He chose one of the two hallways a thug probably hadn't gone down, and as soon as they cleared the crowded main area, he took off running. He saw a sign ahead, and smiled grimly. Perfect. "This way. C'mon."

She started to protest, but he overrode her objections with his superior strength. They ducked into the women's locker room. "They won't look for us in here right away," he said over his shoulder.

A couple half-dressed women uttered startled protests. Julia apologized to them as he dragged her toward a row of private steam rooms. He opened the door of one and peered inside. "Anybody in here?" he asked.

No answer. He stepped in with her and closed the door behind them. The sauna's dimness enveloped them. Much better. Being out in the open like a sitting duck made him way jumpy.

"If they find us here, we're toast," she pointed out nervously. "There's nowhere to run." She turned and nearly bumped into him. Her sexy scent wafted around him again. Damn, that perfume was practically a lethal weapon.

He planted a hand on the wall beside her head and leaned toward her. He smiled with cool anticipation and murmured, "I've got a few tricks up my sleeve. We're far from toast. Trust me."

For just a second, she leaned into him. *Didn't she know he was here to kill her?* Except why was his subconscious straying toward doing something entirely different with her? His gut blazed as the subliminal urge became a conscious thought. His loins surged so powerfully it almost drove him to his knees.

She leaned back a few inches to look up at him. "I know better than to trust you," she replied breathlessly.

He stared at her evenly. It would be so easy to put his hands around her neck and strangle her. Or snap her neck with a quick twist of his wrists. Or pull her body against his, strip off her clothes and savor the sweaty slide of flesh on flesh. An urge to overpower her, to ravish her the way his Viking ancestors would have, broadsided him. The impulse startled him back to reality.

He demanded grimly, "What do you want from me?"

Caution ringed her dark gaze. "This isn't the time or place to talk about it."

"Honey, this is the only chance you get. Start talking."

She wiped away a trickle of sweat from her temple. "Let's get out of these heavy ski clothes before we both pass out."

Stalling, was she? Okay. He'd play along for a few seconds. He took off his coat and bent down to strip off his ski pants. And came face-to-face with her chest. "Sorry," he mumbled.

They fumbled around each other in the tight space, trying to disrobe politely. Their elbows bumped, and then she all but fell into him.

"Tell you what," he suggested, "you go first."

He tried to tuck himself out of the way, but there was just nowhere for his big body to go in the tiny box. He lifted his arms over his head while she squirmed out of her clothes.

She kept bumping against him awkwardly until he finally growled, "Just lean against me. I won't bite you."

But the idea was damn tempting when her rear end snuggled against his groin a second later as she bent down to pull off her ski pants. And then she shimmied out of her tropical yellow and orange ski sweater. In the moment when her face was hidden in its folds, he allowed himself to glance down. Big mistake.

She wore a close-fitting, white silk turtleneck beneath the sweater, and nothing else. It clung to her like a wet T-shirt. Her breasts were small and delicately formed. Atop the gentle swells, a rosy hint of her nipples was visible. Blood rushed in his ears, making a beeline for the other end of his body where his flesh throbbed and hardened to the density of the rocks in the steamer beside him.

His gaze drifted lower. She wore fire-engine-red leggings that hugged her like a second skin. Oh yeah. She definitely worked out. Her thigh muscles were long and lean. They'd grip a guy's waist like steel while he rode her... Stop that! He yanked his gaze away from her knockout body.

She emerged from the sweater and gazed at him expectantly. His turn. Crud. His Lycra shorts weren't nearly tight enough to hide his reaction to her. Ah well, it was either give away his state of arousal or pass out from the heat. He stripped off his sweater and turtleneck, baring his naked chest. A distinct advantage to being a guy in a situation like this. Then he peeled off his ski pants. Her gaze went straight to the bulge in his shorts. He watched in grim amusement as red stained her cheeks.

The dry air burned his lungs. He turned away sharply and ladled water from a bucket onto the bed of rocks. The water hissed as it struck baking stone. He kept at it until a thick cloud of steam swirled around their heads. Better. Now they wouldn't have to look directly into each other's eyes.

She lifted her long, silky hair up off her neck. The movement thrust her breasts out until they all but begged him to take them into his mouth. His lust roared like a Harley with the throttle wide open. Mesmerized, he reached out with a fingertip and caught a drop of moisture that rolled down the side of her exquisite face. She gazed at him wordlessly, her lips parted, her breathing light and fast. Why did this feel so familiar?

A movement outside the tiny window of the steam-room door caught his eye. *A dark silhouette drawing near the glass to peer inside.* Damn, these guys were fast. And thorough. He grabbed her and yanked her down to the floor. He landed on top of her, his elbows braced on either side of her to take his weight. That blasted silk shirt of hers caressed his chest until he thought he was going to embarrass himself on the spot.

He tried to think about something else, but all that filled his mind was the way her belly cushioned his, the way her thighs cupped his throbbing hardness. A need to be inside her, to feel her wet, tight heat around his flesh, to pump away mindlessly until they both came apart nearly overcame him. It was an act of sheer, desperate will to keep his hips from grinding against hers. He clenched his jaw and held his body perfectly still.

He wasn't particularly worried about her pursuer. With Dutch's size, strength and training, there weren't too many people he couldn't take out with his bare hands. But he'd rather avoid a fight until he and Julia talked.

What little light came through the window went dim as somebody peered inside the sauna. *Don't move,* he tried to telegraph silently to her. He let his body sink into hers by fractional degrees, using his weight to hold her still. Ah, sweet God, that felt good. He prayed she wouldn't wriggle. He was so close to the edge that he'd explode if she even breathed deeply. He fought like a drowning man for control as long seconds ticked by.

Finally, the dark shape above their heads eased away. A shaft of weak light penetrated the steam again. He did a careful push-up, easing himself off her luscious body. Her eyes were huge and dark as she stared up at him. She looked like a virgin who'd just been deflowered. Hell, that had been about as close as two people could come to sex without doing the deed.

"Get dressed," he growled. "It's time to go."

"Why not stay put?" she asked breathlessly. "They've already looked here."

Other than the fact that if he stayed here much longer he was going to tear off her remaining clothes and finish what they'd started?

He cleared his throat. "We'd pass out from dehydration and heat exhaustion eventually. Plus, they'll be back. Next time, their search will be more thorough."

She pulled her sweater and ski pants on over her damp undergarments while he did the same. He wiped away the condensation from the tiny glass window and peered outside before he nodded to her.

"Where to next?" she murmured.

"My car. We're getting out of here."

"And going where?" she asked.

"Does it matter?" he asked her darkly.

She answered cautiously, "I'm not going anywhere with you until we talk!"

He whipped his head around to stare narrowly at her. "I don't recall asking your opinion. I'm calling the shots here."

She frowned and opened her mouth, but he stepped out into the locker room before she could argue any more. Being on the move and vulnerable should effectively silence her. Nonetheless, he took her hand lest she try to bolt.

He murmured, "Let's go."

She didn't budge. He tugged on her hand and she dug in her heels stubbornly.

He turned to face her. *Women could be such a pain in the butt.* He murmured darkly, "Believe me. I can't wait to hear what you have to say to me. I'm trying to get somewhere safe so we can have a little conversation."

She frowned, but the pull against his hand abated.

Much better. He ducked down one long hallway after another. Good thing he'd memorized a floor plan of the place before he'd hit the slopes.

He stopped abruptly in front of a door. "Let me know if anybody comes into sight," he muttered.

He fished a plastic card key out of his pocket and shoved it into the lock. With a last look both ways, he pushed her quickly into his room. As he slipped in behind her, he glimpsed a dark shape just turning into the hallway. He closed the door quickly and pressed his ear against the wood. Two pairs of ski boots thumped past at an awkwardly fast clip. The noise faded. He took a deep breath and turned around.

She stood in the middle of his suite, more beautiful than any one woman ought to be. Her chest heaved and her eyes snapped with a fire he could lose himself in forever. He stepped forward into the sunken living room, suddenly aware of a chill across his skin.

But then a flurry of movement caught his attention, jumping at him from the direction of the bedroom. He spun to face this new threat, but he was too late. He'd let Julia's beauty distract him.

He had just enough time to mutter a disgusted curse at himself before something hard slammed into the back of his head. He grabbed for the coffee table that careened into view beside him, but his head slammed into the edge of it. He had no strength to hold back the vast ocean of darkness as unconsciousness consumed him. Julia lurched toward him with her hands outstretched as he fell to the floor.

He fought the drowning loss of self and reached out for her, but her blurry image slipped through his fingers like water. "Help me," he whispered.

And then everything went black.

Chapter 2

The black-clad man leaped out the door and disappeared before Dutch had even hit the floor.

Maybe that guy was in Dutch's room because of some other operation Dutch was involved in. And maybe not. Could she have already been linked to Dutch, only minutes after meeting him? Was her father that all-knowing? Surely Dutch would have been dead meat if he was.

She stared at the big man crumpled on the floor, her first impulse to help him. Her second impulse was to flee. To get away before he could follow through on the fatal promise in his icy gaze. He *had* to listen to her. But what if he didn't? Panic fluttered like a wounded sparrow in her breast.

She couldn't just leave him here, unconscious. Not after what they'd been through together all those years ago. Not after he'd answered her most recent call for help. And not after he'd helped her get away from her father's men. She knelt beside him and touched his shoulder. It felt like freshly forged steel, hard and hot, even through his thick sweater.

She shook him gently. "Wake up," she urged. "We've got to get out of here before they all come back."

No response. A sick feeling roiled in the pit of her stomach. This was the guy who was supposed to keep her alive long enough to save her sister, and he was face-planted on the floor, out like a light.

She looked around the masculine suite, with its hardwood floors, rustic furnishings, rough-hewn oak ceiling and massive stone fireplace. The far wall on either side of the fireplace was glass. The window faced the mountain and framed a postcard-perfect view of snow and skiers. A kitchenette opened up off one side of the living room, and a bedroom lay in the other direction.

She jumped up and raced into the tiny kitchen. She doused a dish towel in cold water, wrung it out and carried it back to Dutch.

She pushed on his shoulder to roll him over. Lord, he was heavy. As densely muscled as he'd looked in the steam room through the wet haze and her own breathless reaction, he was even more impressive than she remembered. Charlie Squad's six-man team was renowned for its crazy level of fitness, but he went beyond fit to flat-out gorgeous.

With a grunt of effort, she managed to turn him on his back. His blue eyes stared up at her glassily under half-closed lids. Ohmigod. Was he *dead?* Frantically she fumbled at his neck, searching for a pulse. Finally, her fingertips found a strong, steady throbbing under his chin.

She sagged over him in relief and held back an urge to cry. It was too much. She was so tired of running. So tired of hiding, of constant fear, of never knowing if the next person she saw would be the one there to kill her.

Utter desperation had driven her to make that phone call two days ago. She had no illusions about how Jim Dutcher would feel about her. He might have saved her life ten years ago, but he wouldn't make that mistake again.

Problem was, there was *no one else* for her to call. Nobody left to turn to for help. Her father's associates were too terrified of him to lift a finger for her. The FBI would arrest her on sight and lock her away for the rest of her life for her part in her father's crime empire. No matter that she'd been coerced into doing his financial dirty work. Even Charlie Squad, the one enemy her father truly feared, would kill her on sight.

She'd never wanted to set up Charlie Squad. Had hated being used as bait to trap them. But her father knew what buttons to push. He always got his way. He'd threatened to hurt her little sister, and Julie had caved in like she always did. She couldn't blame Dutch—all of Charlie Squad for that matter— for wanting her dead. Especially after Dutch's brother got killed in the ambush she'd led them into.

She'd give up this fight to finally break away from her father right now if it weren't for Carina. But her sister's plight left Julia with no choice. She had to keep going. Had to see this mess through. Carina's life was on the line now. And that changed everything.

Julia had raised Carina like her own daughter when their mother died. She'd been eight and Carina two and there'd been no one else to do it. The servants were too frightened to step into a parental role for the children of their violent and vicious employer. Thankfully, Eduardo had never turned that ruthlessness on the two of them. Until now. Until Carina tried to run away and get out from under his heavy thumb.

It still took Julia's breath away to think that her father had actually kidnapped Carina. His own daughter! She was twenty-four years old, for goodness sake. He couldn't control her life forever.

Her mouth tightened at the bitter taste of irony. Eduardo was still in complete control of *her* life, and she was thirty years old. But that was over. He'd crossed the line when he'd put Carina in danger. She was getting both herself and her sister out from under his domination once and for all. She'd even stolen thirty million dollars from him as ransom money for Carina.

All she needed was to trade the money for her sister—and for Dutch to keep her alive that long. She'd planned to buy Dutch's protection by bribing him with the one thing he wanted more than her head on a platter: her father's head on a platter. But first, Dutch had to wake up so she could make the offer.

"Can you hear me?" she asked him with desperate urgency as she pressed the cold towel to his forehead.

Nothing.

"Do you need a doctor?" she asked louder.

Still no response. That guy had knocked him out cold. She pressed her palm against his forehead. No fever. She lifted his eyelids all the way to check his pupils for abnormal or uneven expansion or contraction. She tried to ignore the fact that his eyes were a beautiful shade of blue, a silver-touched sapphire a girl could positively lose herself in.

If he was seriously hurt, she ought to get help. But did she dare call someone? Cause the fuss of paramedics and ambulances and risk drawing attention to herself? Her father's henchmen would spot her in a second.

What she *ought* to do was call a halt to her plans and get the heck out of here before he woke up. All her doubts and fears crowded forward. It was, without question, insane to ask protection from a man who had reason and skill enough to kill her. This scenario had disaster written all over it, and that was before he fell down at her feet. Her fight-or-flight instinct was definitely in full flight mode. Every second she lingered here put her, and by extension, Carina, in more danger. But Julia *couldn't* walk out on him when he was defenseless. She'd led these guys to him, after all.

Marshaling her scant courage, she stretched around behind him, groping for the gun she'd seen him reach for in the coatroom. Cool metal met her touch. She pulled out a blocky, heavy pistol. She'd seen plenty of handguns before—how could she not have, growing up around her father?—but she'd rarely touched one. Eduardo had always been adamant that his daughters not handle weapons of any kind. Maybe he'd known the day would come when they'd finally turn on him, and he'd known better than to allow them to learn skills they could use to take him out.

She sat back on her heels, considering the unconscious man before her. She had to convince him to play ball with her. Convince him not to kill her or hand her over to the FBI. At least not until she'd completed her deal with her father. She *must not fail*. Her sister's life depended on her pulling this off. But first she had to wake him up.

Dutch stirred. He groaned faintly. Thank God.

She scrambled backward, fumbling with the gun, managing to point it clumsily at him while she clambered to her feet. So much violence had swirled around her for so long it made her faintly ill to even touch a handgun. Her heart pounded, and the heavy weapon wavered in her grasp.

She knew the exact second when Dutch regained consciousness. His blue eyes were blank and glassy one second, and the next they glittered with frightening intelligence. His piercing gaze narrowed as he took in the sight of her pointing his pistol at him. He sat up slowly.

"Easy, there. I'm not going to hurt you," he murmured. "We have to talk, remember?"

His voice was deep. Soothing. Tempting her to let go of her terror and trust him. But she knew better. She wasn't some gullible, frightened animal to be lulled into his net.

She took another step backward. "Don't move," she demanded sharply.

He frowned. Focused his attention on the gun. "When I got off the ski lift and saw you, something weird happened to me. But why am I lying on the floor now?"

"There was a guy in here when we arrived. He clocked you on the back of the head. He looked like he was only here to have a look around though."

He reached up and fingered the back of his head gingerly. "Probably here to plant a few bugs. Your father is always looking for ways to infiltrate Charlie Squad. The guy most likely wasn't after you. No big deal. We'll get out of here as soon as you put that gun down."

She ignored the suggestion. "What happened to you on the mountain?" she asked cautiously.

He shrugged. " A blackout or something."

"What caused it?"

"I have no idea," he answered. "I was hoping you could tell me." His gaze was steady and unafraid as he watched her. Like a man who'd had a gun pointed at him before. A lot.

"Well, I certainly don't know why you blacked out!" she retorted. She needed him operating at full strength if he was going to protect her from Eduardo's goons. The only other person she knew who might have the skill to keep her safe was Charlie Squad's commander, Colonel Folly. But the way she heard it, he'd been seriously injured the last time he came to Gavarone—the tiny South American country that was her home—and tangled with her father. Folly was out of the field for good. Eduardo had gloated about his victory for weeks.

Besides. Charlie Squad, as a team, was compromised. She was the banker who cut the cashier's checks for the informant inside the team. She dared not risk being recognized and reported to her father. Eduardo would go nuts if he found out she'd handed herself—and everything she knew—over to his worst enemy.

The mole was probably someone innocuous on Charlie Squad's support staff, someone who'd slipped in beneath the radar. Hence the call to Dutch's private phone and the meeting far from the rest of the team. There was no way one of the actual team members had turned. These guys were fanatics. Committed to truth, justice and the American way to the death. Besides, the payments to the mole were too small to impress a guy like Dutch, who made officer's pay. The amounts were downright modest by comparison to some of the bribes her father dished out to government officials around the world.

Dutch startled her with a question of his own. "Why were those men chasing you? Who are they?"

Odds were they were her father's men. Of course, there was an outside chance the FBI had spotted her coming into the country a couple of weeks ago and hoped to arrest her and make her sing against her father. Not that it really mattered whether the men were FBI or hired thugs. Daddy dearest had the FBI in his back pocket, too.

She shrugged. "Probably my father's men." She ducked his other question about why they were after her.

His eyebrows shot up. "Your old man is trying to capture you? Maybe you do have something interesting to tell me, after all."

She didn't walk through the giant opening he'd just given

her. Now that she was faced with him and his seething hatred for her, serious doubts about her plan were erupting like Mount Vesuvius. She chewed her lower lip anxiously.

He leaned back against the sofa and propped an elbow across one bent knee. Man, he was a cool customer. "So. What are you going to do now? Shoot me? Tie me up?"

"I'm not sure," she admitted in the face of his steel-nerved composure. "I want you to stay over there, out of reach."

"All right," he agreed readily.

What *was* she going to do now? The idea was to forge an alliance. She'd certainly feel safer offering her deal if he was tied up. If her father's rants about Charlie Squad were accurate, Dutch was capable of breathtaking violence in the blink of an eye. Of course, tying him up meant she might tick him off more than he already was.

"Would you mind if I tied you up?" she asked hesitantly.

He blinked, but didn't miss a beat. "Can't say as I'm crazy about the idea, but if it would get you to talk, I suppose I'm game."

It was her turn to blink. What was the catch? She jumped as he began to stand up and she raised the pistol with both hands.

"Honey, would you mind taking your finger off the trigger?" he asked casually. "The safety's off and that pistol's got a real light pull. Just lay your index finger alongside the trigger guard. If you want to shoot me you can reach for the trigger fast, but you won't accidentally kill me in the meantime."

Yikes! She eased her finger off the trigger carefully. She waved the gun toward a sock-draped chair near the fireplace. He'd obviously brought it in here from the kitchen. It looked like the kind of chair people got tied to on TV. He glanced in the direction of her gesture and moved toward the chair. His legs were long and muscular, his hips narrow as he sauntered away from her. His shoulders were a mile wide, and his back formed an awe-inspiring V that tapered down to a lean waist.

He pushed off the damp socks and sat down. "Got any rope?" he asked casually.

She frowned. Drat. She hadn't thought of that.

"You can use a couple of my belts," he suggested.

What the heck was going on here? Why was he being so helpful? "Where are they?" she mumbled, her eyes narrowed in suspicion.

"In the bedroom closet. I'll go get a couple."

He started to get up but froze when she trained the gun on him again. A corner of his mouth quirked up. "You follow at a safe distance, and if I pull any funny stuff, you have my permission to blow my head off."

Blow his head off? She shuddered at the idea. She just wanted to talk to him without all that brawny strength intimidating her half to death. He had to be six foot five. Were he not so trimly fit, he'd look like a nightclub bouncer. Of course, the crew-cut hair and square jaw only added to the tough-guy image.

She followed him into the bedroom, alert for any sort of stunt. But he merely opened the closet and pulled out several leather belts.

She eyed the closet full of clothes suspiciously. "Do you own this place?"

He glanced over at her. "Yeah, as a matter of fact, I do. You didn't sound like you wanted to meet in the conference room at Charlie Squad headquarters."

No kidding. She followed him as he carried the belts back into the living room and sat down. While she watched in no little shock, he leaned over and strapped his own ankles to the chair. He sat up and put his hands behind his back, waiting patiently for her to come over and tie his hands.

"You're sure you're going to let me do this?" she asked him skeptically.

"Yup."

"Why?" she asked as she knelt behind him and wrapped the leather around his wrists and the wooden spindles of the chair.

"Because I want to get this over with."

A shaft of pain sliced through her. Once he couldn't wait to spend time with her. He'd made excuses to talk to her for a few more minutes. She'd lived for those hurried conversations and stolen moments. But all of that was long gone.

She leaned back on her heels and surveyed her work. He *looked* well secured at any rate. Did she dare trust him? He sat quietly, staring back at her, his gaze glacial. This was the most bizarre hostage situation she'd ever heard of.

"Feel better?" he asked coldly.

She frowned at him. "I guess so."

"Excellent. Now maybe you could tell me why in the hell I'm here. I think I've earned that much, don't you?"

She sat down in the armchair facing him. His face could have been chiseled out of granite. His cheeks were flat planes with aggressively slashing cheekbones, his jaw strong, his forehead smooth. He acted completely in control of the situation. Quite the iceman.

"You wanted to talk to me?" he prompted.

She figured her father's financial records ought to be a carrot Dutch wouldn't refuse. Not only could Charlie Squad use them to track down and freeze Eduardo's assets, but they could undoubtedly get a conviction on tax evasion or money laundering or something. She didn't care what, as long as they put her father away for a good long time.

Of course, the trick was to buy herself time now, before Charlie Squad captured her father. Enough to get her father to agree to her proposed trade: the money for Carina. So, she'd leak the financial records to Dutch a little at a time. As long as it took to negotiate Carina's release. Problem was, Eduardo had been surprisingly unwilling to talk so far. He probably expected his men to catch her and bring her in any minute. He had no need to let Carina go. Enter Jim Dutcher.

Belatedly, she said, "I want to make a deal with you."

"I'm listening."

"Do you want my father?" she asked.

His eyes blazed abruptly. "Is the pope Catholic?"

She took a deep breath. "I can deliver him to you. My father, I mean."

Dutch reared back, rocking onto the chair's hind legs. He glared icy daggers at her. His voice dripped sarcasm. "Gee. Where have I heard that line before?"

She closed her eyes in agony as his words pierced her heart like poisoned blades. Reluctantly, she opened her eyes and met his furious gaze. "Okay. I deserve that. But I'm telling you the God's honest truth. I'm willing to give you the information you need to put my father away."

"What information?"

"His financial records."

"Too damn easy to fake."

"Not these. I can give you his private books. The ones he doesn't show anyone."

"And how do you happen to have access to something like that?"

She looked Dutch square in the eye. "I'm his banker. I have been for years. I'm in charge of money laundering, disguising and dispersing his assets, delivering bribe money, you name it."

That dropped his jaw. The silence stretched out between them, along with her nerves. Tension stretched tighter and tighter inside her until it finally snapped. She couldn't stand it anymore. He had to take the bait!

She dug deep for the courage to look him in the eye and say what had to be said. She took a breath and spoke quietly. "I'm not walking you into another ambush here. I'm offering to hand over verifiable and incriminating financial information. Any prosecutor worth his salt should be able to lock up Eduardo for the rest of his life."

Dutch's face went a shade paler and perfectly still. Not a flicker of expression or whisper of movement disrupted his frozen features. He looked like a god captured in marble by some ancient Greek master. She could practically hear him evaluating the risks, weighing the options. But of what? Of killing her after he was untied, or of continuing this conversation and actually contemplating taking the deal she offered?

He asked grimly, reluctantly, "And what do you want in return for this alleged information?"

Here went nothing. "Keep me alive until my father is put away."

"And?" he challenged.

"And nothing. That's it. Just keep me alive."

"What's the catch?" he asked skeptically.

No way could she tell him about Carina. She had cost him his brother, and she had faith he'd leap at the opportunity to cost her a sister. But, she had to tell him something plausible. She'd already decided to appeal to his pride in his skill and his love of a good challenge.

Aloud, she replied, "There's no catch. But in the interest of full disclosure, I must tell you it won't necessarily be easy to keep me alive."

"Does Eduardo know you've contacted me?"

She rolled her eyes. "Are you kidding? He'd have his men kill me immediately if he did."

"So those thugs who are chasing you are only under orders to bring you home?"

She shrugged. "For now. Once they figure out I've come to you, their orders will change."

Dutch stared at her hard, as if he could look inside her head and see the truth. She wouldn't put it past him to do it, either. He'd always been able to read her like an open book. She did her best to concentrate on only what she'd told him. She dared not think about her real reasons for doing this, or Dutch would pick up that she was holding out on him.

Lord, this was a desperate game she was playing. But it was this or death for her sister. The crushing panic she'd been holding at bay for the past few weeks began to build again behind her eyes. She didn't know what to do or who to trust anymore. Where to go or who to turn to. She was so tired of being alone and on the run.

"How do you know I won't just take you into custody and hand you over to the feds? If you're his banker like you say you are, you could go to jail until you're old and gray, too."

She replied dryly, "I think the odds are much higher that you'll kill me outright long before you hand me over to any authorities."

That made him blink.

She continued with a shrug. "But I guess that's the chance I'm willing to take."

Masking her desperation, she stared at him, the challenge plain in her gaze. She was willing to risk her life in this unholy alliance. Was he?

Chapter 3

Her heart raced as he stared at her for a long time, not answering. Too restless to sit there one more second under that unwavering gaze, Julia stood up and headed for the coatrack beside the hallway door, shedding her heavy ski sweater as she went. She'd just hung the garment on a hook, when a quiet knock sounded at the door.

"Housekeeping," a female voice announced. The electronic lock beeped and the handle began to turn.

Dutch shouted from behind her, "No!"

Julia jumped for the door to throw on the interior door lock, but she was too late. The door burst open and two men surged into the suite, lunging at her. She leaped backward, desperately fighting off the grasp of the first guy. The second man circled wide, closing in on her from the back. He grabbed for her legs and she kicked wildly, twisting and turning like a panicked gazelle as they lifted her off the ground.

And then a loud cracking noise split the air. She glimpsed Dutch ripping out of the chair as if it was made of toothpicks. Spindles and chair legs went flying in all directions. He rose like an avenging angel out of the wreckage. He leaped into the fray and delivered a crippling fist to the kidney of the guy trying to grab her legs. Her feet hit the floor and the thug doubled over like a paper doll.

The second man let go of her and turned to fight. Dutch eyed the guy coldly, the promise of death in his eyes. The thug jumped and Dutch slid aside in a blindingly fast move. He stepped forward as the goon spun around to face him and she flinched as he smashed his fists into the man's face with two lightning-fast blows.

The first guy got up and Dutch spun in a blur, kicking him in the side of the head and sending him crashing to the floor. The second guy was back up on his hands and knees. An open-handed chop to the back of his head, and both men were down for good.

"Close the door," he ordered tersely.

She jumped to the entrance and peeked out. The maid— or whoever they'd paid to help them—was long gone. She closed the door with a quiet snick and turned to look at the carnage. Both men sprawled, unconscious, at her feet. A trickle of blood dripped from one guy's broken nose onto the hardwood floor. She stared at Dutch, reeling at the display she'd just witnessed. His eyes were as brittle as ice and danger oozed from every inch of him.

His voice was as cold as his eyes when he stated, "Like I said. I can protect you."

No kidding. Her stomach rumbled with faint nausea.

Silently, Dutch held a hand out to her.

She stared at his big, callused palm. Those fingers were capable of so much violence. But she'd also seen them reach out to her as he went down on the living-room floor, begging for help. Seen him allow himself to be tied to a chair—not like that had ever actually restrained him, as it turned out— so she'd feel less afraid. If she was going to survive the next couple of weeks, she had to trust someone. Why not him? It wasn't as if there was anyone else.

Acting on sheer gut instinct, she stepped forward. Into his arms. In reluctant reflex, he wrapped them around her. Relief unfolded inside her, bathing her in warm comfort. Lord, she'd missed human contact. His sweater was warm and scratchy under her cheek, the man beneath it hard as steel. But in spite of the rigid way he held himself, he made her feel safe. She hadn't felt that way in a long time.

"Do you recognize them?" he murmured into her hair.

"No," she sighed against his chest. "What are we going to do with those two?" It was so nice to let someone else worry about things for a change.

Dutch leaned back enough to look down at her. He actually grinned. "Now we get to have a little fun."

She blinked rapidly. That smile of his still could knock a grown woman right off her feet. "Fun? Are you kidding? These guys just attacked us and there are more of them where they come from!"

Dutch merely stepped over to a kitchen drawer and pocketed a gadget that looked suspiciously like a high-tech lock pick one of her father's men had shown her a few months back. Then he bent over and hoisted one of the guys over his shoulder. He said casually, "Open the door for me and make sure the hall's clear, will you?"

She missed the feel of his arms around her, but the sense of comfort lingered. She did as he requested and stood aside as he hauled the man out. At his head jerk, she followed him down the hallway. They ducked into an alcove that housed an icemaker and a couple of vending machines. Dutch dumped his burden on the floor.

He murmured, "Keep an eye out and let me know if anyone comes this way."

She peeked into the hallway while he worked behind her. She glanced over her shoulder and saw him at an unmarked door, inserting the snazzy, gunlike lock pick in the lock. Apparently breaking and entering was also part of his repertoire. *A man of many talents.* The door opened and he hauled the unconscious thug into what looked like a storage room for the maid's cleaning carts.

"Hold this door open while I go get the other guy."

She nodded and did as he directed. In the eternity he was gone, maybe a minute, she prayed fervently that the goon lying on the floor wouldn't wake up.

"Here we go."

She jumped violently as Dutch materialized beside her. He moved as silently as a big cat on the hunt. He dumped the second man beside the first one. "Grab me some sheets, will you?"

She handed him a stack of linens. With quick jerks of powerful muscles, he tore them into thick strips and tied the men's hands behind their backs. He secured them to heavy cleaning carts on opposite sides of the room from each other and locked the brakes on the cart's wheels. He tied their feet to two more carts. Leaning back on his heels, he surveyed his work.

"Too bad I can't kill these guys on U.S. soil."

She shuddered at the cool calm with which he said that.

He stood up, searching around the room. She watched, frowning, as he grabbed a complimentary pad of hotel stationery and a pen and scribbled a note. He laid it on the floor in front of the door. "There. That ought to keep them busy for a while, don't you think?"

She looked down at the note's block letters and grinned. It read, *Call the police. These are criminals.*

He tore up one last sheet, stuffing pieces of it into each of the men's mouths and tying the gags in place with more strips of cloth. He straightened beside her. Goodness, his height was imposing. Ah, but it was nice to have all that brawn on her side for once.

He plucked pistols out of holsters inside both men's jackets and tucked them in his own waistband. "Let's go," he murmured.

Apparently, he was accepting her deal. He'd just attacked and subdued two armed men on her behalf. She followed him out of the closet.

He looked both ways down the empty hall. "Take me to your room. We're packing your stuff and getting out of here."

That sounded like a great idea. In a matter of minutes she stood by the door with her luggage, watching him go through her room, wiping down the place for fingerprints. They went back to his room and repeated the procedure, and before long, his suitcases stood neatly beside hers.

They carried their bags downstairs to the checkout counter. While she pulled the necessary cash out of her purse, Dutch checked out of his room, as well.

He led her to the parking lot and tossed their luggage into the back of a dark green, late-model SUV. "How did you get here?" he asked.

When her father's men caught up with her in Los Angeles, she'd borrowed a car from her college roommate who lived in Malibu. "I drove."

"A rental?" he asked sharply.

"No. I borrowed it from a friend."

"That's probably how your father's goons found you. We

need to ditch it ASAP. Drive into town and I'll follow you. Park in the grocery-store lot and then come get in my car."

"What about my skis?"

"Leave 'em. It'll make your tails think you fled in haste."

"I *am* fleeing in haste," she retorted testily.

He grinned at her. "We need to be seen leaving separately. Can you go get your car by yourself? I'll keep an eye on you to make sure you're safe."

Of course she could walk to her car by herself. She wasn't *that* helpless. She'd gotten to Colorado by herself, hadn't she? With a nod to Dutch, she headed across the resort's parking lot. Lord, she felt exposed. There were still at least four of those thugs lurking around here somewhere. Her breathing accelerated into a rapid, sucking staccato. Abruptly, a flash of yellow hurtled toward her. She threw herself behind the nearest car, her heart slamming into her throat. A little boy charged past, yelling over his shoulder for his parents to hurry up.

She leaned against the hood of the car while she regained control of her wobbly legs. Two more rows over to her car. She could do this. She was *not* a complete wimp. In an act of sheer willpower, she forced herself to move. One foot in front of the next.

An eternity later, she fumbled at her car door with her keys. She slid behind the wheel, locked the door, and sighed with relief. And then something moved in her rearview mirror. She dived for the seat, laying flat against cold leather. Long seconds ticked past. Nothing happened. She sagged in relief. Her heart couldn't take much more of this.

Sitting up, she checked the rearview mirror. Another movement! But then it resolved itself into a woman skier walking past. Sheesh. *Get a grip.*

She reached for the ignition key and hesitated. Ever since she'd seen her father blow up a rival with a car bomb when she was twelve, she'd had a thing about starting cars. But if her father wanted her killed, she'd be dead already. And it wasn't as though she had any choice about whether or not to start the engine. She had to get this car out of here.

The engine reluctantly coughed to life, not tuned for high altitude and extreme cold. No explosion. Thank God.

As she pulled out of the parking lot, Dutch fell in behind her and followed her down the mountain to town. She pulled into the grocery-store parking lot and stopped her car. Dutch got out of his vehicle several rows over. She was surprised to see him saunter into the store as if he didn't have a care in the world. Should she go now? Wait for him to come back? He'd been specific. Park her car and head for his.

She was developing a real hatred of open spaces. How Dutch lived like this all the time, she had no idea. She'd only been on the lam for a few weeks and her nerves were shot. She walked quickly toward Dutch's SUV, barely managing not to break into a panicked sprint. With a quick glance around—nobody suspicious *seemed* to be watching her—she tested the passenger-door handle of Dutch's vehicle. Unlocked. She slipped inside, sighing in relief as the darkly tinted windows shielded her from prying eyes.

A couple of minutes later, the driver's door flew open without warning, and she jumped violently. Dutch grinned at her and she scowled back at him. His grin got wider as he tossed several plastic bags of groceries in the back seat and slid behind the wheel. "Glad to see me?"

"I'm exceedingly glad you're not the guys who've been following me. Where to now?" she babbled in her relief.

"I've got the bases covered," was his enigmatic reply.

Boy, this guy really bottled his thoughts up tight. Although given her history of conning him she couldn't really expect him to open up. Once burned, twice shy. And she couldn't blame him since she'd done the burning. He pointed the SUV back in the direction they'd just come from. She frowned as he started winding up the mountain once more.

When he turned off onto a narrow road, hardly more than a set of tracks in the snow, she began to wonder. Maybe he had a nice little outing planned for himself out here in the woods—her execution followed by a weenie roast perhaps?

He drove for a good fifteen minutes on a series of trails no better than the first one. Finally, he stopped in front of a tall iron security gate in the middle of nowhere. Dutch leaned out the window, punched in a number code on a keypad, and the gate swung open.

A driveway snaked away into a heavy stand of trees. He followed it for a couple of minutes until the woods opened up before them. In the clearing was a resort unlike any she'd seen in this area before. A cluster of twelve large, log chalets arced around the base of a glorious, snow-covered mountain peak. One large log building stood in the middle, much bigger than the others. A helicopter was parked beside it.

"What is this place?" she asked.

"This is a really private resort. Exclusive with a capital E."

"And how do you know about it?"

"Charlie Squad rescued the owner's son from kidnappers a few years back. Saved the kid's life and saved daddy ten million bucks while we were at it. We have a standing invitation to visit."

And sure enough, when Dutch stepped inside the main building, a woman came out from behind the registration counter immediately and planted a big hug on him. She called out to a man in the back, and in a matter of seconds, he was pounding on Dutch's back effusively. Julia smiled at how uncomfortable the display of affection made Dutch. The poor guy looked ready to turn around and run for cover.

Finally he managed to get a word in between the couple's expansive welcomes. "Do you happen to have a room for us for the night?"

"Of course," the man answered. "Come with me."

He led them outside to one of the chalets. Its interior was as gorgeous as the scenery outside, and they were settled in it in no time. A staff member brought their luggage in and announced, "The first helicopter leaves at 9:30 a.m. tomorrow."

Dutch grimaced. "We don't have skis with us."

The kid answered easily, "No problem. Come on up to the lodge and we'll outfit you. The powder's awesome on the high slopes."

Dutch glanced over at her, and she gave him a hopeful look. She'd never helicopter skied a wild mountain at the higher elevations. She'd heard it was pure skiing heaven. She'd skied the Alps in Switzerland and the Andes in Chile, but her father frowned on extreme sports and had never let her out of the confines of traditional ski resorts.

He looked back at the kid. "Pencil us in for a couple of seats on the first flight tomorrow."

"You've got it, sir. Will you be eating at the lodge tonight?"

Dutch shook his head. "No. We'll cook for ourselves."

The young man nodded and left.

Julia remarked, "I hope you meant you'd be cooking, because I burn water if I try to boil it."

Dutch whistled between his teeth. "Wow. That takes real talent. And yes, I'll cook supper. Why don't you go take a hot bath and relax a bit."

She smiled gratefully at him. The idea of a long, hot soak sounded absolutely wonderful.

Dutch's voice floated to her out of the kitchen, over the sound of steaming water filling the spa tub and its dozen jets. "I figure we've got a couple of days before your tails circle back into this area to look for us. We'll stay here until we figure out what we're doing, and then we can move out."

He sounded so confident. And what he said did make sense. The ever-present burden of fear lifted from her shoulders a bit. It felt great to relinquish responsibility to someone else. Besides, she didn't have anyplace else to go.

Dutch ground a touch more pepper into the pasta carbonara and noted the sound of the hot-tub jets cutting off in the bathroom. Perfect. Supper would be ready just about the same time Julia was done primping after her bath.

Eduardo's banker, huh? Who'd have guessed the bastard would use his own daughter to do his dirty work? But then, maybe it made sense in a sick sort of way. Who else could the guy trust with all his money? Man, he would give his right arm to get a good look at Eduardo's complete financial records. So would half the federal government. That was the *only* reason he'd agreed to postpone his plans for Julia.

He frowned as he tossed the salad. Why had Julia come to him rather than going straight to more traditional authorities?

He didn't buy for a minute the idea that he was the *only* person who could keep her safe. Tickling at the back of his consciousness was the disturbing notion that her being here might have something to do with the feelings they'd once shared for each other. As for him, that most certainly had *nothing* to do with why he was here.

If she was on the up-and-up, the FBI or the Treasury Department would be more than happy to keep her safe in return for her information and her testimony. But, his finely honed sense of intuition smelled a rat. She was up to something.

And the best way to lure her out was to bait the trap with what she wanted: his twenty-four-hour protection.

"Wow. That smells amazing."

He glanced up at Julia as he pulled garlic bread out of the oven. "Hungry?" he asked.

"I haven't eaten a decent meal in weeks."

That would explain the unnatural hollowness of her cheeks, the violet shadows under her eyes, the delicacy of her skin. If she ever met his family, his Swedish mother would plow her under with steak, potatoes and thick, hearty stews, griping all the while about putting some meat on her bones. He found her fragile quality appealing, himself. If she were anyone but Julia Ferrare, it would make him feel…protective.

He'd moved the small kitchen table and two chairs into the living room in front of the fire he'd built, and he'd scraped up a half-dozen candles and put them on the table. He dished up the creamy pasta and burned his fingers slicing off hunks of garlic bread for them. But her sigh of appreciation as he seated her at the table was worth the trouble.

"Now, *that's* romantic," she breathed.

Cripes. The last thing he wanted was for her to think he was making a pass at her. To get her to talk more, he'd been going for relaxing, not romantic. Although romantic might have won him the answers he needed from her, he was not going down that road. Not with her. Even if the thin, white cashmere sweater she wore called up vivid images of her barely covered breasts.

He frowned at the cozy table set for two. It *did* look like a seduction scene. Suddenly he felt like a clumsy, oversize bull, tiptoeing around in a cramped china shop.

Hell, let her think what she would. If thinking he'd traded vengeance for romance would make her talk, so be it. He lit the candles, turned off the overhead lights and decanted a glass of wine for her. He waited for her to pick up her fork before he began eating slowly and carefully himself.

The fire hissed quietly and added its flickering golden

light to the glow of the candles. Outside, darkness was falling fast.

"Mmm, a Chilean *carmenére* grape. Is this a La Playa 2000 vintage? I haven't had this since…"

Dutch carefully kept his expression neutral. Since *when?* And how in the hell did she recognize a rare wine from one of Chile's most famous vineyards? Last time he checked, she supposedly lived in Switzerland. "A wine connoisseur, are you?" he asked casually. Maybe Chile was where Eduardo stashed his millions.

She shrugged. "Not really. I just used to drink it a lot at…a favorite restaurant of mine."

He'd bet his next paycheck she'd never drunk a *carmenére* at any restaurant. The old Bordeaux grape was thought to be extinct until just a few years ago when a few vines turned up in Chile. Wine made from its grapes was still exceedingly rare outside that country and coveted by wine collectors. He'd been amazed to find a bottle at a local wine store when he'd arrived in Colorado. He thought back to the intel reports on his foe. Eduardo was a vodka drinker. Hated wine, in fact. Not the kind of guy who'd stock this stuff in his wine cellar.

So, how did Julia know this wine? As tempted as he was to probe for answers, he steered the conversation into less dangerous waters for now. No sense spooking her when she was just starting to relax with him.

Instead, he moved the conversation forward. They talked about everything from religion and politics to her favorite books and the latest movies. Everything except the details that he wanted. He should have been anxious to uncover the facts, but he wasn't. It was surprisingly easy to talk to her. She was a damn attractive woman. Smart, too. Inspite of her betrayals, he couldn't ignore her gentle, compassionate personality. Or the incisive sense of humor that prevented her from coming across like a sissy.

The sense of déjà vu in talking to her like this was huge. That black gap in his memory pulled at him again. Had he, in fact, done this before? Had they had romantic little trysts where they traded secrets? Was that how she'd wormed her way into the team's good graces and led them like lambs to Eduardo's slaughter?

Tonight, she'd twisted her hair up in a knot on the back of her head, and he kept noticing how long and graceful her neck was. She reminded him of a black swan with her raven hair and dark chocolate eyes. Gradually, as the meal and the wine hit them, her shoulders relaxed and she smiled more often. His gut also began to unclench. Strangely it was getting hard to remember how much he hated her.

Then, without warning, a blindingly bright light flashed in the window. He jumped. But Julia dived for the floor. *A revealing reaction.* Without comment, he knelt beside her and drew her into a protective hug. She came readily, huddling against him like a frightened child. She felt slender and sleek and impossibly soft in his arms.

"Oh God, they've found us," she whispered fearfully against his neck.

"That was the lights on the mountain being turned on for some night skiing. It's okay."

"Really?" she asked in a small voice.

"Really."

"Oh." A pause. "Then I guess I look incredibly stupid, don't I?"

He chuckled. "No, but you sure have great reflexes. Frankly, you look like a frightened woman who needs to tell me more about what's going on with her father so I can protect her from him."

She picked herself up off the floor and sat down in her chair again before she murmured, "What do you want to know?"

Much better. He spread his napkin out on his lap again and picked up his fork. "Where are Eduardo's financial records?"

A turbulent jumble of emotions passed through her gaze, but her answer revealed little. "Hidden. They're safe."

Not going to play ball, was she? Why would she wait to hand over the documents? What did she have to gain? She was definitely holding out on him. Something else was going on between her and her old man that she wasn't telling him.

He sat back and took a sip of wine. Well, now. So she was playing games with him. Why wasn't he surprised? The meal's relaxing effect evaporated like a drop of water on the surface of the Sun. He *knew* better than to let down his guard around this woman.

If he'd learned one thing from their wide-ranging dinner conversation, though, it was that she was no dummy. He'd have to proceed carefully. Appear to play along with her game. See where it led, and keep his eyes open for the trap before she sprang it on him. He needed more information.

"What kinds of legitimate businesses does Eduardo invest in to hide his assets?" he asked.

She shook her head in the negative. Damn. Better lay on more relaxation. He smiled and refilled her glass of wine. He gazed out at the handful of skiers dotting the slope and sipped his wine while he planned his next move.

He leaned back in his chair and stretched his long legs out more comfortably. Hopefully he looked at ease, even though his gut felt like a wet knot being yanked tighter and tighter.

"Okay, let's try something easier," he said lightly. "Why me?"

She studied him for a long time, her eyes black pools of

doubt. Finally she answered, barely louder than a whisper, "Because I trust you."

The words exploded over him like a sonic boom, and sharp pressure built up in his ears and behind his eyes. He gripped the edge of the table while the now-familiar tidal wave of darkness roared toward him. Instead of fighting it this time, he tried a different tactic. He didn't grasp for the memories he sensed lingering behind the veil of black. He squashed his curiosity and merely let the moment roll over him and through him in hopes that this time it would pass him by. It worked. Barely.

He cleared his throat, realizing she was frowning at him. Crap. More relaxation. ASAP. "And why exactly do you trust me?"

Her eyebrows knit into a frown. "Shouldn't that be obvious, given our past?"

Crap. What *was* their past?

She reached across the table and put her hand on top of his. "Are you all right?" she asked in concern, looking him directly in the eyes.

"Hell no, I'm not all right," he bit out.

She flinched at the lash in his voice, but bravely she didn't retreat. He wouldn't have guessed she had such backbone. "What can I do to help?" she asked quietly.

He sighed, the moment of uncontrolled anger past. "Damned if I know."

Compassion softened her expression until he thought he might crawl right into that sweet, melting gaze of hers. "Don't worry, Dutch. I know you'll take great care of me." She pushed back her empty plate and propped her elbows on the table. "Tonight is about relaxing. Let's talk about something else. Where did you learn to ski?"

"Montana. Big Sky Country."

"I hear it's beautiful. I've never been up there."

He smiled fondly. "It's God's own backyard."

She commented, "Ever consider being a professional skier? You looked pretty fast on that downhill run today."

Embarrassment warred with his curiosity over just what had happened up there during his blackout. "Did I..." He didn't quite know how to word it, so he just barged ahead. "Did I say anything, do anything, before I went down that hill?"

"You looked really surprised to see me, which was kind of weird since you were there to meet me. Then you turned and headed straight for the downhill course. I was startled because just about nobody tries it."

He snorted. "For good reason. I nearly broke my neck out there. Why'd you go down it?"

She looked away, then answered reluctantly, "I was worried about you. I got the feeling you might get into trouble on that run."

Rather than delve too deeply into her concern for him, which unaccountably made him uncomfortable, he asked, "Where did you learn to ski so well? It's not like Gavarone has ever seen snow."

She teased, "We took lots of vacations to Switzerland when I was a kid. And I have an apartment there now."

Switzerland. As in the home of secure international banking. That was an interesting, albeit not surprising, choice of residence for a woman with money to hide.

She interrupted his speculations. "Hey, you started asking questions again. It's still my turn."

"Sorry. What else would you like to know about me?"

"Tell me about Charlie Squad."

Now, *there* was a touchy question. Where to begin? And how much to say to the daughter of his enemy? "We still do what we always did. We liaise between the air force and the Special Forces teams from the other branches of the U.S. military. To do that, we're trained the same way they are and can do a broad variety of special ops missions."

"Do you still operate in six-man teams where each guy has a particular specialty?"

"Why do you ask?" he retorted.

"I always wanted to know what you did for Charlie Squad. You never told me."

He smiled without humor. "My specialty's hard to define. I plan missions. I solve problems…creatively. When we're stuck, I'm the guy who leads the team through a brainstorming session to figure out how to get unstuck."

"So, Mr. Thinker. Have you figured out what you're going to do with me after I hand you everything you want on my father?"

"Of course," he answered lightly. "I'm going to kill you."

Her wineglass shattered on the hardwood floor with a musical crash.

Chapter 4

Oh God. Oh God, oh God, oh God.

She should've known that was what he'd say. But to hear the words spoken aloud. With such calm certainty…

She shuddered. Of course, it wouldn't really matter if he killed her or not. Once her father decided she was in need of killing, nothing and nobody would stop him. One way or another, her life was forfeit. She'd known that when she'd started this fiasco. But to die at the hands of a man she'd once loved—that was a cruel blow.

He almost acted as if he'd forgotten the way she used to moon over him like a love-struck calf. Was he playing some sort of sick cat-and-mouse game with her emotions? If so, it was working.

Frankly, it was a minor miracle he hadn't killed her already, regardless of what information she might have on Eduardo. She briefly considered showing him her ace in the hole, the bit of information she planned to hold until last. But it wasn't time. Not yet.

I'm going to kill you.

His words tolled like a death knell, announcing her demise. She should cut her losses and walk out that door this second. Except she had nowhere left to go. Contacting Dutch had been her last-ditch attempt to stay alive long enough to save her sister. Did she dare brazen it out with Dutch and pray like crazy he never followed through on his deadly promise? She knelt on the floor and dabbed clumsily at the obscenely red spill of wine with her napkin.

Dutch towered over her with a roll of paper towels. "Don't worry about that. I'll get it."

She sat back on her heels, too rattled to stand. She watched him mop up the wine and pick up the broken pieces of glass. Quick. Efficient. Thorough.

With a last sweep of paper towel across the floor, he announced, "There. All gone."

Just like her when this was all over. He moved with lethal grace to the kitchen and disposed of the mess. She still hadn't mustered the strength to stand when he came back. He reached down and pulled her effortlessly to her feet. He looked into her eyes, and somehow she found the strength of will to meet the iron resolve in his sapphire gaze. So. The battle was joined. The rules of engagement were understood. This was a duel to the death. To her death, to be precise.

She shivered and rubbed her hands up and down her arms. His gaze drifted to her neck. And then lower, examining her in leisurely fashion, as if measuring her for a take-down. Everywhere his gaze touched her she burned with icy fire, and her shivers intensified. Thankfully he stepped away, and she remembered to breathe again.

He held her chair for her and she sat down weakly. The

combination of terror and intense awareness made it impossible to look up at him, even though she felt his gaze boring into the top of her head.

"I'm not going to hurt you tonight," he said abruptly. "You asked for my protection and I'm giving it to you. For now."

But the day would come when he'd turn on her. She couldn't bear to think about it. She had to leave him. Now. She'd just have to come up with another plan to save Carina. Hysteria swirled around her in a dizzying haze barely held in check. She was trapped. Nowhere to run. Nowhere to hide.

"What's next on the agenda?" she asked, doing her best to mask her agitation.

He jerked his head toward the bedroom. Her brain skipped like a scratched record. He wanted to go in the bedroom with her? The idea fired her imagination in shocking ways.

He remarked, "You need to relax and get a good night's sleep. Your nerves are frazzled, and you're not thinking clearly."

No kidding. For a second there, she'd thought he meant something else entirely. She'd actually hoped he meant something else.

She went into the bedroom with its stone fireplace, picture windows and huge bed. Four normal-size adults could sleep in the thing. She jumped as she sensed a movement behind her.

"Sorry," he murmured. "Didn't mean to startle you. I just need some clothes." He opened his suitcase, pulled out a sweat suit and headed for the door.

"Where are you going to sleep?" she asked.

"On the couch in the living room."

She frowned. "It's not nearly long enough for you. I'll take the couch. You stay here."

"Not a chance. Nobody's getting past me out there. You're safe tonight. Get some sleep."

She couldn't remember the last time she'd been truly safe. Even before she escaped her father's clutches, she'd never felt secure. His enemies, including agents of the various governments he'd flouted, were always waiting to strike. Like the man standing before her now.

"Julia? Are you all right?"

She jerked her attention back to him. He stood so close she could feel the heat radiating off him. No, she wasn't all right! "I'm fine," she managed to force out.

His eyes flashed their disbelief, but he merely stepped back politely and said, "Sweet dreams." His deep voice sent a shiver down her spine. Her cheeks burned.

Startled by the power of her reaction to him, she nodded wordlessly in return. The door closed quietly. She turned away from the knotty-pine panel. Shedding her clothes quickly, she dropped her nightgown over her head. The silk caressed her skin the same sensuous way she imagined his fingers would have if things had been different. She crawled beneath the fluffy down comforter, and its flannel duvet cradled her in gentle warmth.

Restless, she rolled over and stared at the ceiling. Regret pierced her. In another time and place, she'd have loved nothing more than to spend the night with James Dutcher. But it wasn't meant to be. Their worlds had collided before, ending any chance they might have had now before it even began.

She'd catch a nap for a couple of hours, and then she'd leave. As tempting as it was to let him take care of her, she dared not stay with him. He was too smart. He'd figure out what she was really up to, and when he did, she and Carina were as good as dead.

It was dark and silent when she woke up. The mountain outside the window was a black silhouette against the night sky. The bedside clock said it was 3:20 a.m. Perfect.

She climbed out of bed and, shivering, pulled on clothes. She grabbed Dutch's car keys from the bureau and her purse, which contained a few toiletries and her all important cash. Having met him again, having seen his intention to kill her, she simply couldn't stay. She had no right to put Carina's life further at risk. Her little sister had suffered enough. Julia would find some other way to save her.

Carrying her shoes, Julia eased the bedroom door open and tiptoed to the living room in her socks. A red glow came from the remains of the fire, casting a hellish light in the wide space. She made out Dutch's long form stretched out on the couch, as magnificent as a dragon sprawled in his fiery lair. Even asleep, danger radiated from him. Holding her breath, she eased across the floor one careful step at a time. Cold seeped through her socks before she finally drew close to the door. She reached cautiously for the knob.

"Going somewhere?"

She jumped violently and spun around. Dutch loomed directly behind her, his expression stony. How in the world had he gotten right up to her without her hearing a thing?

"Yes, as a matter of fact," she replied bravely.

"Care to tell me where?" Even roughened with sleep, his voice was cool and deadly.

"No, not particularly. I've got to get away from my father's men, and I don't want to endanger you any more than I already have. I'll just be going now." She again reached for the doorknob.

His large hand landed with heavy finality on the door beside her head. "That's a bad idea," he murmured. His breath touched her warmly in stark contrast to the chill pouring off him. There it was again. That strange pull between them. Something about this man called out to her, an odd vulnerability within his steel. It made her want to wrap her arms

around him and hold him, even though on another level he
scared her to death.

She turned under his arm and stared up at him. His face
was an intersecting series of harsh shadows, his eyes pools
of black. She ached to reach up and smooth away the frown
from his forehead. His fathomless gaze narrowed and sexual
awareness abruptly rolled off him. In waves that all but
drowned her. His presence was overpowering even though he
didn't move a muscle. He made her feel so small. Fragile. The
sensation was thrilling and frightening at the same time. Lord,
it was tempting to bury herself in all that strength and masculine appeal. To solve the intriguing mystery that was Jim
Dutcher.

"It's for the best that I go," she murmured.

"Why's that?" he asked.

"Do you really have to ask?"

He leaned even closer, his mouth by her ear. His chest all
but touched hers, and her breasts tingled at the tantalizing
nearness of his body. The lingering remnants of his after-
shave smelled warm and sexy.

He murmured in a lover's endearment, "You're responsible for my brother's death. When you called me you had to
expect that I'd want to hurt you the same way you hurt me.
And it's not like I came looking for you. But now that you're
here, I'm damn well going to see justice done."

A icicle of dread speared her. He wanted to hurt her the
same way she'd hurt him. Oh. My. God. She'd been right. If
he ever found out about Carina, he'd have the perfect tool to
do exactly that—kill one sibling for another. She could *never*
let him find out about her fight to save her sister! If he did,
he'd do whatever it took to get Carina killed. It would be the
perfect revenge.

A violent shudder rippled through her. *Pull yourself to-*

gether! She dared not give away just how scared she was. He'd leap all over her fear and use it to his advantage.

How could she be so drawn to him one second and so afraid of him the next? It made no sense whatsoever.

His other hand landed on the door beside her head, trapping her between his powerful arms. "What aren't you telling me, Julia? I need to know everything if we're going to nail Eduardo before he nails you. What is it?" he demanded softly.

She stared at him in dismay. Busted. As usual, he'd read her like an open book. But now she knew she could never answer that question. Ever. She replied, "I've changed my mind. I don't want your help."

She felt him absorb her refusal to answer like a physical blow. She closed her eyes against the pull between them. She felt like a paper clip in the presence of a high-powered magnet. The haven of his care, the companionship of another human being in her solitary flight from death, his sheer masculine sex appeal were darned near irresistible.

She understood his anger. Could accept it. But she had to get over the past. Had to let go of the feelings for him she'd carried around inside her for all these years like a secret pearl hidden deep within the closed shells of her heart.

She jumped when he trailed a finger down the length of her neck. His voice caressed her like black velvet. "You look like a caged swan. Give me a chance, my desperate Odile. I'll keep you safe."

She blinked at the reference to the black swan from the ballet *Swan Lake* who was tragically manipulated by her evil father. An apt analogy. She let out a slow breath. Even his intelligence was seductive. How was she supposed to get over him?

He pushed away from the door and took a step back.

"Come to bed. It's late and your feet must be frozen. Let's get them warmed up."

There it was again. That natural compassion he lapsed into whenever he forgot to be furious at her. It sent her pulse pounding completely out of control. She shivered, but not from the icy cold seeping between her toes. The inevitability of doom settled around her, but she was powerless to fight it. She followed him back to the bedroom and let him tuck her into bed like a child.

But she lurched when he started to climb in beside her. "What are you doing?" she exclaimed.

"Keeping an eye on you. I'm a very light sleeper. If you get out of bed again, it'll wake me up."

"But—"

"No buts. I'm not letting you run away before Eduardo's behind bars." His voice rang with hard finality.

She subsided against her pillow. A tiny corner of her heart sighed in relief. Was she relieved he'd made her stay because he'd protect her, or was it something else entirely? Something to do with the overwhelmingly male vibes rolling off him as he lay beside her, and the way something instinctive and female inside her responded? She lay there for a long time, staring at the ceiling, beside a man she wanted desperately. A man who had the reason and the resolve to kill her.

What in the world was she supposed to do now?

Dutch paused, listening to the raucous night sounds of the jungle around him. He slid forward a few more steps and paused again, careful not to disrupt the deafening chorus of noise. He was early for the rendezvous with the informant. With Julia.

Even thinking her name sent his heart pounding deep and hard like a bass drum. A totally unprofessional reaction, but she was so beautiful she took his breath away. Every guy on the team had a crush on her, whether they admitted it or not. Hell, even Captain Folly made a point of shaving and putting on a clean uniform whenever he had to meet her.

Dutch grinned. But he was the one she made eye contact with. The one she smiled at shyly. Because she trusted him, he was the one who got to coordinate with her as the sting against her father drew near.

He still had a hard time believing she would help set up her own father. But then, her old man was an incredible bastard.

Eduardo Ferrare was a formidable criminal whose illegal empire had reached far enough into the United States to draw the attention of the federal government. A decision had been made to take him out, and Charlie Squad had been sent to Gavarone to do the job.

He pushed aside a giant fern and peered out at the path ahead. Julia should walk along here in about five minutes. They'd have only a few seconds to exchange information, and then she'd have to move on.

A rustle down the path made him jerk back under cover. Damn. Eduardo's men patrolled this path now and then. If they screwed up this rendezvous, he wouldn't get to see Julia for two more days, until they met at the backup site. Besides the fact that his team desperately needed the information she was going to give them, he also didn't want to wait that long to see her again.

He crouched in the lee of a giant tree trunk, completely still. A lone figure moved into view, and he sighed in relief. He'd know that slender outline and graceful stride anywhere. She was early. He grinned and stood up. Wanted to spend a couple of extra minutes with him, did she?

He stepped out into the path, and even in the heavy shad-

ows, he saw her features light up at the sight of him. Damn, that sort of reaction from a pretty girl made a guy feel good.

"Hey you," he murmured as she drew near.

She kept coming until she'd walked straight into his arms. "Hey you," she whispered back. "I missed you."

His arms tightened around her. "I missed you, too. How was your day?"

"I never thought tonight would get here," she confessed shyly. "I got scared again this afternoon."

This whole business had been hard on her. She was only twenty, barely more than a girl, yet here she was doing the work of a seasoned Special Forces soldier. He stroked her silky hair comfortingly.

She jolted against him as a leopard screamed somewhere nearby. "I hate the jungle," she declared. "I hate Gavarone."

"It's almost over. And then you can get out of here and never come back. I'll take you back to the States myself if you'd like."

She leaned back and smiled up at him. "I'd like that. I'd like to see your Montana."

Her eyes glowed and his heart felt as if it was going to burst out of his chest. The sultry night vibrated around them, alive and breathing with lush life. Julia's lips parted slightly as she gazed up at him, their fullness glistening in what little moonlight filtered down through the canopy above.

He shouldn't do it. He should leave well enough alone. But she flowed like golden honey in his arms, warm and smooth, and he'd wanted to do this ever since he met her. He angled his head down and touched her mouth with his. And sweet God, she leaned into him and all but devoured him back. No hesitation, no coyness. She might be a girl, but she damn well kissed like a woman. Before he knew what he was doing, he'd lifted her off her feet against him and completely lost himself *in her. Her fingers speared into his hair, tugging him closer, and he surrendered to her every bit as fully as she'd surrendered to him. How long they stood there, all but inhaling each other in mutual, desperate need, he had no idea.*

A voice called out her name from behind them. Crap. Her bodyguard!

They broke apart, panting.

She murmured quickly, "My father has a meeting at midnight two nights from now at his compound. It's important. He'll be there for sure."

"How's he going to get there?" he asked fast.

"By car. Two more cars in front of him and one behind. All armored. Twelve to sixteen bodyguards. He'll be a few minutes late and make his visitor wait for him."

He nodded. "We'll meet you behind the gazebo on the south side of the main driveway at 11:30 p.m. Don't be late. Your safety will depend on it."

She nodded her understanding, her eyes huge and frightened.

"Miss Ferrare? Where are you?"

Dutch looked over his shoulder. Time to go. But he couldn't resist stealing a few more seconds with her. He gave her a quick, hard hug and kissed her fast. The fear in her eyes morphed into adoration. He released her and gave her a gentle push toward her bodyguard. "Scoot. I'll see you in two days, and we'll begin your new life, together."

With a last, melting smile, she hurried off down the path. He stepped back quickly, melting silently into the darkness...

He jerked awake, battle ready. Something or someone had just touched him. Dark. Silent. No movement. The bedroom of a ski chalet materialized around him. Julia. Her soft hand rested on his upper arm. Their embrace in the jungle was still so fresh, so raw, he started to roll over and take her in his arms again.

Whoa. Reality check, here. That was a dream. Just a dream.

Or was it?

He could smell the rotten vegetation, feel the mosquitoes landing on his neck, recall exactly the wispy slide of her skirt wrapping around his thighs as they kissed. And that kiss. He couldn't dream up something that vivid if he tried. And that meant...

It was a memory! A piece of that missing month in his life. Julia must have triggered it. Holy cow. If he spent more time with her, would she trigger more recollections? Was it possible for him to regain that entire lost month?

A voice whispered in his head, did he really want to regain that particular month of his life? Did he want to relive the loss of his baby brother, and the loss of a girl he was crazy about, if that dream was accurate?

He stared up at the ceiling in dismay. He'd been half in love with Julia Ferrare? No wonder he was having such a weird reaction to her now. One second he wanted to wring her neck, and the next he wanted to wrap her in his arms and never let her go. Now what in the bloody hell was he supposed to do?

He muttered a curse under his breath.

To most of the people whose lives he entered, he was Death. They could run from him and they could hide, but he'd hunt them down. He always did. The frightened faces of the dozens of criminals he'd nailed through the years floated through his mind. What stuck with him wasn't the moment he killed them. It was always the moment when he first met them face-to-face. When they still hoped to get out alive. Before they realized he was their inexorable fate.

Julia had looked like that when he'd caught her trying to sneak out earlier. Was she a criminal like the others? Disquiet rippled through him. He didn't want to turn the hunter in himself loose on her, no matter his earlier intentions or what he'd told her tonight.

Had that dark, inhuman part of himself that he held in check so carefully finally broken out? Was that what took over his mind during that inexplicable blackout earlier? Was he losing control of the beast within? An unfamiliar emotion rolled over him, choking him until he struggled to breathe. *Fear.* He'd fought for so long to tame the monster, to keep the violent part of himself reined in. The psychologists had warned him it was a delicate dance and that he was skating very close to the edge. But was it too late? Had the beast won?

Julia shifted restlessly, troubled by her dreams. She rolled over and flung an arm and a leg across his body. He froze beneath her. Lust pounded through him, roaring in his ears and demanding release upon the sleek female draped across him with such abandon. The turmoil bubbling in his brain intensified.

It would be so easy to roll over, to pull her beneath him, to bury himself in her sweetness and ravage her mindlessly. To succumb to his baser self once and for all.

No! Forcibly he held himself still, letting her use his body as she would for safety and warmth. He would protect her. Guard her innocence with his life if he had to. He would *not* harm her. Not yet.

The litany replayed itself in his head endlessly as the night stretched out around him. Slowly, slowly, he won the battle against his dark side. One muscle at a time, he gradually let go of his tension, gradually went still in spirit as the beast retreated from his mind. He'd won. This time. Julia's innocence and her life remained intact as she slept on beside him.

But as the light of dawn seeped insidiously between the curtains, fear sidled into his mind once more. What was it about this woman that brought him so close to the brink? Did he dare stay with her? Would keeping his promise to protect her destroy him? Would he take her with him when he went?

With morning came howling winds, blizzard conditions and subzero windchill. He built a fire and made a pot of coffee while Julia slept the deep, hard sleep of someone who'd been on the run for weeks and had finally found a safe place to rest. While the storm raged outside, he pondered the dilemma of the woman in his bed.

Late in the morning she emerged, swallowed in his bathrobe, her hair tangled, and squinting at the bright light. She'd never looked more beautiful.

"Hi," she mumbled shyly.

"Good morning. Sleep all right?"

"Mmm, wonderfully. Sorry about…uh…interrupting your rest last night."

He smiled briefly. "No harm done. Just so long as we're clear that you're staying with me." He got up and headed for the kitchen. "Do you like coffee?" he called.

"Manna from heaven," she called back.

He grinned. "Cream or sugar?"

"Both."

"How much?"

She laughed. "Think coffee-flavored ice cream and you'll have it about right."

He handed her a steaming mug and sat down across from her at the table. He pushed the *Wall Street Journal* toward her and she leaped upon it like a starving dog.

He watched her silently as she devoured the newspaper front to back. Okay, so maybe the banker thing was legit. He was too damn suspicious sometimes. She checked several stock quotes and spent a long time perusing international monetary fund prices. He'd bet his next paycheck that was where her father's illegal money was invested.

Surreptitiously, he watched Julia stand up and do a few stretching exercises. She must do yoga or something similar, for she was as limber as a pretzel. A couple of seriously depraved ideas of what they could with that flexibility of hers flashed across his brain. Damned if that wasn't sweat popping out on his forehead. If he didn't get out of here right now, he was going to attack her like some slavering animal and try out a few of his ideas. "I've got to get out of here," he announced, standing up abruptly.

He had to put some distance between them right now. Otherwise, she'd be in grave danger. From himself.

Chapter 5

"I'm going to take a shower," he growled. "While I'm gone, don't open the door for anybody. *Anybody.* I don't care if Jesus Christ rises up and knocks in person. Don't open it. Got it?"

She nodded, appropriately wide-eyed at his vehemence. He stalked into the bedroom, his adrenaline pumping hard. He needed to do something strenuous to burn it off. Like have sex. Hot, sweaty, wild sex. Dammit. He turned on the shower to cover the noise of his conversation and pulled out his cell phone. He punched out the number for Charlie Squad head-quarters.

"Go ahead."

Dutch recognized the voice of his commander, Colonel Tom Folly. He bit out, "Dutch here. I need a favor."

"You name it. And how's the snow, by the way?"

Dutch answered impatiently, "Packed powder until this

morning. But it's blowing like a big mother out there now. Zero visibility and thirty below zero windchill."

"Bummer. So, what can I do for you?"

"I need to extend my leave for a while."

"Dutch! I'm so proud of you! Your first vacation in five years and you're actually enjoying yourself. Who'd have guessed?"

He flinched at the colonel's mirth. "Can I have, say, another week of leave?"

"Hell, make it two, buddy. What happened? No, wait. Let me guess. You met a girl. She must be a babe and a half."

Might as well let the colonel think it was a woman. And after all, technically, it was. "Yeah, she's gorgeous," Dutch replied.

"Who is she?"

He winced. "Mind if I pass on answering that one, sir?"

Folly chuckled. "Nah, go ahead and be a gentleman. Just don't catch any diseases, eh?"

For some reason, the casual remark set Dutch's teeth on edge. "Thanks for extending my leave," he ground out.

"No sweat," the colonel replied.

Damned if he didn't hear laughter in his boss's voice. Dutch disconnected the phone and tossed it on the bed in disgust. He stomped into the bathroom to take a shower for real. A long, cold one, dammit.

Julia listened to the water turn on in the bathroom. Every fiber in her being screamed for her to take this opportunity to run. But where would she go? What would she do? She believed Dutch without reservation when he promised he'd keep her safe until her father was behind bars. He was nothing if not a man of his word. In the light of morning she could see it was best to go ahead as planned for now. She'd keep trying to contact Eduardo and make a deal.

In fact, now that she had Dutch's protection, it was probably time to apply a little pressure to daddy dearest. And she knew exactly how to do it. She grinned at the idea that had popped into her head when she woke up this morning. She could transfer the money she'd taken from him into Charlie Squad's bank account. Surely they had some sort of quick-draw checking account for use during operations in the field. If she could find that account number, she could tweak her father's nose in a big way. A way guaranteed to draw his attention. Eduardo would rupture something when he found out.

Now, where would Dutch keep something like a bank account number? The sort of offshore account she was looking for typically had up to a twenty-digit number with long access codes, as well. She gave him a couple of minutes to get settled into his shower and then slipped into the bedroom.

She glanced around and spied his cell phone lying on the bed. She reached for it, then hesitated.

What had her decision to run away from her father turned her into? Here she was, sneaking around like a criminal, invading the privacy of a decent guy. She pictured Carina's face. All this was for the sister she'd raised like her own daughter. She had to stop their father, once and for all.

She snatched up Dutch's cell phone and flipped it open. Drat. Not a model that stored dates or notes, or more to the point, bank account numbers. She'd have to look somewhere else.

Thoughtfully, she punched the redial button on Dutch's phone to bring up the last number called. Her hands began to shake as she stared at the digital display. The letters CS glowed up at her. *Charlie Squad.* The phone number burned into her brain. Oh Lord. Had he told his team about her? Called for backup maybe? If so, she'd be in custody or dead within a matter of hours.

Her breathing raced frantically and she grew light-headed. She'd be killed before she ever got a chance to save Carina and the countless other people her father would harm or kill someday. The water in the bathroom turned off and she nearly dropped the phone. She replaced it quickly on the bed and raced from the room.

She buried her nose in a random book from the stocked shelf in the living room. Frozen in terror, she forced her eyes to travel across the page as if she was actually comprehending the book she held numbly.

Thankfully, Dutch paid no attention to her ruse. He spent most of the day reading and resting. She wouldn't call it relaxing, exactly. He varied between states of action and inaction, but he never let down his guard.

The vicious winds finally let up in the late afternoon, leaving behind a blanket of soft powder snow, perfect for skiing. She eyed it wistfully for no more than two minutes before Dutch spoke up behind her. "Wanna hit the slopes?"

She looked over at him eagerly. "Really?" Lord, she could use a physical release of the tension that'd been churning inside her all day. "But won't that be dangerous with my father's men looking for us?"

He shrugged. "This place has its own mountain. A private one. They won't find us." He added casually, "I don't know about you, but I really could use the exercise."

"Let's do it," she said eagerly.

She could swear he checked the small of his back before he ushered her out the door. Armed, was he? His casual gesture restored the constant, edgy fear she lived with these days at the same time that it reassured her.

The resort's ski pro outfitted them for boots and skis and whisked them up the mountain in the resort's sleek helicopter. It landed on the summit and they climbed out into blindingly bright sunlight glittering off pristine snow. Nary a ski track marred its smooth perfection.

Dutch pulled out a pair of mirrored shades and slipped them on, neatly covering his gaze. He grinned, sharklike, and set off down the mountain. At first, it was smooth going, a wide expanse of snow over the gradual slope of a glacier. The occasional mogul and gully made it an intermediate-or-so slope.

But then the trail split. He turned his skis sideways, skidding to a stop and throwing up a rooster tail of powder. "Do you like to live dangerously?" he asked her.

Why the heck not. She was a dead woman walking, anyway. "Sure," she retorted.

He set off to the left, choosing one more isolated route after another. She followed him downward as the mountain got steadily steeper and trickier. Without warning, Dutch significantly picked up the speed. He let his skis race flat out over the snow. She crouched in a racer's tuck to eke out every last bit of speed from her own skis to keep up with him. The slope leveled out, but with their accumulated speed, they managed to keep momentum over the wide, flat area. She'd just started to pole her way forward when Dutch looked over his shoulder.

"How are you at jumps?" he called.

"Not great, but I've done a few," she shouted back.

"Lean back and stay vertical!" he instructed.

And then he disappeared over the edge of a cliff. Without any more warning than that, her skis dropped out from under her and she plunged over the edge of a nearly vertical drop. Had Dutch not said something, she'd no doubt have broken her neck.

As it was, her adrenaline surged and she struggled to keep her weight back as the slope fell away from her in a dizzying descent. She mimicked Dutch, twisting her skis from side to side as she dropped from ledge to snowy ledge. She dodged a nasty rock outcropping and kept on going, doggedly following his red back down the impossible slope.

When her legs were screaming in protest and her nerves at the breaking point, the near cliff gave way to a gentler slope and heavy woods. Dutch pulled up short and waited for her to join him. She schussed over the last couple of moguls and swiveled to a stop beside him.

"Lady, you are one hell of a skier," he panted.

She nodded back, too out of breath from the exertion and the altitude to speak.

"Well, that was fun. Took care of a whole lot of my pent-up energy," Dutch huffed. "How 'bout you?"

She spared a glance over her shoulder for the mountain they'd just traveled, and shuddered. It looked like a nearly vertical cliff, peppered with rock outcroppings and drops. Not the kind of hill approved for any human in their right mind to ski down.

"I must have a death wish to have followed you down that monster," she panted.

"No doubt. You called me, didn't you?" he retorted.

Good point. She'd never considered herself much of a risk taker. The one time in her life, ten years ago, that she'd done something dangerous, it had turned into a total nightmare and a man had died. Ever since, she'd sworn off anything more exciting than transferring funds from bank to bank to hide their origin. Until the last few weeks that led her back to Dutch.

"C'mon," Dutch said behind her. "I'm hungry."

Dutch picked a medium-difficulty, scenic route through the woods. It felt like a walk in the park after that cliff of doom. The snow slid like velvet beneath her feet, soft and sleek as they skied between towering stands of pine and aspen. Dutch stayed beside her, matching his speed to hers. He was smooth and powerful and flowed down the mountain as if he'd been born on it. For a little while, she put aside their dangerous dance of cross-purposes and lost herself in the freedom of gliding between the majestic rows of snowbound trees. They came out onto a prepared ski run. Although the snow wasn't groomed, it was clear that this broad path through the trees was artificial.

A few minutes later, Dutch surprised her by veering off onto a remote side trail. It was a narrow, winding course that traversed an arcing fissure down the mountain face. Long shadows striped it in patches of darkness and light. This trail was quite a bit more difficult than the last one, and she paid close attention to her skiing.

In front of her, Dutch called out, "Follow me."

Oh, Lord. Had he seen something she hadn't? A threat of some kind? Adrenaline shot through her, and her knees went weak. He veered off to the left and she followed him into a side ravine. The trail was barely wider than a single pair of skis, and snow-laden boughs brushed her shoulders. The dim tunnel of trees went on for several minutes. Abruptly, they popped out into a wide clearing. It housed a large, log structure and a nearly full parking lot of cars. They skied up to the building's double front doors.

"Hungry?" he asked.

It was a restaurant! "Famished," she replied enthusiastically. They checked their ski equipment and slipped on felt slippers provided by the restaurant. She padded to their table, a booth, actually, with Dutch.

She slid into her seat, vividly aware of how he completely filled the intimate space. "How did you know about this place?" she asked.

He smiled at her, robbing her of breath. "Like it?"

"If the food matches the decor, I'm going to love it!" The rough, log cabin-style interior, complete with antlers and old-fashioned snowshoes on the walls, belied the understated elegance of the crystal stemware and fine china on the tables. The menu confirmed the gourmet underpinnings of the place. She ordered a stuffed shoulder of veal while Dutch chose the roasted free-range pheasant.

"So, do you vacation here often?"

He shrugged. "Haven't had a day off in five years. Until this week, of course."

"Five years?" She tsked. "Is the world that unsafe for democracy or are you just a workaholic?"

He laughed aloud. The sound was rusty, as if he didn't make it often. "A little bit of both, I suppose. Since I'm unattached, I take extra missions so the married guys can get a little more time with their families."

No surprise there. Since they seemed to be operating under a temporary truce, she asked a question she'd been curious about for years. "Why do you do this job?"

"Because I like it."

How could anybody like the stress and danger of being a Special Forces operative? She prodded, "What's your favorite part?"

He answered without the slightest hesitation. "Saving the lives of innocents."

"Do you do that often?" she asked, surprised.

"Often enough to keep me coming back for more."

She'd never thought about Charlie Squad as a rescue outfit before. She'd always thought of them as more of a death squad. But maybe that was because she'd been working with the criminals.

He startled her by asking a question of his own. "When are you going to trust me and tell me what you're hiding?"

Trust him? Now, *there* was a novel concept. She already trusted him enough to put her life in his hands. For now. Wasn't that enough?

Apparently not, the way his blue gaze was boring into her. "I do trust you. It's just that—"

She broke off as he pinned her with yet another piercing stare. Okay. So she didn't trust him *that* much.

He snapped his napkin off the table and unfolded it deliberately in his lap.

She asked in a rush, "Do you have any idea why I triggered your blackout?"

"Do you?" he challenged. Again that saber-sharp, sapphire stare.

Guilt slammed into her. It probably had something to do with that disastrous ambush ten years ago when her father almost managed to wipe out Charlie Squad. That had been the first time her father had threatened to kill Carina if Julia didn't do his bidding. She'd hated setting up the Americans, but she'd had no choice. No choice at all. The hard edge faded from his gaze and she blinked, startled. *He was afraid of his blackout.* As tough as he pretended to be, as in control as he usually was, he was scared. Alone. How was it that she felt sorry for the man who'd sworn to kill her?

As she continued to watch him cautiously, something desperate flickered at the back of his eyes. She blinked. There it was again! There was no mistaking it. He was terrified. The sight of this man scared unnerved her more than the idea of being chased by a gang of paid killers. A visceral need to reach out to him, to hold him and comfort him, took shape low in her belly.

As if he'd just realized he'd given away too much, he looked off quickly. His phenomenal self-control slammed back into place.

The salads arrived and he commented calmly, as if that raw, revealing exchange hadn't just happened, "So. What have you been up to for the last ten years?"

"Not much. Just running the financial end of a global crime empire," she replied with light bitterness. "It has been a real picnic, let me tell you."

His gaze snapped to hers, his blue eyes blazing in fury for a moment before he clamped down on the reaction. What a pair they made, circling around each other like a couple of prize-fighters, each one waiting for an opening to land the knockout punch.

"Tell me about it," he said quietly.

Right. Like he cared about just how hellish it had really been. The constant danger of discovery, the fear of being murdered by her father's enemies, her anguish over the innocents who were hurt or killed every day by her father's actions and, indirectly, hers. Nobody could understand how she was as much a victim as the people her father killed. They saw her living in a big house with servants and luxury all around her and didn't see it for the beautiful, deadly cage it was. They didn't know about the blackmail, the constant, subtle threats to kill Carina, her beloved Carina.

No, Dutch wouldn't understand. She dug into her salad of baby greens. "How about we enjoy this amazing food and talk about serious things later?"

He nodded briskly and then picked up his water glass. "A toast. To good snow, fine food and beautiful women."

Her face went inexplicably warm as she picked up her glass. Sheesh. It wasn't as if nobody'd ever told her she was beautiful before. Except it mattered when this man said it. She *wanted* him to think she was pretty.

Their glasses touched with a musical chime, and their gazes touched over the sparkling crystal. A hot spark leaped in his eyes and in an instant raised the temperature in the room about twenty degrees. She was too mesmerized to tear her gaze away. For a moment, they were back in the jungle, dark and dangerous, and the beautiful and brave American soldier who'd stolen her heart was coming to meet her. Her heart pounded and the old anticipation filled her.

Ah, to be that young and innocent again. To still have hope that a man like him could fall in love with her and sweep her away to a new life of safety and joy.

The restaurant came back into focus around her. But Dutch's gaze never wavered. The intensity of those azure eyes hadn't changed one bit in the last ten years.

She sighed. As much as she wanted this man, she couldn't have him. Their past had already doomed them. She tore her gaze away and blindly cut into her salad.

"So," he said painfully politely, "tell me about your hobbies."

And just like that he bottled up all that sizzling sexual attraction. She'd give her right arm to know how he did it. But at the same time, a kernel of pity for him formed deep in her heart. What must it be like living that way, always shut off from his feelings, isolated from the rest of the human race?

True to his word, Dutch steered their conversation strictly to inconsequential subjects. Nonetheless, he had interesting opinions and observations on everything from Cuban art to international lending practices. His raw intelligence and body of knowledge reached the point of being downright frightening. How was she ever going to outsmart or outmaneuver this man?

As she savored a scrumptious crème brûlée to top off the spectacular meal, he murmured, "It's later."

"I beg your pardon?"

"You said we'd talk about serious things later."

She stared down at the crisp, golden layer of caramelized sugar coating her custard. Composure. Breathe. Living with her father for so long had taught her how to lie convincingly. She could do this.

"What do you want to know?" she managed to ask.

"What are you hiding from me?"

Well, obviously, she thought, I'm not going to tell you every detail of my life. Just as you're not going to tell me every detail of yours. "I'm not keeping anything from you that will affect our deal. I swear. You keep me alive, and I'll give you my father's financial records."

"Why haven't you handed over the records to me already?"

"Because I have to get them first," she lied.

"Where are they now?"

"I uploaded them onto a secure Internet site. I have to retrieve them."

"So all you need is access to an Internet-capable computer and we're finished?"

She gulped. "It's not quite that simple. They're hidden behind several layers of encryption. I can break through it, but it'll take a little while."

"Define a little while. Are we talking a couple of days, or are we talking weeks?"

She looked him square in the eye. That was one she could answer with total honesty. "I don't know. I wish I did."

He leaned back, studying her with laser intensity. She had the distinct feeling he wasn't buying her line for a second. But she had to play out this farce. And in his own way, so did he.

"Where have you lived all this time?" he fired at her.

"Gavarone. I travel some in the course of managing Eduardo's money, but mostly he keeps me close by."

"Wants to keep an eye on you, does he?"

She snorted. "More like an iron fist over my head."

Dutch said nothing in response to that one.

The silence deepened as she waited for him to cook up some other horribly awkward question. Her father always said the best defense was a good offense. Maybe it was time to borrow a page out of Eduardo's book. She leaned forward and fired off a question of her own. "So. What have you been up to for the last ten years?"

Dutch's frown deepened. He shrugged enigmatically. "The same old thing. Doing my damnedest to keep the world safe for democracy."

She remarked, "That's become quite a tall order in the last decade."

"If it's not one thing, it's another," he replied. "My kind aren't ever going to be out of work."

The conversation lapsed. She ought to keep him talking. Keep him distracted. But she was so relieved to escape the charge of the conversation, she didn't push.

The tension between them must have been thicker than she realized, because she noticed a guy several tables over looking at them. As soon as she made eye contact with him, he jerked his gaze to his plate. Creepy kind of fellow. So boringly plain and brown he practically faded into the background and became invisible. Eating alone.

She murmured to Dutch in quiet concern, "A guy over there was just looking at me."

Dutch's lips curved in a wry smile. "I expect most of the men in this restaurant have been looking at you. You're a beautiful woman."

Flustered by the comment, she made a production of folding her napkin beside her plate.

Dutch said under his breath, "Let's get out of here. I'll have a look at the guy on the way out."

He paid for the meal with a credit card, and she eyed it

speculatively. A person could access a bank account via plastic, too. She ought to check his wallet for debit cards. She might be able to trace the Charlie Squad account number from one of them.

Dutch ushered her outside. Night had fallen while they ate. How in the world were they supposed to ski back to the resort up that narrow, dark trail? But Dutch set off confidently, leaving her to follow dubiously. He didn't take the same trail they'd used before. Although as narrow as the last one, this trail sloped downhill away from the restaurant.

Initially, the trail passed across reasonably open terrain and she could see the path in the moonlight. But then flanking walls of black pines closed in, casting the trail into pitch darkness. Her right foot lurched. She flailed but managed to maintain her balance. Her ski had caught on something and her binding yanked loose, separating her boot from her ski.

She called out to Dutch, who was pulling away from her rapidly, "Wait! I popped a binding."

Dutch turned around and muscled his way back up the incline toward her. "Can you step back into it yourself?"

"Tried already. There's something wedged in the bottom of my boot and I can't knock it loose."

"Hang on." He made his way to her side and leaned down, touching her leg just above her knee. She jumped at the uncanny familiarity. His big palm slid down her leg and cupped her calf. "Use my shoulder to steady yourself," he murmured.

He pried loose a piece of broken tree branch and guided her boot back into her ski. The binding closed with a solid click. He started to stand up but froze halfway to his feet. Abrupt tension flowed through him under her hand. She froze as well. He eased by slow degrees the rest of the way to vertical. Silence settled around them in a dim, fluffy blanket of black on white. And then something else. The sound that must have made Dutch freeze in his tracks. A sound of something slick, synthetic, rubbing on branches. Like a nylon ski jacket.

Dutch's powerful arm swept around her waist, and he tipped her over, half burying her in a deep snowbank. A light dusting of crystalline snow showered down upon her.

She shook her head to clear the snow off her face and Dutch's hand clapped over her jaw, halting the movement. His arm lay over her chest, and his body half covered hers. Warm breath touched her ear, and she felt the snow there melt against her skin. She lay in the embrace of the snow and the man, paralyzed by the heat inside her and the cold without.

A chill began to seep through her clothing, the deep painful kind that went straight to her bones. She did her best to suppress the shivering that set in, but her body had other ideas. She shook like a leaf beneath Dutch and found herself abruptly grateful for his weight pressing down upon her, holding her still.

And then she heard another swishing noise. This time from skis cautiously sliding across snow. If it was possible, Dutch went even more still. She held her breath and made like a tree. A nice, warm one that didn't shiver.

Swish, swish…

Her entire being hummed with terror as the noise passed by them, not more than a dozen feet away. Dutch eased away from her and looked down. His intense gaze met hers. He didn't have to say anything aloud. She was to stay quiet, follow his instructions and not do anything foolish. He nodded fractionally and then stood up slowly as complete silence descended upon them again. He stood there for a long time before he finally held a hand down to her.

She was numb with cold and fear as he pulled her to her feet. Who had that been? Just another tourist making his way back to the resort after supper, or someone more sinister? Her gut said it was the latter. Dutch's gut must have told him the same thing, because his jaw all but rippled with tension.

"Let's go," he breathed in her ear. "We're going to give this guy a head start to get well away from us. When we go, we'll move quickly and quietly. No talking. Keep up with me or stay as close as you can. If we get separated, I'll meet you at my car in the parking lot. Don't go back to our chalet by yourself. Got all that?"

"Yes." And then she asked the question burning a hole in her tongue. "Did you see who that was?"

His terse answer chilled her worse than any snowbank ever could. "That was your admirer from the restaurant. If I had to guess, that's one of Eduardo's men."

Chapter 6

Julia staggered and might have fallen if Dutch's arm hadn't gone around her. As he pulled her close to his side, she shuddered against his solid warmth. She didn't know how long she stood there, absorbing his body heat and silent reassurance.

"Talk to me." His voice was low and urgent against her temple. "Who was that guy?"

"I've never seen him before. He's not one of my father's regulars," she answered into his chest.

"Tell me what you know about these jokers so I know what I'm up against here," he urged.

"I can tell you this much. The only contract guys my father hires to do his dirty work are the very best money can buy."

Dutch's gaze bored into her, measuring the truth of her words. "Give me the financial information now. I'll call in the authorities and we'll take your father down. Then we can nab this guy and call him and his team off."

She whispered, "It's not that simple—" Her voice broke.

He gazed at her in entreaty. "I swear, I can help you if you'll let me."

How was she supposed to answer that? He'd already declared his intention to hurt her the same way she'd hurt him. She *could not* tell him about Carina's situation. She stared back at him wordlessly, watching in dismay as his compassion slowly changed to frustration.

"I want to help you, Julia, but I can't if you won't let me."

His disappointment rolled over her, too much after the emotional drain of the last few weeks, not to mention the last few minutes. She didn't have the strength to fight him. Nor did she want to. Gazing up at him, she absorbed his terrible tension into herself. Long seconds ticked by. Ever so gradually, the rigidity in his shoulders eased and the flat line of his mouth relaxed.

He finally asked, his voice low and pained, "Are you afraid of me?"

"Should I be?" she whispered.

He stripped off his gloves and his bare hands came to rest on her neck. She shuddered at her vulnerability as he cupped her neck in his powerful grip. His fingertips trailed lightly over her skin to her nape, and his thumbs pressed lightly under her chin, tilting her face up. She fought an urge to let her eyes drift closed and simply accept the caress or the strangling to come. She stared up into the fathomless darkness of his gaze as he battled some private demon.

"You're trembling," he finally murmured. He was so close his breath felt warm against her lips. And then his mouth touched hers. Lightly. Again, with a little more authority. And then he was really kissing her, his mouth moving across hers with a finesse that was almost reverent. Her knees melted into jelly, and her hands came up to cling to his broad shoulders as his arms swept around her.

The last ten years melted away in an instant, leaving her feelings as raw and vulnerable as they'd ever been where this man was concerned. Faint echoes of a jungle pressing in around them, all sound and steam heat, rang in her ears.

She moaned low in the back of her throat as he dragged her up against him. The heat of his body seared her, even through their ski clothing. His head slanted and she met him halfway, seeking and finding the best angle to meet his tongue with hers, to devour him as voraciously as he devoured her.

His hands roamed up and down her back and her entire being vibrated with the need to get closer to him. She surged against him, and one of his hands slid under her hair to the back of her head. The other slid lower, cupping her buttocks, lifting and tucking her snugly against him. Were it not for the heavy ski boots she wore, she'd have wrapped one of her legs around his waist, so great was her instinct to feel the hard length of him against her feminine softness.

His tongue plunged inside her mouth and she ran her tongue around his, sparring with him to see who could eat the other alive first. The short hairs at the back of his neck slid under her fingers, and the solid muscles there corded with tension.

And so it was that she felt the moment that his rampant lust shifted into reluctant self-control. No! She wanted more of him! Reluctantly, she forced herself not to cling as he eased back from the embrace. His kisses lightened and then retreated completely, and somehow she found the strength to let him go. It was one of the hardest things she'd ever done.

He stroked her cheek lightly with his thumb. His brooding gaze captured hers in the scant light. He stared at her for a long, pensive moment.

"Maybe you *should* be afraid of me, Julia."

A shiver snaked down her spine. Maybe she should, indeed.

* * *

Holy hell and damnation. What had he been thinking to kiss her like that? He was *not* some raw recruit who let his crotch compromise missions.

Of course, Julia was doing her damnedest to compromise this mission all on her own. What was it going to take for her to give him the information he needed to unravel what the hell was going on? He could smell the currents flowing around her like smoke, but he couldn't *see* them.

Her soulfully delivered story of the last decade was all well and good, but she was leaving out all the important parts. Why did she still refuse to trust him? He'd been steadily taking care of her, setting aside the past and protecting her just as he'd said he would. What more did she want from him before she started helping him?

He realized he was skiing aggressively, shooting down the trail with reckless abandon. He slowed so he wouldn't lose her completely. But when he emerged onto the main trail, she was right behind him. Hell of a skier. Either that or she didn't give a damn if she broke her neck.

She'd told the truth about one thing though. The guys trailing them were pros. How in the hell they'd even found this place, let alone figured out he and Julie were here, baffled him. The United States was such a transparent country it was damn hard to hide for any period of time. But twenty-four hours? How had Ferrare's men tracked them down so quickly?

Was there a radio tracker in her personal possessions? It would explain a lot. He'd have to check when they got back to the hotel. Surely his gear was still clean. They couldn't have connected him to her. Unless—

He completed the thought reluctantly. Bitterly. Unless she was setting him up again.

He swore under his breath. He'd always scorned men who let beautiful women turn their heads and wreck their lives, but damned if his neck didn't feel twisted around like a corkscrew right about now. He was a fool, and that's all there was to it.

Usually he was the master of knowing when to cut his losses, of knowing how to bend without breaking, of giving up the small defeat now in favor of the greater victory later. But this situation with Julia completely stumped him.

Near the bottom of the mountain, they skied into the lights from the night run at the resort. He let his speed build, burning off a fraction of the rage and lust pounding through him. That kiss had been one for the record books. How could any guy not want more where that came from? He was only human, after all. Looked like another cold shower in store for him tonight.

He headed for the dark side of the main lodge, and made Julia lurk in the shadows with him for nearly half an hour before he was satisfied it was safe to approach their chalet. Either her goons weren't around, or—scary thought—they were better than he was.

He rushed her inside and tore through all her gear after a hurried apology for what he had to do. Once he told her what he was looking for, she stood by without complaint and let him have at her things. The underwear and lingerie brought unexpected heat to his face. But he gritted his teeth and made it through the exercise without dying of embarrassment.

"All clean," he announced a couple of minutes later.

"Thank God," she murmured.

"Time to get out of here," he announced.

To her credit, she didn't utter a single syllable of complaint. She just sucked it up and repacked her things in about five minutes. Another five to wipe the place down for fingerprints,

and two more to call the owners, thank them for their hospi-
tality, and let them know about their abrupt departure.

Dutch scouted around outside while she waited in the dark
for long minutes. Finally, he motioned her to join him outside. He tossed her bags in the back of his SUV but conspic-
uously left his on the ground. Time to call her bluff.

Julia stared at Dutch dubiously. *Now* what was he up to?
He held out his hand and she looked down at it. His car keys
lay in his palm.

"You want me to drive?" she asked in confusion.

"No. I'm giving you a chance to run. You've been itching
to get away from me, and I'm going to let you go."

Her gaze snapped up to his. He was letting her go? Why?
And why was her stomach sinking in dismay and not soaring
in elation?

He forged on grimly. "You could've left me lying on the
floor when I hit my head, but you didn't. You stayed and took
the time and risk to make sure I was okay. I owe you one."
He jingled the keys lightly. "Go on. Take them."

Her hand moved toward the keys. Then fell back to her
side. She looked up at him regretfully. "I don't want to leave
you. I feel safe when I'm with you. I *am* safe when I'm with
you. If only you'd—"

He jumped all over that one. "If only I'd what?"

She winced. "If only you'd promise to give me some time.
I won't take any more than I need. I swear."

"How long do you need?"

"I have to stay alive until—" She broke off, horrified at
what she'd almost blurted out.

"Until what?" he asked urgently.

"I'm sorry, Dutch. I can't. It doesn't involve you."

He ground out, "Look. I've been busting my butt to keep

you safe. Everything about you is my business right now. If you can't give me the answers I need, then I can't do my job. You and I are finished."

Her gaze snapped to his. That meant he was free to follow through on his promise to kill her. Not yet! Carina wasn't free!

He had her between a rock and a hard place, and they both knew it. She sighed. "Okay. Fine. I'll tell you more. But not here. Not now. We're standing out in the open with my father's men poking around very nearby. Let's get somewhere safe and then we can talk."

Thankfully, he didn't split hairs over her choice of words. She hadn't promised to tell him everything. Just more. That left her a lot of wiggle room.

"Please," she pleaded.

He stared at her for a long time. Finally, he answered heavily, "What you're asking of me goes against my better judgment."

She retorted desperately, "I'm *asking* you to save my life. And I'm offering to hand you my father. None of that has changed."

Another long pause. A sigh. "All right. You can have some time."

Thank God. Without thinking about what she was doing, she flung herself against him with all the abject relief of a death-row inmate who'd been given a last-minute reprieve. He caught her in his arms and held her close, sheltering her with his strength the way he always did.

"But you have to promise me something, too," he murmured against her temple.

"What's that?"

"You won't try to run away from me again."

She'd be crazy to run from the one person who could keep her safe. Even if he did pose a real threat to her safety when this was all over. What a choice. Probable death now without him, certain death later with him. She mulled over the idea for a moment. Ultimately, she'd rather face Dutch's wrath than her father's hired killers.

Although his condition did raise the question of why exactly it was so important to him that she not leave him. Was there more going on in his heart than met the eye? Did he still harbor feelings for her? Interesting. All the more reason to stay. She answered solemnly, "I promise. I won't try to run away."

He wrapped her tightly in his arms, burying his face in her hair for an instant. So fast she wasn't entirely sure he'd done it.

He murmured, "We probably ought to get going."

She sighed and let go of him reluctantly.

With a last, reassuring squeeze, he let her go and unlocked the passenger door, holding it for her as she climbed in. He climbed into the driver's seat and put the key in the ignition, but he paused before starting the car.

He looked over at her grimly. "Last chance to leave me, Julia. Once we go to ground, we stay together until this thing is over."

She gave him a grim look of her own and nodded her understanding. "Let's do it."

Dutch drove south for a couple of hours, stopping at the first decent-size hotel they came to in Durango, in southern Colorado. He checked in quickly and parked around back. His need to hide her from her pursuers was overpowering. It went far beyond professional concern. *And that was a problem.*

Somewhere along the way tonight, he'd come to a realization. He didn't feel nearly the burning need to kill Julia that he had a scant twenty-four hours ago. He still wanted to get

justice for his brother, of course, but he had set aside his
wrath for now. Just for now, he assured himself.

He hustled her through the door to their room, breathing
a sigh of relief when its darkness enveloped them. He felt her
move beside him and caught her hand in midair as she reached
for the light switch. For caution's sake, he pushed her down
into a crouch by the door, and in the scant light creeping
through the curtains, signaled her to stay put. She nodded
fearfully, and he reached for his gun.

Bending over at the waist, he raced silently across the
room and plastered himself beside the bathroom door.
Crouching, he spun into the room, pistol first. Quick scan. No
targets. Same treatment to the tiny closet. All clear.

He stowed his pistol and flipped on the lights. In the spill
of yellow, Julia looked like a scared rabbit huddled shivering
by the door. He strode over to her, picked her up, coat and all,
and carried her to the couch. He sat down with her in his lap.

She felt like an ice cube and was shaking like a leaf. He
held her close for a long time, gifting her with his heat until
her trembling subsided. But then he made a tactical mistake.
He buried his nose in her silky hair, inhaling the spicy scent
of her until the fantasy spinning out in his head made it all
but impossible to sit still beneath her. Business, dammit! It
was an act of sheer will to drag his mind back to the situation
at hand.

"Okay, Julia. Talk."

"Before I give you my father's books, we have to figure
out which federal authorities you're going to hand them over
to."

"I'll take them to the FBI, of course. And they'll take it to
the IRS, Treasury Department, Justice Department, and the
Secret Service, depending on what the records reveal."

Julia frowned. "That's what I thought, but here's the thing.

The FBI's compromised. My father's got a man on the inside. He could foul up the legal process. Make an intentional mistake to get the case against my father thrown out or something."

He lurched. "How in the hell do you know Eduardo's got a mole in the FBI?"

"I'm my father's banker, remember? I write the checks."

"Jeez. Who is it?" he demanded, fury simmering in his gut. He and his teammates busted their asses every day in the name of defending their country, while some schmuck at a desk was selling it out behind their backs? Make that fury *boiling* in his gut.

Julia answered, "I don't know who it is. I wire the money to an offshore account in the Bahamas. I can give you the account number, I suppose. Your people could track it down and probably get a name."

"If you'll get started retrieving your old man's books, I'll figure out where to go with them. And you can damn well be sure I won't hand them over to any traitor. They'll stay within Charlie Squad completely if they have to. Nobody's screwing up this case."

She flinched. Did the idea of Charlie Squad handling the entire case scare her? He *had* announced that he was going to kill her; she had good cause to be scared of the whole squad. He shouldn't have threatened her. He'd put her on the defensive, dammit. He knew better than to let his personal feelings get in the way of the mission. Now that he needed her trust, she wasn't about to give it to him. How was he supposed to earn it back?

He asked as gently as he could, "Tell me a little bit about what you do for your father."

"If it involves his money, I do it or he does it himself. Nobody else touches it. Ever."

"How does he make his money?"

"I imagine you know about most of his activities. Drugs, arms sales, smuggling, human trafficking. If it's ugly and illegal, he does it."

He frowned at her. "Why wait for his financial records? If you turn state's evidence with what you know about Eduardo, you ought to be able to get full immunity from prosecution right now."

"I just can't."

He cursed under his breath. They were back to that black hole she wouldn't let him see into. What in the hell was she hiding? If he didn't have to stay glued to her side, he might be able to investigate it, figure out what she was holding back. Maybe he should call his boss…see what the squad could scare up on her. Right. Like that wouldn't send up every red flag in the book back at HQ. He'd have some tall explaining to do about why he didn't tell the squad the moment Julia had called him to set up their meeting.

He tensed when Julia laid her head on his shoulder, but then he set aside his turbulent thoughts to focus on the woman sitting in his lap. Shockingly, he gradually found himself relaxing. He allowed himself to savor the show of trust from her. A soft hand crept up to his opposite shoulder, her fingers toying absently with the neck of his sweater. He swore to himself. This woman's slightest touch sent his hormones raging completely out of control. He was rapidly becoming dangerously, excruciatingly aroused. Faced with either embarrassing himself or moving, he chose the latter and disengaged himself from beneath her gently.

She curled up on the couch, as graceful as a newborn colt with her long legs folded beneath her. He was careful to sit on the far edge of the bed, well out of arm's reach of the temptation she represented. But he couldn't help imagining her sprawled on satin sheets beneath him.

As she lost herself in thought, her features relaxed, became more vibrant. Youthful. He blinked. And stared. An absolute certainty came over him. *He'd seen her sit just like that somewhere before.* But where? It tickled just beyond the edges of his consciousness. The way the light was playing across her skin…the dreamy expression in her eyes…damn! *Why couldn't he remember?*

What was it he'd blocked out with the help of all that booze? For surely that night ten years ago he'd drunk himself into a stupor with the intent to forget something.

A chill of foreboding rippled across his skin. Why was he suddenly afraid of the gaping hole in his memory?

A dull headache began to throb at the back of his neck. It beat a painful rhythm in time with the lust still demanding release elsewhere in his body. He felt crazy enough to climb the walls and hang cackling from the ceiling like a madman.

If she weren't sitting there, he'd be pacing the room like a caged lion. Of course, if she weren't sitting there, he wouldn't have reason to pace. He wouldn't be rock hard with no prospects in sight for some seriously gnarly sex to relieve the discomfort.

He shoved to his feet and growled, "I'm gonna go take a shower. You know the drill. Don't open the door for anybody."

When he emerged, blue with cold and only marginally less randy, Julia was curled up on the bed, reading a magazine. He picked up a day-old newspaper, but didn't see a single word of it as he surreptitiously watched her.

When she finally retired at midnight, the thought of her in bed beside him all but broke him. He headed for the minibar in the refrigerator and tossed back a double shot of vodka. It burned a modicum of sanity into his brain. For about a minute. And then he did give in and pace. As her breath settled into the steady rhythm of deep sleep, he prowled back and forth restlessly.

She was the one who'd set up this meeting in the first place. Why, almost as soon as she met him, did she change her mind and try to get away from him? Surely it wasn't his threat to kill her. She had to have known before she ever picked up the phone to contact him that he would blame her for his brother's death. So what changed after they met? It was damn hard for a guy not to take something like that personally.

He needed to get some rest if he was going to be sharp in the morning and stay one step ahead of both Julia and her pursuers. As much as he ought to stay on the couch, he didn't want to.

Girding himself to do battle with his baser instincts, he pulled on a pair of gym shorts and a T-shirt and joined Julia. Her slim shape barely disturbed the covers in the bed, and her breathing was soft and steady in the dark. The warmth generated by her body wrapped around him under the covers and the sleepy, sexy scent of her wafted over him.

He tossed and turned for what seemed like hours. But eventually, he fell asleep.

He was the forward sniper, which meant he'd been lying under a gillie net for almost two days, motionless. His nappie, as the undergarment was fondly called, was almost full. The next time he took a leak, his leg was gonna get wet. Despite drenching himself in bug repellent, the effects of the chemical were wearing off, and gnats pestered him incessantly. It was an exercise in sheer torture not to reach up and swat them from his face.

Night had fallen and the relentless heat of the jungle had begun to ease, but under his mesh blanket woven full of grass and leaves, he still sweltered. Miserable work, but he'd get the first shot at Eduardo Ferrare.

And tonight was the night, here at Ferrare's plush, South American estate. Security conscious and crafty as hell, he'd been a hard man to find, let alone kill. Without Julia's help in pinning down his location, they'd still have been back at square one.

Captain Folly's whispered voice came over Dutch's headset. "Movement on the road."

He eased the sight of his sniper rifle to his eye, only a few inches, but it took upward of a minute to complete the motion. A limousine sprang into focus. Four men stepped out. The smug, smiling face of Eduardo Ferrare moved into the crosshairs. Bingo. Dutch began a slow, steady squeeze on the trigger, cold and precise under his index finger.

And then all hell broke loose.

The jungle lit up around Charlie Squad with muzzle flashes from all directions. There must be twenty positions firing at them! A moment of indecision—did he move and reveal his position or hang his life on his gillie net, concealing his location?

If Ferrare's thugs were using IR equipment—infrared scopes that painted heat—he was toast. Screw it. He rolled and fired behind him at the black-green wall of jungle over his shoulder. Dammit, the whole place was lit up! How the deadly carpet of lead had so far missed him was a mystery.

A cry over his radio. "I'm hit. Gut shot. I'm in trouble here…"

The nightmare spun away from Dutch, lost in the mists of his subconscious. Who in the hell was hit? He struggled to recall the dream, to pull it back into the front of his mind. He had to know! But it slipped away from him like a mysterious

whale, only partially glimpsed, sliding slowly and majesti-
cally into the blackness of the abyss, where no man could follow.

Hell, they'd all been hit that night. Not a single man on the
team had escaped with less than two gunshot wounds. He'd
brought out four lead slugs. He didn't have to remember that
part. He'd seen the scars he and his teammates bore from that
ambush.

A hand touched his shoulder. He jumped, ready to take out
bare-handed whatever bastard of Ferrare's had found him.

"Julia." He sagged back to the mattress and his hands fell
away from her neck. He was soaked in sweat and breathing
like a marathon runner. The aftermath of the nightmare re-
ceded slowly, reluctant to give up its thrall over him. But gradually, awareness of his present surroundings overtook the
heat and darkness of that elusive jungle. The violence remained, though. And the unreasoning terror.

Julia lay half across him, her small breasts smashed against
his chest and more out of the top of her nightgown than in it.
Her hand smoothed his hair, and she murmured a string of
soothing nonsense sounds. Her raven hair fell in a dark curtain around them, blocking out the rest of the world, narrow-
ing down his reality to her smoky, dark eyes and the husky
murmur of her voice.

He watched her lips move, moist and full, mesmerized by
the dark magic she spun around him. He reached up. Pulled
her head down to him. Took her mouth more roughly than he
should have. But she just moaned deep in her throat and gave
way before the raging storm he unleashed upon her. Like a
willow, she bent but did not break, beneath his onslaught. He
rolled over, pinning her beneath him, expecting fear from her
but unable to control the fury ripping through him. Instead,
she smiled. And reached up with her slender arms, twined

them around his neck and opened her thighs to cradle him against her.

Earth magic flowed from her, warm and welcoming. It embraced his rage, containing it but not quenching the fire. Like a drowning man, he stared into her eyes, clinging to the thread of hope she'd thrown to him. Fist by excruciating fist, he hauled himself back from the void, up the lifeline she anchored. And when he finally saw light once more, his spirit soared. For a split second, he knew infinity as all of Nature came together in her.

He drew a shuddering breath, and the beast within retreated. Just like that nightmare colossus, it pulled back slowly into the depths of his mind. He gazed down at her in silent awe. Her mouth curved into a smile, without a doubt the most beautiful sight he'd ever seen.

"Welcome back," she murmured.

He rolled onto his back and flung and arm over his eyes. "Christ, I'm sorry."

She rolled over, propping herself up on his chest. "Whatever for? You had a nightmare and woke up a little disoriented. There's nothing to apologize for."

He pulled his arm down to stare at her. "I damn well do owe you an apology for nearly strangling you, not to mention kissing you."

"But you didn't hurt me," she whispered with aching gentleness. "Maybe you need to lose control more often."

He snorted. "You have no idea what you're suggesting."

She reached up to stroke his cheek, and he felt his whisker stubble abrade her delicate fingertips. "You might be surprised, James Dutcher," she murmured.

"Trust me, you couldn't handle it. I'd hurt you."

Her eyes gleamed with warmth and inner strength. "You didn't hurt me just now."

"Yes, I did. You're lying to be polite." He carried her palm to his mouth and kissed it. "I'm sorry."

A dimple winked in her cheek. "I'm telling you, you didn't hurt me. But, if it'll make you feel better, apology accepted."

"Thanks," he mumbled gruffly. He cleared his throat. "And about kissing you—"

She cut him off. "I'm not accepting any apologies for that. Period. Got it?"

He grinned at her and stroked back her silky hair. "Got it," he murmured.

Lord, he wanted to make love to her right now. Not slick, slamming, sheet-tangling sex, but something slow and easy. Sensual. A give-and-take. The mere thought of it sent a shiver of anticipation up his spine. This was a woman to savor like a fine wine.

What was he thinking?

Julia spoke into his shocked stillness. "It's pretty late. We probably ought to get a little sleep. Lord only knows what tomorrow will bring."

He closed his eyes for a pained moment, forcing back his lecherous thoughts. She was right. And he was a horny bastard. He pulled her down into the crook of his arm and tucked her head on his shoulder.

"Tomorrow will take care of itself," he growled. "We'll worry about that in the morning. Sleep now."

She snuggled against him like a sleek, contented kitten, and promptly went back to sleep. He sighed and settled in for a night of unfulfilled lust, but surprisingly, found himself relaxing into peaceful slumber.

His last thought before he went unconscious was that he and Julia were racing down the fast track to disaster. But who the hell cared? It was going to be one incredible ride.

Chapter 7

They slept late, and Dutch awoke to a gorgeous, sunny morning, refreshed from a no-kidding, decent night's sleep. He couldn't remember the last time he'd had one of those. Only a faint residue of his nightmare remained, tainting the bright light of morning with its ominous shadow. He'd been trained in how to deal with violent thoughts and memories, and with a little work he was able to put the horror of his nightmare into perspective. However, the exercise left behind a deep restlessness within him.

They got in the SUV and he drove like a man on the run from something that scared the hell out of him. Truth be told, he *was* scared. Scared of what Julia did to his head.

And of what she did to his heart.

He drove until late that night, heading west this time, into New Mexico. The first order of business was to ditch whoever was following them. Then he'd worry about getting Julia access to a secure computer and an Internet connection.

What was it about those snippets of memory that had him so freaked out? He knew the high points of what he was starting to recall already. It's not as if any big shocks awaited him. Too damn many unanswered questions were floating around in his head, and not only about his lost memories. He was ready for some solid answers.

He felt like a runaway train, gathering more and more speed as he rolled toward a terrible calamity. Since this crazy mission had begun, it seemed as though the only glue holding him together was the gentle, frightened woman beside him. Frustration rumbled through him. How could she be the cause of his problem and the cure? It made no sense.

He glanced over at Julia. She'd been silent for much of the day, staring out the car window, her eyes dark and troubled. If he could only get inside her head! But she steadfastly held him at arm's length.

Which was just as well because he needed to focus all his attention on what he was doing. He wasn't used to operating inside the United States. Most of his work took place overseas in nasty corners of the world with little or no technology, archaic telecommunications systems, and in some cases, barely any electricity. This country was a whole lot harder to hide in.

It was late, he was getting tired, and the winding mountain roads were treacherous in the dark. He was going to get them killed if he pushed too much harder. He started looking for someplace to stop for the night.

The unrelenting darkness of the mountains began to give way before the lights of civilization, and gift shops and hotels became abundant. They were getting close to Santa Fe and its dense tourist population. Perfect. He randomly picked one of the many midpriced, medium-size hotels in the area and checked in. Hopefully, he and Julia would get lost in the sheer volume of people in a place like this.

He parked so his vehicle wasn't visible from the street and led Julia in a side entrance. He took a quick look at the layout of the building as they headed for their room. Standard H. Two long halls of rooms connected by a crossing hallway in the middle. Elevators, ice machines and stairwells in the middle, fire escapes at the end of each leg of the building.

He dumped his jacket on the bed, its pockets stuffed with a toothbrush, toothpaste, and a razor he'd pulled out of his bags. Julia dropped her oversize purse, similarly loaded, and flopped down wearily on the bed beside his coat. They needed to be able to move fast from here on out, so he'd vetoed unloading any cumbersome luggage.

Though he knew he shouldn't, he sat down beside Julia and reached over to massage her shoulders, rolling the muscles under his hands and working loose the accumulated kinks of stress and fatigue.

She groaned in pleasure as he worked his way down her back and then up each side of her spine with his fingertips.

She mumbled, "Where did you get so good at this?"

He smiled. "It's part of my first-aid training. We get sore after some of the wilder stuff we do."

She looked over her shoulder, grinning widely. "You guys give each other massages like this? I can't say as I pictured that of you big bad Special Forces soldiers."

An errant image of the guys in his squad all sitting around giving each other back rubs popped into his head. He snorted. "Hardly. But our team has a medic who's a miracle worker at keeping us in fighting condition. I've picked up a few things from him over the years."

She turned her head, giving him better access to her neck.

"Well, I'm not complaining about it one bit. This is pure heaven."

He grunted. More like pure hell. The way her skin slid like satin under his palms, the little moans she was making in the back of her throat, the sheer sensual pleasure she allowed herself to feel... Oh yeah. Definitely an inner circle of hell.

He lifted his hands away from her. "A hot shower should take care of the rest," he managed to grit out.

"Thanks," she murmured as she headed straight for the bathroom.

Sure. No sweat. He worked himself into unsatisfied sexual frenzies all the time for fun. No problem. He'd just go over and jump out the window now. He fell back on the bed and groaned in utter frustration.

He lay there for several minutes, doing his damnedest to think about anything except hot water sluicing down that delicious body of hers, turning her skin all rosy and forming rivulets between her breasts, heating up the flesh between her thighs... Hell, maybe he *should* go for the window.

After nearly a half hour, the water finally cut off in the shower. He slitted one eye open lazily and glanced toward the bathroom. Both of his eyes popped open. Julia'd cracked the door open, no doubt to let out the clouds of steam billowing forth, and he had a clear view of the bathroom mirror from where he lay. A vague, honey-colored shape moved sinuously in the foggy glass. *Hello.* His senses leaped to full alert. If he were a gentleman, he'd turn away. But he was just a soldier. And he wanted her worse than he wanted to draw his next breath.

A square of white joined the dusky reflection, gliding across the shapely form. The condensation on the mirror evaporated a bit, and he was able to make out slender arms wrapping languorously around her body as she dried herself.

More detail came into view as the fog cleared. God bless the dry, mountain air! As she bent over to towel her legs, her back was long and graceful. Black, wet hair streamed down it. His hand ached to fist itself in that dark mass and pull her down on top of him, trapping her body against his.

She turned around, and he made out the outline of her breasts. They weren't large, but sweet Mother of God, they were beautifully made. They'd arch up into him so sweetly, with their little hard buds rubbing his skin...

Her face looked foreign, exotic, with her hair slicked back, as her high cheekbones and big, dark eyes came into focus. She fiddled with something on the counter, and then she propped a foot up on the toilet. The mirror cleared a bit more and one long, slender leg came into view. He watched greedily as she smoothed lotion over her thigh, already feeling its sleek smoothness wrapped around his waist. Her hand slid down over the shapely curve of her calf with almost pornographic appeal.

She gave the same maddening treatment to the other leg, and then she reached for another towel. She glanced into the mirror. And froze. Her gaze locked with his in shock. He didn't look away. Couldn't. He was a cad, but he was absolutely mesmerized by the sight of her.

She stared at him for a long moment, and then wrapped the towel absently around herself as she continued to hold his gaze. She felt for the doorknob and pulled it the rest of the way open. And then she was looking at him directly, her eyes smoky with passion.

A step toward him. And another. He willed her closer with his gaze, his male flesh pounding with desperate need to have this cat-eyed beauty. Right now. She put one knee on the bed.

And then he lost his formidable control. He surged up, wrapping her in his arms and tumbling her on top of him. Her skin was hot and damp, and she burned him alive with the fire in her eyes. He tugged at the towel. It slid from between them and he flung it aside.

Her hungry mouth captured his, as incendiary as the rest of her. Ah, good Lord, her breasts felt exactly as he'd imagined against his chest. And then her tongue was inside his mouth, swirling and dancing around his. Somehow, he managed to want her even more ferociously. His lust was downright painful as he dragged her higher against him, devouring her mouth like an addict way overdue for a fix.

Her silken legs straddled his hips and he groaned as her burning flesh rubbed against him. He was dangerously close to exploding. She laughed deep in her throat, a husky, throaty sound that was pure sex. Who'd have guessed that inside sweet Julia lurked such a tigress? She was driving him plumb out of his mind!

But the further he spun out of control, the more fear gripped him. Finally, drenching terror overwhelmed his lust and made him break out in a cold sweat. Control was the one thing he must not let go of. Dared not. The beast within surged, clawing at his sanity. A driving need to do violence roared up like a volcano from deep within him. No! Not to Julia!

He tore his mouth away from hers, panting wildly in his struggle to wrestle down the strange, primitive urge inside him. How long he fought it, he didn't know. But gradually he became aware of her soft hands cupping his face. Her dark, worried eyes gazing at him.

Dammit! He'd almost lost it completely, and he hadn't even had a blackout or a nightmare! Dread coiled like a viper lurking in the detritus of his mind. He had to get control of himself. And having sex with Julia sure as hell wasn't the way to do that.

He rolled out from underneath her and stood up, pushing his hand through his short hair. He swore viciously, reining in his disgust at himself enough to mumble, "Dammit, I'm sorry, Julia. I'm a bastard."

He stumbled to the shower and turned on the hot water full blast. He braced his hands against the cold tile, his head hanging low. He hardly felt the water's scalding needles stinging his skin. What in the hell was he going to do? His career, his *life*, was slipping through his fingers like sand, and he couldn't seem to snatch a single grain of it back.

Julia lay naked on the bed, stunned. What had just happened? To her and to Dutch? One hot look from him, and she'd walked straight into his arms and his bed without a second thought. Was she crazy? She knew better than to let down her guard with him. Every time he looked deep into her eyes, she lost another piece of her heart.

He obviously wanted her so bad he could hardly stand it. She was sure of that. How any guy in his right mind walked away from a woman who was as eager as she was to jump into the sack, she had no idea. But the self-discipline he could muster up was nearly beyond her comprehension. Thank goodness for it, or heaven only knew what kind of mess she'd be in now. She had no business even contemplating sleeping with a man, much less one who planned to kill her.

Abruptly aware of her nudity, she hastily pulled on her clothes. She fished around in Dutch's coat pocket and found his keys. She needed his Internet-capable computer. It was time to end this game.

She slipped out of the hotel room and hurried down to the parking lot. She found his laptop in the back seat, next to a plastic grocery bag of food. She grabbed both and headed back to the room. She slipped the key card into its slot and pushed the door open. And only managed to gasp before a hand slapped over her mouth, cutting off all her air. Panic slammed into her almost as hard as the big, hot body behind her did. *Dutch.*

He must have recognized her in almost the same instant she recognized him, because the iron hand fell away from her mouth and she stumbled as she was abruptly released from his powerful grasp.

He demanded, "What the hell were you thinking, going out by yourself? You could've been jumped and snatched before I had any idea there was a problem."

His jaw rippled with tension. She sighed. He was right. She hadn't stopped to think about her safety before she'd raced out to get the computer.

"And for God's sake," he lectured, "if you do get separated from me, announce yourself before you come barging back into the room. I could've broken your neck!"

She looked up into his eyes and asked gently, "Do you honestly think you could ever hurt me?"

His anguished blue gaze met hers. His answer sounded torn from his throat. "I don't know what I'm doing half the time anymore, dammit."

"I went out to the car to get the laptop so I can get to work on downloading Eduardo's records."

He nodded grimly. "I'm gonna go shave and finish getting dressed. Have at it."

She noticed for the first time since he'd nearly scared the life out of her that he was shirtless. His stomach and chest were a breathtaking mass of muscle. He was so beautiful to look at it practically made her ache.

Somehow, she tore her gaze away from him and sat down at the room's desk. She plugged the computer into the phone jack the hotel provided. Finally. Access to his computer.

Maybe she could find the Charlie Squad bank account number while she was at it. Bypassing the minimal security on his machine was a piece of cake. It was designed to keep out a casual hacker—not a banker and security expert like her. She scrolled down through the directory of files on the machine, looking quickly for one that might have the bank account number in it.

"So tell me something, Dutch," she called through the open door of the bathroom. "How come a good-looking guy like you is still single?"

A snort over the sound of water running in the sink. "No time."

No sign of the information she was looking for, although there was a cluster of encrypted files. Probably not a good idea to break into them right now when he could stroll out of the bathroom anytime and see what she was doing.

She asked aloud, "Meaning you don't have the time or you don't make the time?" Her fingers raced over the keyboard, signing the system on to the Internet. No answer from Dutch. She glanced up and saw him staring at her in the mirror.

"Why do you ask?" he rumbled warningly.

She typed in her password to the server she usually used. A welcome message flashed on the computer screen. She shrugged. "Just trying to get to know you a little better. I mean," she added, "it's not like it's any surprise to me that you're single."

The water cut off abruptly. Damn. He stepped out into the bedroom, shaving cream smeared all over his face. "Why's *that?*" he demanded indignantly.

She grinned to herself and, accessing a search engine, typed in a search command for Eduardo Ferrare and a bank in Hong Kong.

For the last few weeks she'd been methodically searching

every major bank in every major banking city in the world. That account was out there somewhere. She'd find it eventually. It was only a matter of time.

As the computer hummed, performing the search, she looked up from the keyboard. And leaned back in her chair, captivated by his reaction to her comment. His shoulders were all bunched up around his ears, and she could see his jaw muscles moving, even under a layer of shaving cream. Oh, he was really annoyed. Didn't like having his romantic prowess questioned, did he?

Amused, she answer lightly, "Well, you're such a control freak, I can't imagine any woman putting up with you for too long."

"A control freak?" he all but bellowed.

She bit back outright laughter. "Well, yes."

He spun and stomped back into the bathroom. She watched him in the mirror pick up his razor and begin slashing at his face with it.

She commented blandly, "Be careful, there. You wouldn't want to slit your throat by accident."

She caught his glare and looked away hastily before she could laugh aloud and further bruise his ego. She noticed information was beginning to scroll across the computer screen. She leaned forward eagerly, scanning the information rolling down the screen.

Bingo. She typed commands furiously and more information popped up. It was true. Eduardo did have a bank account in Hong Kong that he'd tried to hide from her. Her ace in the hole.

She'd stumbled across the account number and password inside Eduardo's private address book by accident a couple of years ago. That mistake was the only reason she even knew about the account's existence. What she'd lacked was the name of the bank. She'd had no way to search for it without being traced through her father's computer system.

For the last few weeks, she'd searched furiously for the information. With access to that account, plus the thirty million dollars she'd stolen, she could exert enough financial pressure on Eduardo to force him to release Carina.

Today, she'd found the bank in Hong Kong. It had an account in the name of Eduardo J. Ferrare. It had to be her father. How many people with the name Ferrare had VIP bank accounts in Hong Kong, for goodness' sake?

She entered her father's password and asked for the total current value of the account. The computer blinked, accessing the information.

She jumped as Dutch turned out the light in the bathroom and stepped into the room behind her. Crud. She had to go. She couldn't risk Dutch seeing this information. Not yet.

She reached for the power switch to turn off the computer, and as her finger approached the button, an answer popped up on the screen. She stared at it for a millisecond of utter disbelief and then hit the power button.

Oh. My. God.

Chapter 8

*D*utch thrashed against the tangle around his legs. The damned gillie net wouldn't let go of him. He had to get moving. One of their guys was down, and a hail of lead was flying over his head.

"Report!" he bellowed into the throat mike over the sound of the gunfire. "Who's hit? Where are you?"

"It's Simon. I'm at your—" a gurgling gasp "—ten o'clock. Don't come—" another liquid rasp "—over here. Too hot."

That was a death rattle if he'd ever heard one. Dutch cursed foully. Not Simon. Not his kid brother. "Hang in there, you little twerp," he yelled in his mike. "Don't you die on me!"

He jumped up and took off running in Simon's direction. The green-black jungle seemed to stretch on forever around him, slow-motion flashes of hot lead zinging past in a red laser pattern all around him. He zigzagged and leapfrogged *side to side as he fired randomly to his left at the unseen ambushers.*

A scream from in front of him. He hit the dirt, rolled, and came to a skidding halt in a firing position with his rifle against his cheek. The scene before him came into focus just as one of Ferrare's men leaned down, knife in hand, over Simon's prone body. Dutch barely felt the bullet slam into his own leg, so intent was he on the macabre scene playing out before him.

"Nooooo!" he screamed. He pulled the trigger over and over until the rifle clicked, empty…

Dutch lurched awake, bolt upright in bed. He rubbed his palms across his sweat-soaked face and realized his hands were shaking. Bad. His whole body was shaking, in fact.

Simon. An agony of loss ripped through him. He'd always known his brother died a violent death. How in the hell could he have forgotten the way his brother had *suffered?* The way Julia Ferrare had set him up to suffer? A need for vengeance sliced through him, as cold and sharp as an assassin's stiletto.

Her body language at the computer earlier shouted that she'd found some or all of what she'd been looking for. She'd almost suckered him in again. Almost convinced him she was basically a decent person who was just the victim of her father's machinations. But look what she'd done to his baby brother. Only a viper of the worst kind could do that to another human being and live with themselves.

Julia rolled over and mumbled something at him. God, he needed to hurt her. To make her feel the pain Simon had felt. He literally shook with the effort to hold his hands still at his sides. How long he fought himself, he couldn't say. By the time he finally beat back the violence humming through him, he was drenched with sweat. Exhausted.

Still breathing hard, he tried desperately to remember more

about the ambush, but nothing came back to him. Just a flood
of memories of Simon when they were kids, raising hell and
becoming men together. Entering Charlie Squad together.
He'd always protected his little brother. Taken care of him.
Until that night in the jungle. He'd failed Simon big-time then.

He must have dozed off, because he woke with another
lurch some time later. He was startled to see light creeping
around the curtains. He'd slept through the rest of the night?
Thank God. Maybe a couple hours' sleep would hold at bay
any more of those blasted nightmares. Were he not in the habit
of being so brutally honest with himself, he'd pretend he
wasn't scared of the damn things. But he was. And it galled
him. What kind of soldier was afraid of his own brain? *A crazy
one about to be out of a job.*

He slid out of bed quietly. Julia was still sleeping peace-
fully on her side of the king-size bed. Lord, she was beautiful. How could she be responsible for so much hurt and
betrayal? A fleeting taste of last night's rage soured his tongue.

He pulled on his pants and a shirt and shrugged into his
coat. He'd slip out and get some breakfast for them. He let
himself out of the room quietly, strode down the hallway and
trotted down the stairs. He reached for the handle of the exit
door and froze.

He spun away from the clear glass, plastering his big frame
against the wall. Out of sight of the four men peering in the
windows of his SUV.

Son of a—

He slid along the wall slowly, easing away from the door.
When he was clear of the men's sight line, he turned and
sprinted for the stairs. He burst into the room and Julia lurched
awake. He ordered sharply, "Get up. We've got to go. Now."

Her eyes were huge and black as she stumbled out of bed
and pulled on her clothes. He stuffed what little gear they had

into his coat pockets. No time to wipe down the room for prints. Besides, the bastards knew they were here. No need to cover their tracks.

He tucked the laptop under his arm and headed for the door the second Julia's head emerged from her sweater. He eased the door open and peered out into the hallway. Clear. He stepped out with her close on his heels and headed for the front of the hotel, away from their pursuers. They approached the crossing hallway. The elevator dinged, announcing its imminent arrival on the second floor. A gut instinct honed over years of fieldwork exploded a warning in his brain. He reversed course rapidly, grabbing Julia by the arm and spinning her around to run beside him in the opposite direction.

"Where to?" she gasped.

A long hallway stretched before them. He dared not return to their room. A maid's cleaning cart stood at the far end of the hall. It was a long distance to cover in a few seconds, but an open doorway stood beside it. If they could just make that door…

He put on an extra burst of speed, stretching his long legs into a full sprint for their lives. He half lifted Julia, propelling her along beside him.

"Jump!" he ordered at the last second before he went airborne.

They dived for the door. He twisted and landed on his shoulder. Julia landed on top of him and he absorbed the impact with a grunt.

He looked up and saw a maid drawing breath to scream. Crap. And then Julia was talking low and urgent in rapid Spanish.

She clambered off him and he climbed to his feet beside her. He listened as she quickly explained to the maid that the two of them were running from Immigration agents who were after her. The maid nodded sagely, pulled her cleaning cart all the way into the room, and closed the door behind her. Damn, Julia could lie like a pro.

The woman eyed Dutch critically. In Spanish, she said, "He will be a close fit. But I think we can get him out the usual way."

The usual way? What the heck had they stumbled into here? Some sort of underground railroad?

Julia frowned and gave voice to his thoughts. "The usual way?"

The maid smiled. "You are far from the first illegal to come through here. We take care of our own."

Julia thanked her with warm sincerity and a graceful offer of compensation for the risks the woman was offering to take. Dutch's Spanish was fluent, but Julia was working the woman so well that he kept his mouth shut. The maid was visibly responding to Julia's gentle, compassionate nature. If he didn't already know Julia's *true* nature, he'd buy her act hook, line and sinker. Here was full proof that he was standing before a truly accomplished actress.

He tuned back in to what she was saying. "...so we ride in the cart to the hotel's laundry and then a couple of the maintenance guys will carry us outside? Are you sure they can pick up my friend? He's pretty big."

Dutch sighed. The bane of his special-ops career—his size. Sometimes it was damn hard to hide six and a half feet of muscular body.

"Where will they take us once we're outside?" he murmured to Julia in English.

She turned to the maid and relayed the question. He blinked at the maid's answer. A Dumpster? Could be damn dangerous if a trash truck came along and tossed them in its crusher. But the maid went on to explain that they'd signal the driver by tying a cloth to a handle on the Dumpster so he'd know he had human cargo.

Not a bad scam. "What's it going to cost us?" he asked under his breath. "I've got about two grand in cash on me."

Julia smiled and turned to the maid. "Is a thousand dollars cash thanks enough to all of you for the risk you will be taking?" She added apologetically, "It's all we can spare at the moment, but we can get you more if you need it."

The maid's gaping mouth was answer enough. They had their escape route. A few last details were worked out quickly. This maid would leave now with Julia hidden in the bottom of her cleaning cart. Another maid would be by in a little while to pick him up. He didn't like being separated, but it seemed to be the only way. He pulled the cash out of his wallet and handed it to the maid.

He put a hand on Julia's arm and stared down at her. "Be careful," he murmured. "And don't go anywhere without me."

She smiled up at him. Healing warmth spread through him whether he liked it or not. She had the damnedest effect on him.

"You, too," she murmured. A pause. "It's going to feel strange being separated from you."

He nodded tersely. "Time to go."

She clung to his hand for a moment and then stepped back resolutely. He helped her curl up in the compartment that usually stored buckets and other miscellaneous cleaning equipment. How in the hell he was supposed to fit in that tiny space, he had no idea. But he'd find a way. Damned if he was getting left behind. He shut the compartment's door and nodded at the maid. She opened the hallway door and slipped out with her secret cargo.

And then he was alone. Oddly enough, it felt as though part of himself was missing. Restless, he peered around the edges of the drawn curtains. As he'd expected. One of Julia's pursuers from the ski resort was patrolling the parking lot. He had a big fat black eye.

Dutch shifted his surveillance to the hallway door's peephole. It only took about five minutes for the pair of guys who'd jumped Julia in his hotel room that first day to come into view. They looked grim. Determined.

Dutch pulled his eye away from the peephole once they were past. He felt pretty grim right about now, too. How in the *hell* had these guys found him and Julia so fast? He'd used his nontraceable credit card issued by the government for when he was on Charlie Squad missions to pay for their room. Did Julia's pursuers have police contacts? Maybe Eduardo's FBI mole? Who else could have found them this fast? His estimation of the threat to Julia notched up yet another level.

Where were the rest of the guys who'd been chasing Julia? Surely they were around here somewhere. His hackles lifted at the thought of more of these jerks roaming around without him knowing where they were.

The good news was, the thugs couldn't bust into every room in the hotel looking for him and Julia. The bad news was, they might convince the manager to let them into his and Julia's original room. Then the bastards would know how close behind the two of them they really were. And there was nothing more persistent than a bloodhound after it acquired a fresh scent.

The pair of men patrolling the hallway passed by twice more. Definitely scouting. Not much he could do now but sit tight and wait for his ride.

He looked around the hotel room. Comfortable as cages went. A strong sense of déjà vu broadsided him as he paced the confined space. He'd done this before. In similar circumstances.

His head started to hurt. He shut the curtains to block out

the painful sunlight and stretched out on the bed. He closed his eyes against the throbbing in his temples.

The room's walls began to close in on him, and abruptly he was sitting in another hotel room, in another place and time. He'd been waiting for Julia then, too. Waiting to give her final instructions for leaving Gavarone in case she couldn't get outside before Charlie Squad sprung its trap and she missed her rendezvous with the team.

He'd been too impatient to sit still. So eager to see her he couldn't think straight. Too in love to breathe.

Whoa.

Dutch sat upright abruptly, back in New Mexico in a rush. He'd been in *love* with her? He knew better than to get involved with a target on a mission. He never let his emotions interfere with his work. He was the iceman. The one everyone accused of being a robot because he held his feelings so tightly in check. Even after his brother's death.

He subsided against the pillows, shaken. The longer he lay there, the worse his head hurt. He squeezed his eyes shut and clenched the headboard until his fingers ached. He focused on the pain, concentrating with all his might on holding back the insidious certainty that, on that particular mission, he hadn't been a robot. Hadn't frozen out his feelings. Had let a woman inside his guard. *And it had cost his brother his life.* He couldn't possibly have been in love with Julia!

But the lightness in his heart whenever he'd thought of her was real. The way he'd craved her presence, the way everything had seemed more vivid when she was with him…it wasn't his imagination. And dammit, some of those reactions lingered even now, any time she was near. This very second, her absence rubbed at him, a raw spot that demanded relief.

What sorcery had Julia Ferrare performed to get to him

back then? Whatever it was, she was doing it again. How could he simultaneously love and hate a woman like this?

His control was slipping, inch by inch. He had to fight it. To fight her! But how? He'd sworn to protect her until this was over.

He ought to just kill her now and be done with it. Except breaking his word rankled. Stupid, but that was just the way he was. He'd promised.

The abyss retreated. He felt it hovering near, though, laying in wait for another chance to strike at him.

As the wait for his escape dragged out, his normally prodigious patience stretched thinner and thinner. In his line of work, it wasn't uncommon to sit in the same spot without moving for two days at a time, doing surveillance or waiting for a target to step into his rifle sights. But this separation from Julia was driving him nuts. An overpowering need to see her, to make sure she was safe, rode him.

It was almost two hours later, and he was on the edge of certifiably insane, before a knock finally sounded on the door and a female voice announced, "Housekeeping."

Thank God. He leaped to his feet, stopping only long enough at the peephole to verify that the woman was alone. He let the maid in. The girl was young and very scared looking. "Relax," he said to her lightly in Spanish. "This will be a piece of cake."

She smiled timidly, but it didn't reach her eyes. Great. He didn't need her panicking on him at the worst possible moment. "What's your name?" he asked her as he helped her empty out the bottom of her cart.

"Maria," she mumbled.

"Pretty name. My mother's middle name is Maria. After my grandmother. They're two feisty women. They chased a bear out of our strawberry patch once with an empty shotgun and a golf club."

It was a patent lie, but it brought a real smile to the girl's face, and the terrified set of her shoulders eased a bit. "I bet your mother and grandmother are real fighters, too," he commented. "Takes courage to let your baby girl come to the United States to make a better life for herself."

The girl's shoulders squared even more. Much better. He said briskly, "We're clear on the plan, right? You just wheel your cart from here straight down to the laundry and leave it there. The maintenance guys will take it from there."

She nodded.

He got down on his hands and knees and paused in the act of levering himself into the cramped space. "Thanks," he told her sincerely.

"Piece of cake," the maid replied in halting English.

How he crammed his entire body into the storage space, he had no idea. It was such a tight fit the girl had to stow his laptop computer in the laundry bag at the end of the cart. He recalled his claustrophobia training in survival school and did what he'd been taught. He located the airhole and did his best to relax and slow his breathing. Long before he'd succeeded fully, the hallway door opened and the girl wheeled him out.

The cart stopped in front of the service elevator, waiting for a ride to the basement and safety. A male voice from off to the left asked the maid to stop. Dammit! She mumbled in Spanish that she spoke no English. The guy tried again, in louder English. Not a Spanish speaker, apparently. *Stay cool, Maria. Keep your head.* He willed the girl to hear his thoughts. The elevator dinged. The guy raised his voice even more, and the maid, bless her heart, burst out in a spate of rapid, upset Spanish.

Dutch registered vaguely that her outburst had to do with this guy slowing her down and how much work she had to do and that he was going to get her fired. But what really held his attention was that she pushed the cart on to the elevator as she railed.

The elevator door closed, shutting out the sound of the maid, still protesting the man's interference vociferously. Whew, that had been a close call. What a gutsy girl. As slick a move as he'd ever seen.

He held his position in the cart when the elevator doors opened again. In a few seconds, someone came to investigate, and a hushed female voice asked, "Are you there, señor?"

"Yeah," he murmured back.

"Where is Maria?"

"A man is questioning her upstairs. But she managed to get the cart on the elevator before they could stop her. Does she need help?" Dutch asked urgently.

"I'll go up and check on her."

"Thanks." The last thing he needed was that girl on his conscience.

Thankfully, the cart lurched into motion again. His hamstrings were starting to cramp up, and it was getting damn stuffy. The doors opened abruptly and he squinted at the flood of bright light.

"Quickly, *señor*," said a male voice. "Into this crate."

Dutch rolled out of the cleaning cart and eyed the wooden box before him. It was substantially larger than his previous hiding spot, at any rate. His limbs only half cooperating, he snatched his computer and climbed into the box. A lid clamped down, and darkness wrapped around him. The crate tilted onto a dolly and someone grunted as they pushed him into motion. A minute later a male voice counted to three and he was heaved up into the air. He braced himself as best he could, but rolled wildly in the box as it tumbled to a soft landing.

And then an overpowering stench hit him. Rotting trash. *Ye gods.* He was definitely in a Dumpster.

A man's voice nearby. "The garbage truck will be here in about fifteen minutes. Sit tight until then."

He might die of asphyxiation before then. And Julia. How was she standing the hideous smell? He waited several seconds and heard nothing at all.

"Julia?" he whispered.

Nothing. He tried again. Panic surged in his chest. What had they done with her? So far, the hotel staff had done exactly as they'd said they would. Should he trust them? Should he blow this escape and break out to go look for her?

Eduardo's goon would still be patrolling the parking lot. He'd have to take that guy out, which would probably draw the attention of his buddies. And then the bastards would know Julia was still nearby. At least she'd *better* still be nearby. If she'd cut and run on him…

He didn't know if he'd be terrified or disappointed. He'd been relieved beyond belief when she'd agreed not to bolt on him yesterday. Made his job a hell of a lot easier. Right. That was why he'd nearly puked in relief when she'd agreed to stick with him. It had nothing to do with the feelings that were tearing him apart. Man, he was a mess.

He stayed put for ten minutes and then he couldn't stand it any longer. He had to go find her. It was a royal pain twisting around in the box until he could plant both feet on the top of his crate. But he managed to make like a pretzel and position himself. He drew a deep breath and prepared to kick out the lid when, suddenly, he heard two male voices approaching.

He froze, straining with all his might to listen. His heart started beating normally again when they came close enough for him to hear them speaking in Spanish. He jostled as they carefully set something in the Dumpster. *Julia.* His relief was so intense he momentarily felt light-headed. They'd spared her the long wait in the fetid pile of trash.

Sure enough, the men's voices had barely faded when the loud rumble of a truck approached. "You with me, honey?" he murmured.

He heard a sob in her voice. "Thank God you're here."

"I promised I wouldn't leave you," he chided gently.

The Dumpster lurched just then and her only answer was a soft cry of surprise.

"Hang on," he instructed. "Brace yourself as best you can." He did the same as they slowly tipped over. His crate tumbled over twice and came to a rest. If possible, the stench was even worse in here. The truck drove away and proceeded for about five minutes. And then, thankfully, it stopped. A man's voice called out low to them, instructing them to keep talking until he found them. Julia spoke a steady stream of thanks for this man's assistance. Her voice retreated as she climbed out of the truck.

"Your turn, *señor*," the man said.

In a matter of seconds, the lid cracked open and he climbed out onto a soggy, disgusting mound of filth. And then he was over the side, crushing Julia in a spontaneous hug of relief. If she smelled any worse than him, he couldn't tell, but he didn't care in the least. Her smile was the sweetest sight he'd seen in years.

She wrapped her slender, strong arms around his waist and held him every bit as tightly as he was holding her.

"I don't ever want to be apart from you again," she murmured fervently against his chest.

"Me neither." The words were out of his mouth before he even realized what he'd said. *Me neither?* Sweet Mother of God, what had he gone and done?

Chapter 9

The only thing in the world Julia wanted worse than a shower was for Dutch never to let go of her. But she felt him tense abruptly. Now what crisis threatened? She eased her grip on him reluctantly so he could do his job. But oddly, he didn't pull away. Rather, he stared down at her for a long time. She could swear that was fear lurking behind his hooded gaze. What in the world did he have to fear from her?

He sighed and looked away. Practical as always, he asked the truck driver for directions to a motel where they would be safe. Where they'd be anonymous. He also arranged with the guy for the driver's brother to pick up his SUV after her pursuers left and deliver it to them.

Dutch paid for the new motel room with cash. The clerk asked for no ID but did leer knowingly at them. Julia didn't care as long as she could get this smell off her skin and out of her hair.

Profound relief washed over her as they stepped into the tiny room and its giant bed. Lord, it felt good to be off the street and safe from prying eyes. *For the moment.* But this, too, wouldn't last. She tried not to think ahead, to stay firmly focused on the present. After all, it might be all she had.

A tear escaped and rolled down her cheek.

Dutch was there immediately, his arms wrapping reassuringly around her. "It's okay to let go now. You're safe."

"For how long?" she mumbled against his chest.

His arms tightened around her. "I said I'd keep you safe until Eduardo's put away, and I will."

He made it sound so simple. But there was a big bad world out there, full of her father's men. And then there was Dutch. He was merely biding his time, waiting for his turn to kill her. He'd kill Carina, too, if he got the chance.

"I wish it all was that easy," she sighed.

"Aw, baby. It is. Just trust me. I'll take care of the rest." His cheek came to rest against the top of her head and his heart beat strong and steady beneath her ear.

Then his hand slid under her hair to massage the back of her neck, and—for now—it all suddenly *was* that easy. The tension melted from her body, taking every last ounce of her resistance with it. He'd laid his neck on the line for her yet again today. How many times was he going to have to save her before she accepted the fact that Jim Dutcher was the real deal? He'd keep his word and not hurt her. At least not until this was all over. Here he was, patiently taking care of her, steadfastly upholding his end of their bargain. Again. Maybe she'd spent so long living in the shadow of a monster that she couldn't see a good man when he was standing right in front of her.

And with that thought came comfort. Security. Her feelings for him, tightly held in check until this moment, unfolded as naturally as breathing. A warm, peaceful sense of in-evitability came over her that loving him was meant to be. She blinked. *Loving* him? She was *not*—

Her thoughts completely derailed as his mouth found hers. She didn't stand a chance against the warm union of their mouths. She exhaled on a sigh and lost herself in the kiss. He surrounded her in his heat and strength, overwhelming her without suffocating her. It reminded her of being caught up in warm ocean surf, carried away from the safety of shore but cradled in its soothing embrace. Except this time she was lost already. There was no need to fight her way back to land. For once, she allowed the current of his hands and mouth to sweep her away.

He lifted her off the ground and spun her around slowly as he kissed her half senseless. Her head spun twice as fast and she wrapped her arms around the immovable column of his neck. She sought the heat of his mouth, tasting the warm musk of his smooth lips, and then she sought even more. Her tongue slid inside his mouth, and he opened for her, giving himself up with a groan. She slanted her head, gorging her-self on the hardness of his body and the wet, devouring heat of his mouth.

And then she was bent backward over his arm, his mouth tearing away from hers to travel down her throat and toward the cleft of her aching breasts. She pulled his golden head closer, desperate for the fire. His free hand came up to cup her throbbing flesh, and she groaned with the exquisite tor-ture to sensitized nerves.

With a quick flex of his biceps, he righted her, backing her up against the wall as his kisses turned voracious. She wrapped her right leg around his hips, and he rocked against her core. Wet heat flooded her and her left leg practically col-lapsed from the drowning pleasure of it. Her nipples felt tight

and swollen, and his clever fingers plucked at them until she
threw her head back, banging it against the wall. Dutch
winced and she laughed, grabbing the back of his neck and
pulling his mouth down for more. Straining upward, she met
him halfway, consumed by a blaze that all but incinerated her
soul.

The room spun around her, and she had no idea if Dutch
had lifted her again or not. Everything fell away but her driving need to reach inside his very soul, to feast upon every cell
of his being, to *have* this man. And then her clothes started
to fall off, drifting away like smoke. She tore at his shirt, surprised that his buttons survived the attack as she ripped at the
fabric in her haste to get to naked male skin. And then her
palms encountered the raw silk of his flesh, sliding over slabs
of rock-hard muscle. Pure animal need to feel him thrusting
deep inside her drove her onward, clumsily peeling away the
rest of his clothes.

A hum started somewhere behind him, and cool air from
overhead struck her skin, not even putting a dent in the inferno consuming her. And then his arms were under her legs,
scooping her up. He strode swiftly into the bathroom and de-
posited her on her feet in the shower. A quick flick of his
wrists turning on the water, and then he was kissing her again,
his hands and mouth roaming all over her body as he claimed
every inch of her for his own.

His onslaught was merciless, leaving no quarter, nowhere
to hide. She opened herself to him as water sluiced across her
skin. Hot or cold, she couldn't tell and didn't care. Steam rose
around them and then he was washing her, his hands soapy
and slippery on her body, driving her out of her mind with
the exquisite sensation of it.

His hand slid down her front, down the smooth slope of
her belly and into the silky softness between her legs. He

"Hey," he mumbled back. If he wasn't mistaken, he'd just made a colossal fool of himself.

"Feeling better?" she asked simply.

"Feeling human." And he bet she had no idea how monumental an achievement that was, either. He frowned up at her. "Are you okay?" He had a vague memory of terror blossoming on her face, of her fleeing from the beast.

"Me? I'm fine," she answered lightly. But something else vibrated in her voice.

He freed a hand from the blankets to run it through his short hair. "God, I'm sorry. I scared you, didn't I? Look, if you want to leave me, I'll call in someone else from the squad. I have a buddy on the team who'd help you, no questions asked."

She looked long and hard at him, unfathomable thoughts flitting through her dark gaze. Finally she whispered, "I don't want anybody else. Just you."

He met her gaze candidly. And something passed between them. An understanding. An agreement of sorts. Recognition that there was something powerful between them, and if they both lived long enough they'd explore it.

"Some pair we make," he remarked ruefully.

"You've got that right." She grinned briefly. "Hungry?" she asked.

In his line of work, a guy never turned down a meal. Some ops got so hot or so covert that he might go for days at a time without eating. "What did you have in mind?"

"Pizza? There's a delivery joint across the street." She smiled and that damn mirage swam forward again. Something about seeing that water running over Julia's face had triggered the memory. But the harder he reached beyond that one image, the more he felt it slipping away.

Enough was enough. He threw back the mound of covers

and swung his feet to the floor. And realized he was naked. He swore under his breath. He glanced up to see if he'd shocked Julia, but she was smiling at him, and damned if that wasn't unabashed appreciation he saw in her eyes.

He yanked on his shorts, which reeked to high heaven, but they were all he had until his SUV got delivered. Much better. He felt more in control now. Somehow, he'd managed to fight off the beast one more time, barely.

The pizza was average but filling. When they'd both eaten all they wanted, he pulled out his faithful laptop computer to see if it had survived the day's shenanigans. He plugged it into the wall and the screen lit up as usual.

Julia collected the paper plates and went into the bathroom to throw them out. He felt her approach, looking curiously over his shoulder. "What are you up to?" she inquired.

"I've got to find out what's happening to my head."

He typed, logging on to the Internet and initiating a search on blackouts, flashbacks and nightmares. His attention riveted on the medical information scrolling down his screen. He read article after article and they all said the same thing. No doubt about it. His symptoms were consistent with someone harboring a repressed memory. A freaking huge one that was trying to surface.

No surprise there.

One thing he was sure of. Julia was the trigger to release it.

Chapter 10

A quiet knock on the door in the wee hours of the morning swung Dutch out of bed and into a defensive crouch, gun in hand. Julia quickly rolled out of bed on the other side and onto the floor. A voice outside said low in Spanish, "I brought your car."

"Anyone see you?" Dutch asked through the door.

"No. The INS, they left a couple hours ago."

The Immigration and Naturalization Service? And then Dutch remembered their cover story about Immigration agents chasing Julia. He didn't hear any stress vibrations in the guy's voice to indicate someone had put him up to knocking on the door or was watching him from afar.

Dutch left the chain on—not that the flimsy thing would do a damn bit of good, but it might buy him a couple of seconds in a pinch—and opened the door a crack. A young Hispanic man nodded and smiled at him.

The kid held the SUV keys to the crack. "Sweet set of wheels. It's parked around back."

"Thanks," Dutch replied. "What do I owe you for your trouble?"

"*Nada.* My brother's share of the money you paid will feed his kids for a month. You be careful, dude. Those men, they were really hot to find your lady."

"Thanks." Dutch watched the young man through the window as he disappeared into the night. All was still outside. The kid wasn't followed, as far as Dutch could see. He eased the curtain back into place and slid into bed beside Julia, who also crawled back under the covers.

Her breathing was shallow and rapid. As much as he'd like to think it was because he turned her on, he knew it to be nothing more than abject terror.

He rolled on his side and opened his arms. "Come here," he murmured.

He gathered her cold, board-stiff body close, sharing his heat with her until she began to thaw out and relax. God, she felt good in his arms. Like she belonged there.

This was bad. Very, very bad. He'd watched half the guys on his team go down this road before. It was always a nightmare to get involved with a woman on an op. Maybe they got their girl when it was all said and done, but they paid in blood in the meantime.

And here he was, rolling around in the sack with Julia Ferrare. Worse, she made no secret of the fact that she wanted him. They were headed for some seriously hot and sweaty sex in the near future if he didn't put on the brakes. And the situation couldn't get much messier than that.

All he had to do was unwrap his arms, roll over and go to sleep. *Go ahead. Do it.* His arms didn't budge. *Sever the link, you coward! Put this op back on track where it belongs.* Nothing. His body flatly refused to cooperate.

Dammit.

Distance. Emotional distance. Think detached. She was just an informant. He should work her over for information and then bring her in. He should do it now and walk away from this. Walk away from her. But there he lay, berating himself up one side and down the other. And he didn't move a damn muscle.

Julia drifted off to sleep and turned to soft silk in his arms, but he lay there, ramrod stiff for hours, watching the clock tick away the minutes until he had to get up. Until he had to unwrap his arms and let her go. One minute before the alarm was set to go off, he kissed Julia awake. She stretched like a sleek kitten in his arms, and his heart clenched.

"Time to go, sleepyhead," he murmured.

"Ugh," she groaned. He tickled her neck and she laughed up at him. "No fair. I'm still half-asleep. Do we have to go so early?"

He sighed. "Yup. Roads are deserted at this hour. Nobody'll follow us without me seeing them."

With nothing to pack but the laptop and some cold pizza, they were out the door in a matter of minutes.

Julia headed for the passenger door of his SUV, but he murmured, "Change of plans. Help me get our bags."

She frowned, but came around back and picked up her suitcases.

He looked around the parking lot, scoping out a decent target. Over there. A heavy-duty Jeep. It would handle the mountain roads and the snow that was in today's forecast.

"This way," he murmured.

Julia followed him, a perplexed look on her face. He dug out a pouch of tools, lay down underneath the front end of the Jeep and disabled the vehicle's alarm system. It was a bit of a trick to reach, but he managed to snip the necessary wires.

He shimmied out from under the car. Using a Slim Jim, a flat metal tool that unlocked car doors from the outside, and a pocket reference book on how to jimmy different models of cars, he popped the Jeep's locks.

He tossed their bags in the back and held the passenger door for Julia. Her eyebrows hovered in the vicinity of her hairline as she slid into the vehicle silently.

Hot-wiring the Jeep was kid stuff, and he had it running in about thirty seconds. He pulled out of the parking lot and headed for the highway, keeping a close eye on the rearview mirror for tails.

"And we just stole a car why?" she finally asked, nearly a half hour later.

"Keeping our tail clean," he replied.

She looked over at him in dismay. "Don't you feel any twinge of conscience over stealing somebody's car?"

He glanced over at her, surprised. "I'm doing my job. The owner of this vehicle will get compensated by Uncle Sam when this is all over."

She didn't look convinced. And for some reason, he actually gave a damn about what she thought of him. He sighed and explained, "If it comes down to a choice between you and me staying alive or taking some guy's car temporarily, which would you choose?"

Her gaze wavered and slid away.

He shrugged. "It's not pretty or clean, but that's how it goes in my line of work."

Her dark gaze swiveled back to him. "That's why I'm glad I found you. I could never do what it takes to stay alive on my own."

"Oh, I don't know about that. You were doing okay when I found you."

She laughed shortly. "I was at my wit's end and would've been caught and perhaps killed within a few hours if you hadn't come along when you did."

He tensed when she reached over, put her hand on his arm and squeezed it gratefully. Sparks leaped between them, and the temperature in the Jeep went up noticeably. Good thing there wasn't a rest area just ahead, or he'd pull off and make love to her right this very minute. By main force, he dragged his attention back to his driving.

Sometime later, Julia asked around a yawn, "Where are we going?"

"Montana."

"As in where you're from?"

"Yup. To my home turf. Let's see if those bastards can move around unseen in a place where every single person knows everyone else, and a rancher would rather shoot you himself than bother calling the cops."

"Sounds like the Wild Wild West."

He nodded, "It's isolated country. Folks up there look out for each other. I can't think of a safer place to take you."

Dutch kept one eye peeled on the rearview mirror as he put New Mexico behind them. Nobody followed them. He breathed a sigh of relief.

He drove until the sun rose, and now and then he saw a frown flicker across Julia's face. Finally, he asked, "What's got you looking so worried?"

"Are you taking me to your family's house?" she asked hesitantly.

"No!" he answered in sharp alarm. He would never insult his parents by introducing them to the girl who'd set up Simon.

Julia replied fervently, "Thank goodness. I couldn't live

with myself if they were endangered on my account." She paused and then added miserably, "I've hurt your family enough already."

His gaze snapped to her. She sounded genuinely remorseful. Was that all part of her act? He wanted to believe her. Wanted to think she wasn't an unfeeling monster.

He said quietly, "My dad has a hunting cabin in the mountains above our ranch, and I'm heading for it. I know the area around it like the back of my hand. We'll be safe there."

Silence fell between them. The morning was gray. Low, heavy clouds scudded along the mountain peaks as they made their way higher into the Rockies. He eyed the sky warily. Those were snow clouds packing in. The kind that dropped truckloads of white stuff hard and fast.

He stopped for gas at midmorning and loaded up on emergency provisions: food, candles, matches, blankets, batteries and a portable radio.

They started out again and the wind began to pick up. By noon, it howled around the Jeep and he was forced to slow down lest they be blown clean off the narrow, winding mountain road. If they could've hopped onto an interstate highway without being spotted, they'd be crossing into Montana by now. But by traveling these anonymous back roads and taking a circuitous route, they were still hours away from their destination in the high Rockies, near the Canadian border.

The snow started around two o'clock. At first a few sparse crystals fell and then they thickened rapidly into big fat flakes. The snow, driven against the windshield by the developing blizzard, all but blinded him. He was forced to slow down even more.

Because of the rotten visibility, the dark blue, full-size sedan was almost in his back seat by the time he finally caught sight of it. His internal alarm system went wild. Almost as fast as the car had run up on their rear fender, it slowed down and disappeared from sight. Oh yeah. Definitely Ferrare's men. The bastards got close enough to make his license plate, but the second they knew it was him and Julia, they backed off to wait for reinforcements.

He swore under his breath. How did those jerks find them way out here in the middle of blessed nowhere? They must have heard about a stolen vehicle in the parking lot of the hotel where his SUV was parked. Definite police contacts, then. Dammit. He pressed down on the accelerator on the assumption that this Jeep had more guts than that sedan.

He drove in grim silence for nearly half an hour. He didn't see the blue car again, but he had no doubt it was back there somewhere. He jolted when a cell phone rang shrilly. That wasn't his...

He frowned as Julia lurched and dug her cell phone out of a coat pocket hastily. She put it to her ear and said a nervous hello. She listened in silence for several seconds, then mumbled a couple yeses and noes. As the call progressed, the color drained out of her face, leaving it a sickly beige shade. She disconnected the phone silently. He watched without comment as, with shaking hands, she stowed the instrument in her pocket.

"Who was that?" he asked.

"Nobody," she answered quickly. Too quickly.

He swore under his breath. He'd lay odds that had been her father. What had they been talking about? Had the guy been threatening her? Demanding that she give back his financial records? Or perhaps, were they working out the details of an ambush to finish off what they'd started ten years ago?

Why in the hell couldn't she just be straight with him and not put him in this blasted position of *not knowing?*

He braked hard just beyond a big curve and crawled along

until the blue car careened around the hairpin turn, skidding behind them and barely missing rear-ending the Jeep.

He said tersely, "Don't turn around. Use the mirror in your sun visor to look back at the car behind us. Can you get a look at the people inside it?"

She peered into the mirror for a moment and then visibly jumped. "It's them!" she gasped. "Two of the guys from the ski resort! How did they find us out here? Oh God. What are we going to do?"

How did they find her, indeed? Hell of a good question. Especially in light of that phone call. How much to believe? Had that call actually scared the hell out of her?

He cut across her building panic, real or otherwise, by stating mildly, "The first thing we're going to do is stay calm."

She sat back in her seat.

"The next thing we're going to do is use the power of this Jeep to put some distance between us and them." To that end, he leaned on the accelerator and picked up the vehicle's speed significantly, even though the roads were starting to get slick. The blue car was already dropping back. He'd bet the driver had to clean out his pants after that near miss back there.

Over the next few minutes, he gradually sped up until the Jeep was going near the speed limit once more. Fortunately, its four-wheel drive and snow tires held the road. He pushed the speed some more.

"Don't you think we should slow down a little?" Julia suggested nervously.

He glanced over at her grimly. "Nope. I've got to get far enough ahead of these guys so I can lay a trap for them."

"A trap?" she asked in surprise. "What kind?"

"I'll know it when I see it." He didn't say more because the car was really becoming a handful. The wind buffeted them, and the road was a strip of featureless white. Worse, dark was falling prematurely, and these roads weren't anywhere near adequately enough marked to be safe at night in a snowstorm. The good news was they'd climbed up into the high elevations where the Jeep's robust engine could really show its superiority to that of the car following them.

On the downhill slopes, he punched the accelerator, putting on extra bursts of speed to keep their pursuers from making up lost ground. They were flying down one such hill at a suicidal pace when Dutch nearly lost control of the Jeep. It began to slide toward the empty space of a drop-off, and there was no guardrail to stop them. Praying hard, he yanked his foot off the accelerator and stopped his impulse to go for the brakes. That would've done them in for sure. Thankfully, the antiskid system kicked in and the tires caught traction once more. He straightened out the car carefully and steered back onto his own side of the road.

Surely he'd bought them a few minutes' lead by now. He began to keep his eye out for a good spot to ambush the blue car, and in the meantime, kept the pedal to the metal. He'd need every second he could buy to pull off the plan taking shape in his mind.

It took about five minutes and two more hair-raising rises and falls of the road before he found what he was looking for. A switchback turn on a steep downhill part of the road in a heavily forested area. Hell, he'd barely made the turn himself. He stopped carefully and backed up the couple hundred feet to the curve.

"Stay in the car," he ordered Julia.

He grabbed his coat and shrugged into it as he stepped out into the storm. He guessed it would be dark in another ten minutes. Perfect. In the gray dusk, he searched the sides of the road until he found what he'd glimpsed on the way around the bend. A medium-size, freshly fallen tree with most of its branches intact.

He grabbed the top of it and dragged it around until it lay perpendicular to the road. Then he put his back into it and heaved, pulling it up toward the road. It moved about twelve inches. Again. Inch by inch, he worked it out into the road. But it was taking too long. And the left lane was still open. A person could swerve around the tree. The blue car would be here any second.

And then a movement beside him. Julia put her hands on one of the branches and leaned into the tree with him. Together, they were able to move the thing a few feet. Two more big heaves and they had it all the way across the road just beyond the curve. The blue car would come around blind and have no chance to stop.

He was sick of these jerks picking up his and Julia's trail over and over as if he were some rank amateur who couldn't shake a tail. A few hours sitting out here in a blizzard should cool their jets. The sound of an engine coming down the mountain caught his attention.

"Run!" he shouted at Julia. They took off down the hill, slipping and sliding toward the Jeep. They weren't going to make it. At the last second, he yanked her down behind a bush at the side of the road.

The blue car careened around the corner the way he had, barely holding the road. It didn't stand a chance. The tree popped up in front of it completely without warning. The driver swerved and slammed on the brakes, but he plowed into the tree, driving it and the car toward the ditch on the side of the road. The tree's round trunk rolled under the car's front wheels and sent its front end flying into the air. The vehicle did a half revolution and came to a sickening halt on its roof, half buried in snow.

"Julia, get in the driver's side of the Jeep. If I don't come back to it alone, leave. You hear me?"

She nodded, but hesitated. He gave her a little push toward the vehicle, then turned and ran back up the hill. Now was his chance to find out exactly who these guys were. He pulled out his pistol and approached the flipped-over car cautiously. In the failing light, he made out two men hanging upside down in their seat belts. Deflated air bags draped around them both.

They looked unconscious. He ordered them to show their hands, and neither moved. The driver's-side window was broken but visible, while the passenger's door was completely buried in snow. He eased closer slowly. And nudged the driver's shoulder with his foot. No response. He crouched down and looked across the car. A big bruise was starting to form on the passenger's forehead. But he was breathing.

Holding his gun to the driver's temple with his left hand, he searched the guy's coat with his right hand. He pocketed the Glock pistol he found. He reached between the guy's rear end and the seat and pulled out the dude's wallet. He wanted a name. He came up with a cell phone instead. On a sickening hunch, he punched the menu and brought up its most recent outgoing call.

And stared in shock at the name and number displayed.

Julia Ferrare.

This guy had made that phone call to Julia a little while ago! She was in direct contact with Ferrare's men? This chase *was* all a ruse! To dupe him into another trap. Son of a *bitch!*

It sure explained how these guys kept popping up over and over when any normal thug would have been way out of the picture by now. No wonder he couldn't shake the bastards. Great. Just freaking great.

He stabbed his hand behind the guy's back and grabbed his wallet this time. He slipped the warm leather into his own pocket and backed away from the car.

He stormed toward the Jeep and the oh-so-innocent-seeming woman inside it. The second they got out of this damn blizzard, he and Julia were going to have a little talk. And this time she was damn well going to tell him exactly what was going on—if he had to wring it out of her with his bare hands.

He opened the driver's-side door. She took one look at his face and all but leaped over the center console to her seat.

He growled, "When we get to the top of the next mountain and have clear cell-phone reception, call nine-one-one and report the accident. Be vague about the exact location."

He started to drive. She must have picked up on his tightly controlled fury, because she did as he ordered without any questions.

The snow continued to fall, and he pressed on in stony silence. Drifts began to form across the road. Even the sturdy Jeep struggled to punch through the deepening snow. Like it or not, they had to get off the road soon and find someplace to wait out the storm.

He kept an eye out for a driveway or a mailbox, anything to indicate that a house might be nearby. He drove at a bare crawl, peering into the blackness. The snow was falling so thickly in the headlights that he could hardly see the road, let alone the side of it.

He thought he glimpsed a break in the trees. He stopped and backed up carefully to the spot. It looked like a driveway sloping down away from the road. But it was buried in snow. He'd probably be able to make it down the lane, but they'd never make it back up. If he was wrong and it led nowhere they'd be stranded.

What the hell. He was too mad to feel anything but reckless, and the roads were beyond impassable. He pointed the Jeep at the gap in the trees.

"Hang on," he bit out.

He punched the engine and blasted through the first snowdrift. The narrow lane must have gone on for several hundred yards, but it was hard to tell, given that he could only see a few feet of the thing at any one time. And then, without warning, it came to an end. Just like that. A wall of trees surrounded them on all sides.

He pushed the car door open, moving aside a hefty pile of snow in the process. He got out of the vehicle and waded out into a good three feet of snow to take a look around. There. Tucked back into a stand of towering pines. A dark, low shape. Rectangular like a cabin.

He busted a path to the front door of the log structure. Holding his flashlight in his teeth, he stripped off his gloves and picked the door lock. His fingers were clumsy with cold, but he managed to force the thing open. He felt around on the wall inside the door and found a light switch. He flipped it on. Nothing. Damn. The power was either out from the storm or cut off for the winter. No help for it at the moment, though.

He trudged back to the Jeep to collect Julia and their gear. His footsteps were already half-full of snow. What a blizzard. The way snow was accumulating on the roof and hood of the vehicle, he wasn't going to have to worry about hiding the Jeep from view. It would be buried before long.

Julia followed on his heels as he slogged to the cabin. He dropped their supplies inside the front door and thrust his flashlight into her hands. "Have a look around while I try to find some firewood," he ordered.

Any self-respecting cabin in this part of the world had a good-size woodpile that was kept stocked at all times. It was a matter of survival. Sure enough, around back he found another door and a big stack of split wood buried in snow beside it. He brushed off enough snow to grab a huge armload of the stuff. Right about then, the door opened. Julia poked her head out.

"Good timing," he grunted under the pile of wood.

She helped him maneuver it inside, and he dumped it in the little mudroom attached to the cabin's main room. Julia had found and lit a lantern. A soft, golden glow filled the space. He had a quick look around. The one-room cabin was well equipped, snug and neat, albeit freezing cold at the moment. But it would keep them dry and out of the wind, and after he built a big fire in the stone fireplace, they'd be warm enough.

While he laid the fire, Julia poked around in the cupboards and supplemented their food stores with some canned baked beans and fruit cocktail. Not exactly gourmet fare, but a far sight better than going hungry. The tinderbox beside the fireplace was fully stocked with dry twigs and resin-soaked fatwood, and in no time, he had a thriving fire crackling.

It took about an hour for some canned stew to get hot and ready to eat. The air was still bitingly cold. It would probably take all night for the stones in the fireplace to heat up enough to take the chill off the room. Again, not ideal, but a hell of a lot better than freezing to death in the car. They ate, wearing their coats, seated in a pair of bentwood chairs near the fire.

Dutch bided his time until Julia set aside her empty plate. He did the same. But then the infuriated soldier within him could be patient no more.

He leaned forward, skewering her with a saber-sharp stare. He spoke with cold precision. "We need to talk. Or rather you need to talk. Why don't you start with why your father's men were calling you. You can finish with telling me what in the hell is going on. *All of it.*"

Chapter 11

The noose that had been tightening around her neck gave one final yank. And from the looks of him, he was about to kick the chair out from under her feet.

That call this afternoon had put her off balance, and now Dutch was calling her bluff. This day kept getting better and better. Maybe she should bolt out the door and disappear into the blizzard. It would solve everyone's problems. Except Carina's, of course.

She sighed. It always came back to her little sister. That's what she got for loving someone. Her feelings for Carina tied her down, locking her into an inevitable course of action. No wonder Dutch had never fallen in love. Guys in his line of work couldn't afford the vulnerability and limitations that emotional attachments placed on them.

She shuddered as she recalled the voice of her father's hired killer trying to disguise his snarl as charm this afternoon.

Eduardo must have given the man her cell-phone number. She just didn't buy the goon's offer to let her live if she gave her father his money back immediately.

She'd been evasive in response to his demand, of course. With Dutch sitting right beside her, she couldn't very well engage in a negotiation for Carina's freedom. She'd made it clear to the thug that she couldn't talk right now and that he or her father should call her back later.

Had the guy gotten the message? Would his orders change when he delivered the message to Eduardo that she'd refused to return his thirty million? Were the thugs in that blue car chasing her with an eye to killing her? If not now, then they would be soon.

She'd been profoundly relieved when Dutch flipped over her pursuers' car. Lord, they'd been close. Literally on her heels. Even with Dutch's formidable skill, he was barely managing to stay ahead of these killers.

Time was running out. As much as she wanted to delay the inevitable, heck, just to stay alive a few more days, it was time to launch the endgame. Time to show her cards to Dutch and face the fallout. Dutch wanted to know everything, did he? Fine. Then that's exactly what he'd get.

She took a deep breath. "Here's the problem. Someone else is at risk. I can't afford for you to do anything to jeopardize their safety."

Dutch replied tersely, "Tell me who this person is so I can take their safety into account as I make decisions."

He didn't have any idea what he was promising, but she wasn't above holding him to it. "Do you swear you'll do whatever's necessary to keep this person safe?"

"Is he an innocent?"

"Yes," she answered firmly. "Absolutely."

He shrugged. "Then I promise."

She stared at him doubtfully. Did she dare hang Carina's life on his word? She might be willing to put her own life on the line that way, but her sister's?

He added, "Honest. On a stack of Bibles. Just tell me who he is."

She nodded slowly. It wasn't as if she had any choice at this point. She would have to trust him not to take revenge by hurting her sister. Her father's men were practically on top of them. She had to have Dutch's help to stay away from them until she could finish this. "It's not a he. It's a she."

"Who is she, then?"

"My sister. Carina. My father has kidnapped her and is holding her hostage until I return the copies of his financial records."

"And what makes you think she's in danger?"

"He told me he'd kill her unless he got the records back."

"Why hasn't he killed her already, then?" Dutch demanded. She could swear there was a trace of suspicion in his voice.

"Because I took something of his to make sure he wouldn't kill her."

"What did you take?"

She sighed. In for a penny, in for a pound. "I transferred thirty million dollars in cash out of his checking account and into another bank account he knows nothing about."

Dutch went perfectly still. Like a carved block of ice. He asked flatly, "And you're hoping to do what? Trade the financial records and the thirty million for Carina's freedom?"

"Yes."

He gritted out, "So you never had any intention of handing over Eduardo's financial records to me? This was all a ruse to get me to keep you alive until you could blackmail your old man?"

She flinched. Put that way, it made her sound like the worst sort of self-serving human being. "I have multiple copies of the financial records. I was planning to give a set to you. That way I can keep my word to both of you."

"How's your father supposed to be assured that you haven't made copies?"

She looked Dutch square in the eye. "He's just going to have to trust me."

Dutch snorted. "Fat chance. He won't buy it for a second."

She shrugged. "It's not like he has any choice. I have thirty million reasons for him to take me at my word, whether he likes it or not."

He shook his head. "It's a risky gambit." He sprang up out of the chair with unnatural energy, but gave no other hint of his agitation. "I have to make a phone call."

She'd bet he did. She closed her eyes briefly. She'd barely climbed aboard, and already this train was out of control, careening toward a spectacular wreck. Dutch hit the speed dial on his satellite cell phone.

A few moments later, he said, "Patch me through to the colonel."

Oh God. Charlie Squad headquarters! She leaped to her feet, alarmed, and said frantically, "What are you doing? You haven't figured out what triggered your blackout! You'll lose your job if you go in now!"

He shrugged. "So much for my job. Some things are more important than my life, and nailing your father is one of them."

She closed her eyes, distraught. He was throwing away his career. It was more than his job. It was his life! She'd never meant to cost him so much by approaching him for help.

"Don't do it," she whispered, more to herself than to him.

"It's a done deal, babe. They're patching me through now."

A command post somewhere would be linking his call to Colonel Folly's home phone, or wherever he was tonight. More to the point, a command-post controller would be doing it. She lurched with renewed urgency.

"Dutch, don't say *anything* unless you're on a secure line! You have to make sure nobody else is able to monitor the call!"

He frowned and nodded shortly. He spoke into the phone again. "I need a secure line. This is a Tango One."

Whatever the heck that was. But, it got him through to his boss in a matter of seconds on a line that audibly shrilled a series of electronic noises through Dutch's cell phone into the cabin before it settled into silence once more. She listened as he and his boss traded verifications that this was a secure line and a classified conversation.

Then Dutch said, "You'll never guess who's sitting beside me right now." A pause. "Way better than that. Julia Ferrare."

She could practically hear the exclamation of surprise at the other end of the line.

Dutch again. "She's got Eduardo's complete and accurate financial records for the last ten years and is willing to hand them over to us. But there's a hitch. Ferrare has kidnapped the younger sister and is threatening to kill her if Julia doesn't return the goods."

Dutch glanced at her as he spoke. "I thought you'd feel that way, sir. I'll bring her in as soon as we get out of this blizzard. We're snowed in right now. In northern Wyoming. An empty cabin I broke into for shelter."

Julia blurted out, "I'm not going anywhere. Especially not to Charlie Squad headquarters!"

Dutch relayed her statement to his boss. A pause. Then, "She claims to have all sorts of juicy stuff. Says she's been making funds transfers to someone in the FBI via an offshore account."

Dutch listened for a moment, then looked at her again. He lifted the phone away from his mouth and spoke to her. "If Charlie Squad can mount a successful rescue of your sister, will you come in from the cold and turn state's evidence against your father?"

She stared in disbelief. "You guys can't just waltz in and snatch her! She's inside my father's compound in Gavarone. It's an impregnable fortress!"

Dutch shrugged. "We've been chewing on ways to get in there for a decade. It's not entirely impregnable. Is it a deal?"

It was more than a deal. It was a dream come true. If Carina could be freed *and* her father put away, her life would be perfect. Well, maybe not *perfect*. Truly perfect would involve staying alive and having Dutch in her life for a very long time.

She nodded slowly. "Give Colonel Folly a message for me. Tell him he can't take Carina to Charlie Squad headquarters once he has her."

"Why not?" Dutch asked sharply.

She dropped the bomb without fanfare. "My father has a mole inside Charlie Squad's support team, and Carina wouldn't be safe there."

Dutch's jaw dropped. He mumbled into the phone, "Did you catch that, sir?" A pause. "No, she's serious." Then he asked her quietly, "Julia, who is Ferrare's informant near the squad?"

She answered honestly, "I don't know his name. I do know he's in the military, and he always knows where Charlie Squad is operating at any given time."

Dutch flinched at whatever his boss said to him next. Then he said, "I'll do my best, sir." Then he listened for a long time, apparently receiving a string of instructions.

She'd bet they involved wringing her like a washcloth for information and not letting her out of his sight at all costs. He turned off the phone and turned to her.

"As soon as this storm breaks, the rest of the team will head for Wyoming. We'll hook up with them and they'll help escort you to safety. Then they'll go get your sister. Ferrare's thugs aren't getting anywhere near you again until you testify against that bastard."

And once she'd done that, then the whole squad could gleefully kill her as a team sport. Lovely.

Now what was she supposed to do? Should she continue trying to contact her father and make the trade? Wouldn't it be better to buy Carina's freedom than count on Charlie Squad to force her out of Gavarone in a pitched gun battle? The very thought of Carina being subjected to the same terror she'd experienced that night a decade ago sent shivers rippling through Julia. She *had* to protect her baby sister from that.

At the end of the day, nothing had changed. She still had to proceed with her plan to ransom Carina away from Eduardo.

At least by involving his boss in this mess, Dutch wasn't in as good a position to intentionally kill Carina in order to get revenge for losing his brother.

The other good news was that since the thirty million hadn't come up in Dutch's conversation with the colonel, she still could use it safely to ransom back Carina.

Dutch paced several laps around the small room. Finally he stopped. "I know you. You're still not telling me everything. What else is there?"

Dang, he was good. She'd only seconds before decided to go ahead with her negotiations, and he was already smelling a rat. She needed to throw him off the scent.

She answered simply, "Haven't I told you enough? I got your brother killed. Now you have the power to get my sister killed. You must be tickled pink."

He stared at her for a long time, his gaze inscrutable. She'd dearly love to know what he was thinking.

Finally, he asked, "What makes you so sure your old man will actually kill your sister? I mean, she's his daughter, after all."

She shrugged. "He killed his wife. Why not his daughter?"

Dutch lurched. "Jeez. What a slimy mother—" He broke off the epithet and flopped in a chair, thinking hard.

She girded herself for the next leap in his logic—the one where he remembered how she'd set him up once before, and started questioning whether she was doing the same thing again. But he didn't bring it up.

Instead, he said, "It's going to get colder before morning. I need to bring in more wood to get us through the night."

She hauled a bucket of melted snow into the tiny bathroom, poured it in the back of the toilet and prayed fervently that the pipes weren't frozen. It flushed just fine and she made her way back to the lone bed in the main room.

Dutch carried in three big armloads of wood and stacked them on the hearth. He threw a pile of logs on the fire, and then he joined her in the cabin's bed.

It wasn't the king-size affair she'd gotten used to in hotels, and Dutch's big body seemed to swallow the whole mattress. But when he rolled on his side and tucked her body against his, spooning around her backside for warmth, it was pretty darned comfortable. A little heat reached her from the fire, and all in all, she was fairly cozy for being in an unheated log cabin in the middle of a blizzard. Exhausted by the day's events, she fell asleep quickly.

Dutch woke up to the vibration of his watch a few hours later. He crawled out of the cocoon of blankets to throw more wood on the fire. By morning, the stones should be warm enough to heat the whole room to a comfortable level. But for the moment, his breath hung in the air, testament to the chilly temperature. He headed back to bed.

His thoughts full of nailing Eduardo Ferrare once and for all, he drifted off to sleep.

The jungle closed in around him, steamy even at midnight. He lay on the ground where the bullet had knocked his leg out from under him. The dull glint of a long, fanglike knife blade arced down. Into Simon's gut.

Simon's scream echoed his own silent howl of rage and all but ripped out his guts, too. Agony exploded inside him as if he was being eviscerated instead of his brother. He shoved to his feet. Damn, his gut really did burn like fire. He glanced down. A red streak slashed across his stomach. A bullet must have creased him. Didn't feel as if it had penetrated. Probably just grazed him. Not that anything was going to stop him from getting to his little brother.

A crackle on his radio. "Dutch, get down! You're squarely in the crossfire. A sitting duck!"

"Can't," he grunted back. "Simon—"

"You can't help Simon if you're dead. Get down. Now! That's an order."

He dropped. Automatic reflex reaction to an order, dammit. But he kept crawling toward Simon and the bastard who was now crouching beside his brother, stabbing Simon repeatedly.

He kept pulling the trigger of his empty rifle as if more bullets would materialize in the chamber and drop the bastard. Another reflex he had no control over.

"Retreat!" Captain Folly bellowed over the radio. The din of a burst of gunfire nearly drowned him out. "Fall back. Into the jungle. Proceed due south for a hundred yards, then regroup on my position."

Out of the corner of his eye, Dutch saw his teammates following the order and moving off toward his left in a fighting retreat. His brain felt wrapped in fog. He was supposed to go with them.

"Simon..." he protested into his throat mike.

"There's nothing we can do for him now," Folly bit out. "Fall back."

"We don't leave our own behind," Dutch snapped back.

"We do this time. We've got to regroup. We'll come back for him in a little while. I swear. But we're all going to die if we don't get out of the line of fire and get a head count and position fix on what we're up against."

Simon was less than a dozen yards ahead of him now. Just a few more seconds.

And then Simon turned his head and looked at Dutch. The kid was still alive! By some miracle, his eyes were open and aware and staring straight at him. Beseeching his big brother not to leave him here to die alone.

The bastard reached for Simon's hair. Took a handful of it and yanked Simon's chin up. The bloody knife descended slowly toward his brother's jugular.

Orders be damned. All in one move, Dutch leaped up and flung himself forward. He caught the fist holding the knife, twisted the weapon still in the guy's grasp, and drove it into the guy's throat in a lethal blow.

And then another scream caught his attention. A high-pitched keening that had to come from a female throat. His head whipped around. He swore violently. Julia. What the hell was she doing running down the front lawn toward him? She was supposed to be hiding in the gazebo, safe on the other side of the house from this fiasco!

"Stop! Stop!" she screamed over and over. She was coming straight at him. She wanted him to stop? Not a chance. Simon's intestines might be spread all over the front yard, but he was getting his brother out of here if it was the last thing he ever did. Hell, it probably would be the last thing he ever did.

"Dutch. Julia's coming right at you. Get her out of there."

He blinked at Folly's orders. Glanced down at Simon. Looked up at the panicked girl racing toward him. But his brother...

He knew his duty. Get the innocent civilian out. He knelt down. Tore off his shirt. Awkwardly bundled the slippery mass of Simon's intestines in the cloth and set it on top of Simon's gut. He knew better than to stuff them back in his brother's body before they were cleaned and repaired. Otherwise, peritonitis would kill Simon for sure.

God, he looked like an angel lying there. Almost otherworldly in his pale, blond perfection. So damn peaceful. Simon opened his eyes. Looked up at him. "Thanks, bro," he murmured.

Something hot and wet ran down Dutch's face. Stung his eyes like hell. Burned his cheeks. His heart felt as if it was cracking in two. "Don't you die on me, you little punk. Fight, dammit!"

Simon's hand lifted an inch or so, then fell back to the ground. Dutch grabbed it, and Simon tugged on it so weakly he barely felt it. Dutch ducked as a barrage of lead flew close to his head and he put his ear next to Simon's mouth. A bare whisper of breath touched his skin.

"Love...you..."

Folly's voice cut into his other ear, sharp. Desperate. "Dutch, get the girl and get the hell out of there before I shoot you myself!"

He ignored his boss's order and lifted up enough to look down into Simon's clear, sky-blue eyes. Tears ran unchecked down his face, dripping onto Simon's pale cheek. "I love you, too, little brother."

And then Julia was beside him, tugging on his arm with frantic urgency. "Get out of here! They'll kill you, too," she *pleaded, close to hysterical. He heard the words, but they passed by him, not really touching his consciousness.*

And then he heard a thud, and Julia toppled into him as if something heavy had just hit her and knocked her over. He caught her as much to keep her from crashing into Simon as to steady her.

"Go…" Simon gasped. A bubble of spit and blood formed at the corner of his mouth.

And that one word finally penetrated his brain. The lightning-and-thunder fury of an all-out gun battle slammed into him in a rush, along with awareness of the mortal danger that he and Julia were both in.

Julia. The innocent young girl he'd half seduced into helping them set up this nightmare. He had to get her out of here. If he didn't, she'd lucky if all her father did was kill her.

He glanced up at her. And blinked at the crimson stain spreading on her shirt along her right side. She'd been hit!

He glanced down at Simon, whose eyes were closed now. He looked unconscious, but just in case, Dutch called down to him, "I'll get you out of here in a couple of minutes, Simon. I've got to get Julia under cover first. And then I'll be back for you."

A groan of agony at leaving his brother's side escaped his throat as he grabbed her left arm and took off running, all but dragging her across the expanse of lawn toward the wall of black that was the jungle and safety…

"Please, Dutch! Wake up!"

He swam up through the layers of horror still clinging to his mind. Bit by bit, a cabin took shape around him, replacing the humid rot of the jungle. Something hot and wet still burned his face. Grief tore at him, as raw and fresh as if it all had just happened. An impulse to rip the agony out of his body by main force nearly overcame him. An urge to claw out his eyes, to tear at his flesh, rocked him.

He heard a moan of anguish. Had that sound come from his throat?

A curtain of dark hair fell around his face and darker eyes captured his gaze, holding it as forcefully as the slender but surprisingly strong hands grasping his shoulders.

"You're safe. You're with me, now. I love you."

Who did those eyes, those vaguely heard words, belong to?

Pain so deep he thought it would kill him seared its way through his gut. Something shifted nearby, and his head was lifted. Gently set down on something soft. Warm. A hand stroked his hair. His face. Wiping away the tears.

Oh, God. It hurt. Simon…

The lap cradling his head rocked back and forth gently. Slowly, slowly, the motion soothed him. The soft hand wiped away more tears. And gradually, meaningless murmurs of comfort eased the suffering in his heart. Not a lot, but enough for him to breathe again. He reached up. Captured one of the hands and pulled it close, tucking it against his cheek. And finally, he slept.

He woke up some time later and sat up slowly. He ached all over. Where was he? He felt wrung out. Drained to the last drop of emotion. What in the hell had happened? He looked around in the dim firelight.

The air was cold, hanging brittle around him. The fire was down to a pile of glowing embers. By rote, he got up and stacked a half-dozen stout pieces of wood over the coals. Lord, he was tired. He felt as if he'd been worked over with a baseball bat. So exhausted he could hardly stand, he stumbled back to bed and crawled under the covers.

He curled around Julia's body heat, huddling against her reassuring warmth. He hadn't felt this lost in years. She was the only solid thing in his life, and he clung to her like the lifeline she was.

He ought to pull away from her. Stay away... But for the life of him, he couldn't remember why right now. She was so inexorably intertwined with his pain and its relief that he barely knew where the dream ended and she began.

He slept fitfully through the remainder of the night. He woke up once more, mumbling Simon's name, and immediately felt Julia's hands on him. He stumbled out of bed to pile more wood on the fire and then collapsed back into her arms again. He let her guide his head down to her chest. He shouldn't need her like this, but there wasn't a damn thing he could do about it. He sank into her. Accepted the loving comfort she offered. The steady sound of her heartbeat was the last thing he remembered before he went comatose.

By morning, the little cabin had warmed up to a civilized temperature, and the pot of water he'd hung by the fire the night before simmered hot enough to make a passable cup of coffee.

He felt like hell, but somehow the wan light of day pushed the terrors of the previous night back to the margins of his consciousness. He had a blurry memory of Julia holding him, talking him back from the edge while he was snared in his nightmare, deep in the throes of his darkest hours. He got the distinct impression that, had it not been for her, he'd have been in serious trouble last night.

She'd said something important. But it was as lost to him as the rest of the night's details. If he could only remember! It tickled at the edges of his mind, tantalizing him with its nearness. But it wouldn't show itself.

Frankly, he didn't want to remember more. If he could halt his memory's return, he would. Better the black void and the frustration of not knowing what had happened that fateful night in the jungle than trying to live with the ghastly details flooding back into his mind so relentlessly now.

The snow let up in the afternoon. He went outside in the bitter cold to restock the woodpile and made a trip through chest-deep snowdrifts to the Jeep to fetch the laptop computer.

He wanted to touch base with Charlie Squad headquarters. He'd already tried his cell phone today, but the battery was getting weak. Charlie Squad should have moved into this general part of the country by now, and as soon as he and Julia got out of this cabin they could get her into proper protective custody and get on with the business of putting away Eduardo Ferrare once and for all.

He went inside, shook off the snow, and warmed up, then he signed online via a wireless connection and checked his e-mail quickly. No word from Charlie Squad reporting their movement yet. That was odd. Unless this blizzard was more widespread than he'd realized and had shut down travel to this entire region of the country. Nonetheless, a prickle of foreboding crawled down his spine.

Julia had been unusually subdued all day, withdrawn almost. Had he said or done something last night in his sleep to frighten her? God, he hated these nightmares and what they did to him.

He mumbled, "I'm going to go outside and have a look around. Do you need anything from the car while I'm out?"

She shook her head.

"Okay, then. I'll be back in a few minutes."

He went outside and scouted the area. His biggest find was a storage shed behind the cabin. Or more to the point, his big find was the pair of snowmobiles inside the shed. Excited to tell Julia about his discovery, he headed back to the cabin.

He was just stomping the snow off his boots when he heard the faint sound of his cell phone ringing. He reached inside his jacket to answer it, but it wasn't there. He patted his pants pockets. The noise stopped after the third ring. That was an awfully quick hang-up. Everyone who had the phone number knew to let it ring seven times until his voice mail kicked in.

He heard Julia's voice murmuring from inside the cabin. Ah. He must've left his cell phone inside and she'd answered it for him. Crap. He opened the door quickly and was just in time to see his cell phone tumble from her fingers, clattering to the floor. Julia collapsed into one of the chairs in front of the fireplace, her face ashen.

He was in front of her in a flash, kneeling with his hands on her knees. "What's happened?"

Julia shook her head, her eyes black with fright.

"Talk to me," he ordered urgently.

"Colonel Folly just called. They were too late. My father moved Carina last night. To his beach house."

Dutch frowned. And why did that provoke such a terrified reaction from her? "And?" he asked aloud cautiously.

She gazed up at him in anguish. "There are sharks like crazy off that stretch of beach. They devour anything protein-based that gets thrown in the water."

Okay. He was missing some major piece of information here. He frowned, confused.

Julie explained in a choked voice, "It's where he always takes his victims to murder them."

Chapter 12

This was bad. Very bad. Dutch leaned down and picked up the phone, putting it to his ear. He heard only the hum of a dial tone.

He thought fast. How in the hell did Ferrare know to move so quickly to kill the sister? It had to be that damn informant inside the squad. If they'd needed any more proof that this person existed, they'd just gotten it. Furthermore, they now knew the bastard had access to the team's classified telephone logs. He swore violently under his breath.

His brain went into overdrive calculating the implications. Would Julia still testify? Could the squad get permission to launch a major rescue op for the sister? How was he supposed to keep Julia out of harm's way with informants lurking behind every bush?

Julia interrupted his turbulent thoughts. "I can't do it, Dutch. I can't testify against my father as long as Carina's life is in danger."

"We'll get your sister out safe and sound. I promise. And in the meantime, I need you to be tough. Stay strong for Carina."

She reached up to stroke his cheek. She whispered achingly, "I'm so sorry I got you involved in this mess."

He shrugged. "No need to apologize. I'm just glad to get a shot at taking down the Ferrare organization once and for all."

Julia recoiled. She was part of that organization. The venom of his words—intentional or otherwise—spread to every corner of her soul, paralyzing her with guilt. Would that night never end? It had dominated her life for the last decade, and it wasn't showing any signs of releasing its stranglehold on her. She'd give anything to take back her betrayal, to undo it if she could.

She'd never forget Simon's screams. The very thought of them still made her faintly ill. He was just a kid trying to serve his country. Trying to be one of the good guys. To make the world a better place. And she'd gotten him murdered slowly and horribly.

How Dutch didn't just kill her and be done with it, she had no idea. The depth of his pain last night had been a scourge that bloodied her soul. She'd absorbed it into herself as much as she could, but it would never be enough. She could never make it up to Dutch. Holding him through the dark hours of the night was a single drop of water in the ocean of what she owed him.

Maybe this was some cosmic evening of the scales. Her penance was to take upon herself the suffering she'd caused the man she loved.

"I'm so sorry," she choked out.

A finger touched her chin. It lifted her face until she gazed at him reluctantly.

He said grimly, "Don't agonize over the atrocities committed by bastards like Eduardo Ferrare. Just help me put him away and stop him from hurting anyone else."

A shudder ran through her, of dread, and of hope at the possibility of finally ending the web of Eduardo's threats and coercion. She couldn't remember a time when she hadn't been afraid of her father. In fact, Dutch was the first man she'd ever known who made her feel safe. What an irony that even he held a terrible threat to her locked inside his heart.

Poor Carina. She must be scared to death. And angry, too, if Julia knew her spirited sister. She sighed. She knew what she had to do.

She took a deep breath. And looked Dutch square in the eye. "I'm sorry. This changes everything. I can't risk testifying."

He stared at her incredulously. "You're going to cut and run at the first sign of trouble?"

"I'm no coward," she flared. "I came this far, didn't I?"

He sighed. "Yes, you did. And you're in the home stretch. Just hold the course a few more days, and it'll all be over. Don't worry about my threats. We'll catch your old man and you and your sister will be safe. You'll get your life back."

She threw her hands up in frustration, too agitated to accept the concession he'd made. "Don't you get it? It's not about me and my safety! It never has been. This has always been about protecting my sister, protecting the other innocents Eduardo will harm. I don't matter at all."

Dutch stood up abruptly and pulled her to her feet. His hands rested on her shoulders, pinning her in place before him. His sapphire gaze burned into her like a laser. He growled, "Yes, you do matter."

She shook her head, denying his words, rejecting his message.

His fingers tightened painfully on her shoulders. "You matter to me. A lot. More than a lot, dammit."

It couldn't be. It wasn't possible that he returned her feelings. But there it was, clear as day in his eyes, for just an instant before he reasserted his rigid self-control. How he could shut down his emotions like that she'd never know.

"Let go, Julia. Trust me."

"You're one to talk! You never let go of your heart, not for a second."

"I... But... It's complicated," he mumbled.

She huffed, frustrated. "You meet a girl, she's crazy about you, you're crazy about her. What's so damn complicated about that?" She was completely fed up with his ever-present restraint. His withdrawals. The walls of ice locked around his heart.

His eyes blazed momentarily at her words, but still he held his cool. That infuriating, unshakable self-discipline of his. What was it going to take to get through to him?

What the heck. Nothing else had worked. Maybe going on the offensive might. "What's the matter?" she flung at him. "Afraid of a weak little woman like me?"

"I'm not afraid of you," he ground out.

"Then what is it? Why won't you let yourself *feel* something? Anything!" He turned away, but she continued to batter at the walls he barricaded himself behind. "What are you punishing yourself for?"

He paced a lap around the small room but still refused to rise to the bait.

"Don't tell me you're beating yourself up because you lived and your brother died in that ambush all those years ago," she declared in dawning enlightenment.

"What would it matter if I were?" he flashed.

Ah. Better. Definite anger. She pressed on. "Oh, *puhlease.*

All of you guys know the risks going in. Simon knew full well he might die in the line of duty. It was his choice to be there. Not yours."

Dutch didn't answer.

Agony tore through her at the mountain of pain she'd caused him. Was causing him now. All these years, all this private hell… She owed it to him to take this burden off his chest, to help him make peace with the chain of terrible events she'd helped set in motion. She stepped in front of him, into his line of sight. She reached up and took his face in both her hands, forcing him to look at her. "Did you do your best that night?" she asked.

"Yes. No. Hell, I don't know," he mumbled.

"Dutch, I've seen you react to some tough situations. And never, ever, have you done less than your utmost. It's not in your nature to do a halfway job. You have to believe you did the best you could that night. But other forces were at work. People and events you couldn't control. *And that's not your fault.*"

She looked deep into his eyes and saw a desperate wish to believe her flickering in their dark, wounded depths. "You have to believe me. Let Simon go. He wouldn't want his death to destroy you like this."

Dutch ran a distracted hand through his hair. "I don't know how to let go. I've held on so tight for so long… Aw hell. I don't know what I'm talking about."

She stepped close and let all her feelings for him flow through her, praying they reached him. She whispered, "Let me help you."

He stared down at her, a struggle for self-control etched on his face. Doubt warred with desperation. Fear wrestled with need. His innate strength clamored for a moment's rest. And behind it all, she saw a lonely man tremendously in need of love. What she was contemplating was terribly dangerous. Not only did she chance cutting loose his emotions, but also his violence. She dared not go there. Except how could she not? She knew in her heart he needed to heal. To feel again. To rejoin the human race. She owed it to him. She'd cost him ten years of his life. And that was enough. It was time to right the wrong she'd done to this man. Even his subconscious was screaming for release by sending him torturous dreams.

She reached up to stroke his cheek. "Give us tonight," she murmured. "Forget everything else and live in the moment for once. Just one night."

He continued to stare down at her, motionless.

She stepped closer, leaning into him with her whole body. "Can't you feel the fire between us?" she coaxed. "How can your heart stay frozen in the face of that?"

She took a step back and reached for the hem of her sweater. "I'm not letting you retreat behind your stiff jaw and walls of ice anymore, Jim Dutcher. It's high time you came out of your cave."

She lifted her sweater over her head and tossed it aside. She kicked off her shoes and shed her turtleneck shirt, only breaking eye contact with him when the fabric passed over her face. His hooded gaze revealed nothing of his thoughts. Determined to break through his emotional fortifications, she reached for the zipper on her jeans.

She shimmied out of the soft denim and felt his gaze sweep down her body. Clad only in her lacy underwear, she straightened, silently daring him to take what she was offering.

Blue fire flared in his eyes, tinged by a hint of savagery. Trepidation whisked down her spine, touching her with a chill that had nothing to do with the cool air. But there was no turning back now. Once and for all, she was going to break down the walls around his heart or make a complete fool of herself trying.

She reached behind her back for the hook in her bra. The lace gapped away from her skin, and she pushed it down over her arms. The scrap of fabric dropped to the floor.

She stepped forward and reached for the hem of his sweater. She tugged it over his head and he didn't resist. But neither did he respond. His cotton turtleneck followed suit, and then she reached for his belt. He sucked in his breath as her fingers touched the hard slab of his stomach, but he gave no other indication that she was affecting him.

The leather belt slithered from around his waist. Girding herself to continue in the face of his stony silence, she reached for his zipper. The backs of her fingers rubbed a massive swell of hard flesh as she tugged the zipper down.

The man of steel wasn't completely impervious to her, after all! She slipped her hands inside the waistband of his jeans to push them down, and abruptly, her wrists were encircled in the twin vises of his powerful grip.

"Enough, already," he growled.

"No, it's not enough. I meant it. I'm sick and tired of you bottling up all your feelings. One of these days your head is going to explode. Tonight's the night you let go."

"By what right—" he spluttered.

"By this right," she interrupted, standing on tiptoe and wrapping her arms around his neck. Oh Lord, that felt good. Skin on skin. Silk on satin. The heat and hardness of his chest against hers almost brought her to her knees. She tugged his head down to where she could kiss him, pausing an inch from his mouth. "If not me, then who? Who else cares about you enough to break down your walls? Let me do this for you."

He stared at her for a long time. He was so close she could see the individual flecks of silver within the sea of midnight blue of his eyes. She palpably felt the battle raging inside him.

She murmured, "Stop fighting yourself. You and I were meant to be, and you know it as well as I do."

He held out for another second, and then without warning, his arms swept around her, lifting her completely off the ground. His mouth descended to hers, and he kissed her almost violently. Passionately. Overwhelmingly. And she was lost.

She ought to make him admit she was right, ought to make him admit his capitulation. But as his hot mouth moved across hers and his strong arms plastered her against his body, she didn't care. All that mattered was this moment. The electricity zinging back and forth between them, scorching her from the inside out.

Maybe it was the recklessness of living outside the law. Maybe it was the danger of knowing that any second Dutch's emotional control could shatter and transform into violence. Or maybe he just drove her out of her mind with lust. But his touch lit a fire in her that raged completely out of control. She kissed him voraciously, his face, his eyes, his mouth.

His lovely mouth. So mobile and expressive, be it clamped shut against the emotions churning inside him, or moving restlessly across her lips. She searched out the fire blazing beneath the icy surface of the man, plunging her tongue into his heat, slanting her mouth to fit more closely to his.

Their lips and tongues clashed as they devoured each other, his ice to her fire, his yin to her yang. She tore at his jeans, frantic to feel his skin, to taste his flesh, to wrap herself around him, to take him inside her body and her heart.

He ripped her panties off, and they stumbled to the bed together, kicking aside shoes and laughing as they tripped over clothes. They fell in a heap onto the mattress. He disentangled himself long enough to fish a foil packet out of his wallet and slip on a condom, but she gave him no mercy, kissing her way across his body while he did so. He gathered her close in a tangle of heated limbs and loomed over her, pushing her hair back. He captured her gaze with his. "Is this what you want?" he asked roughly.

"No. I want a great deal more than this from you," she replied, dead serious.

Frustration flickered in his beautiful eyes. "I don't know if I can give you more."

She reached up and tugged at the back of his neck, pulling him down toward her. "I want it all. I want all of you."

She wrapped her legs around him, pulling him close with her entire body. He stole her breath away with all that magnificent, naked flesh against hers. Where the blazing glory of his body stopped and hers began, she had no idea. She just knew that she wanted him inside her. Now.

Thankfully, he was as impatient as she. He plunged into her softness, burying himself to the hilt. She gasped at the glorious sensation of being impaled upon a fiery sword and arched up into him, seeking everything he had to give and more. He groaned and surged again, and she arced in a tightly strung bow of ecstasy.

His forehead landed on her shoulder, but she tugged at his hair, forcing him to raise his head and look her in the eyes. There'd be no hiding between them tonight. She looked deep into the azure ocean of his gaze and dived in. What was that Melville quote? Beneath the icy seas ran the hottest blood of all?

The words drifted away as he surged again, unleashing a veritable inferno of pleasure within her. His mouth dipped to hers, never breaking the soul-baring lock of their gazes. There would be no escape for her, either, now that the battle was joined.

He invaded every corner of her body and her soul. Not one

inch of her was safe from his explorations as he took her to-tally. He lifted her hips to fill her more completely, he sucked and teased her breasts until they positively ached for more. His hands roamed over her, seeking and finding the most sensitive parts, plucking at her and playing her like a fine vi-olin until she fairly sang for him.

And all the while, that mind-blowing slide of flesh on flesh, the stretching fullness of him, the throbbing pleasure pulsing through her blood, driving her closer and closer to the edge. His fingers entwined with hers, dragging her hands up over her head. He pressed her deep into the mattress, his body pinning hers in place, claiming her irrevocably and unmistakably as his.

His gaze never wavered from hers, locked in a mesmeriz-ing dance of desire and possession. She stared up at him, hyp-notized by the play of emotions raging through that beautiful sea of blue. He demanded all she had to give, but in return, he laid his heart completely bare.

He released one of her hands to reach down between them. He stroked her most sensitive flesh, already engorged with pleasure and on the verge of exploding. He touched her again and she fell apart in his hand, shuddering with ripples of drowning pleasure around him.

A groan of soul-deep gratification escaped his throat. And still he stared at her, willing her to feel what he did, to expe-rience the mind-numbing explosion along with him. His jaw rippled, and with a last apocalyptic thrust into her very core, they detonated together like a nuclear blast.

She released a shattered breath while the fallout rained down around her. Gradually, her breathing slowed and she focused on his face. He remained seated deep within her and contin-ued staring down into her eyes. But now his gaze was filled with something new. Something she'd never seen from him. *Joy.*

Thank God.

Completely wrung out by the experience, she could only smile at him in speechless awe.

Dutch stared down at Julia, struggling to form a thought. But words floated through his head disjointedly. Inadequate words like *amazing. Beyond amazing. Phenomenal.*

He propped himself up on one elbow and pushed damp tendrils of hair off her forehead. Were those tears in her eyes? For a second, he jolted in alarm, until he noticed the brilliant smile unfolding across her face. He knew the feeling exactly. No more walls stood between them. Brick by brick, she'd torn them down, ripped them away with her bare hands. How a gentle soul like her had managed to do it, he had no idea. She'd asked him to open himself to her completely, and like a tamed lion, he'd docilely gone along.

Not that he was complaining about it. He'd never experienced anything remotely like what they'd just shared. Never had he let another human being inside his guard so totally, nor had anyone ever given herself to him so without reservation. He was humbled by the gift.

He rolled over onto his back, tucking her against his shoulder. She snuggled close to him, and he reveled in the sleek length of her body against his. He drifted on gentle waves of pleasure, and gradually regained awareness of their surroundings. But the delirious haze of joy remained.

He glanced down, and a faint smile still curved her mouth. Contentment unfolded deep in his soul as he looked into the face of the woman he loved. The thought didn't even panic him. She was right. They were meant to be and he'd known it from the very beginning. Why he'd wasted so much time and energy fighting it was beyond him. He stroked her hair lazily, enjoying the silky slide of it beneath his fingers.

"I hope you're prepared to have a lot of kids," he murmured. "I want a houseful."

She twirled the hairs on his chest lazily and murmured, "Me, too. I want a home chock-full of noise and laughter and love."

"I assume there wasn't much of those in your home growing up," he replied.

"No. My mom died when Carina was two. I was eight. When she went away, the light went out of our lives." She propped herself up on his chest to look down at him. "Until now. You've changed my life."

You've changed my life. The words swirled around him, glowing in the air. He'd heard those words before.

The room spun around him, growing indistinct, no more than revolving shadows of light and dark. And at the center of it, a pair of dark, seductive eyes, luring him ever onward toward the abyss.

The towering, black wall of memory smashed into him with such force he thought it might shatter his skull. He gasped for air, drowned in cloying darkness. Cold. So terribly cold. He shuddered uncontrollably, frozen until his body was tortured by a thousand ice picks of agony.

Dear God, what was happening to him? Was this what it felt like to die? To drown in the depths of the abyss that was his soul? He struggled against the thick, suffocating weight of it, fighting desperately to surface. To *breathe.*

An image slammed into him. A jungle. Lit up by gunfire. Simon, lying in a pool of black blood across a suicidally wide expanse of lawn, his body gutted, his throat slit. There'd been no question who was going to make the run to recover him. Not only was the downed man his brother, but Dutch was the biggest, strongest man on the team, and his wounds were the lightest. Doc had hastily patched up the worst of his bleeding, duct taping a pressure pad over his leg wound and pants.

Under a withering blanket of suppression fire from the rest of Charlie Squad, he'd sprinted out of the jungle and picked up Simon like a baby, cradling him in his arms. Miraculously, Simon was still alive. The bastard who'd sliced him to shreds was apparently motivated more by rage than actual skill at gutting human beings.

Every step of that endless run was agony as Simon gasped for air, drowning in his own blood. Between ragged, sobbing pants for breath, Dutch had begged Simon to hang on for a few more seconds. He had no memory of zigzagging across the lawn, but he must have done it. Either that or Providence had looked out for him as he rescued his brother, for he took no more bullets even though Ferrare's men were firing everything they had.

Back under the protective cover of the rain forest, Doc was waiting, his trauma kit unpacked and ready to go. A pitifully small assortment of medical supplies to throw against his brother's staggering injuries.

Doc had worked frantically, swearing and imploring and finally shouting at Simon to live. But it wasn't enough. Simon's shock was too deep, he'd lost too much blood, his body was too mutilated to repair. Doc finally rocked back on his heels. He had looked up at Dutch and shook his head in mute apology.

Dutch remembered the soft squish beneath his knees as he had dropped to the ground beside Simon.

It was only a few seconds. A couple of shallow, rattling gasps, and then it was over. Simon was gone. Quietly. Without any fanfare.

And Dutch's heart had broken in two.

Funny that now Simon was gone he'd had no tears to shed. Dry-eyed, he'd looked up at the four men and one woman standing silent watch around him. "We've got to get out of here. Ferrare will send his men out looking for us once he figures out we blew all our ammunition on that last barrage."

Captain Folly's hand had come down. Landed on Dutch's shoulder for just a moment. A quick squeeze, and then it was gone. A promise that there'd be time for proper mourning later.

Folly spoke briskly. "Howdy, Mac, you help Doc rig up a litter and the four of us will carry Simon. Dutch, you stick with Julia."

Painfully, like an old man, he'd stood up. Turned. And saw his immense suffering mirrored in her dark gaze.

Behind him, Folly murmured quietly, "Time to move out. We'll take the lead. You two follow."

More dead inside than alive, he'd nodded. Heard the faint rustle of the others heading into the jungle.

"Let's go," he had mumbled to the woman before him. She was the one decent thing to come out of this nightmare. The one tiny spark of light in a great, black void that made him believe someday life would be worth living once more.

She'd whispered, "I can't go."

He hadn't heard her right.

"C'mon," he'd insisted. "It's time to get out of here. Your father's men will be here soon."

"I know. You need to leave. Quickly."

"I'm not going anywhere without you." He had felt dense, dumb. What was she talking about?

"Dutch. I'm not going. I'm staying here. With my father."

"But he'll kill you. You set him up."

Her gaze had been desperate. Cruel in her urgency to get through to him. "No, Dutch. I set *you* up. My father made me do it. I'm so sorry…"

He'd stared, dumbfounded. She stepped close and gave him a little push. "Go! Get out of here before he finds you and kills you, too!"

She'd betrayed them? Set them up? His brother died in an ambush she led them into? Understanding finally exploded across his brain like a supernova. The pain of it pierced his eyeballs until he nearly reached up and gouged them out.

Rage roared through him.

And something else. Something insidious that burned a hole in his soul.

He'd known.

There'd been hints all along. Little slips of the tongue. Furtive glances when there should have been direct stares. Evasion when there should have been honesty. She'd given him all the clues that should have told him it was a setup.

And he'd been so damn besotted with her he'd refused to see it all right in front of him.

Like a lamb to the slaughter, he'd let her lead him and his whole team into Eduardo's trap.

He'd betrayed Charlie Squad.

Chapter 13

She didn't know exactly when he slipped away from her, but she became aware of a creeping rigidity in his body.

Alarmed, she propped herself up on an elbow to look down at him. His gaze had turned inward and gone empty as it had during that first blackout back at the ski resort.

"Dutch?" she murmured.

Nothing. He'd gone from her. She lay back down beside him, continuing to hold him, to share her presence and her body heat with him. Maybe at some level, it comforted him. She snuggled close to wait it out.

One moment he lay there, stiff and unmoving, and the next, awareness vibrated through his body. She sagged in relief. *Thank goodness.*

But no sooner had the thought entered her mind, than she knew something was terribly wrong. He was squirming beneath her, scrabbling away from her toward the headboard, struggling to get away from her touch as if she were a leper. Wildness glinted in his eyes and it frightened her. She'd never seen him like this before. He looked left and right, as if seeking an escape route.

"Dutch! Come back to me!" she cried out.

Instead, in a blindingly fast move, he reversed their positions, looming over her, his hands pinning her shoulders flat to the bed. Cold fury filled his gaze. Death glowed, inhuman, in his eyes. She recoiled from the sight of it.

His voice terrible, he snarled, "You made me betray my teammates."

Julia's mouth went bone dry. Oh God.

His hands flexed against her shoulders, as if he was seriously considering putting them around her neck. Fear blasted into her. Her breath came short and fast.

He was acting like he'd just realized who she was and what she'd done. But how could that be? Unless…that blackout on the mountain…those odd little gaps in his memory…was it possible? Did he suffer from some sort of memory loss? It made sense.

She jumped as he leaped out of bed and snatched up the pistol he'd left laying on the kitchen table.

She stared into the tiny black bore of the gun and knew he'd have no compunction whatsoever about pulling the trigger. Arguing with him was useless. Finally, it was all going to come full circle. The man to whom she'd entrusted her body, her heart, her very life, was now going to betray that trust. As she'd betrayed him.

There was a certain poetic justice in it. Inexplicably, a sense of calm came over her. Maybe this was why she'd sought him out in the first place. Maybe she'd known at some deep, subconscious level that it would all come down to this in the end.

She sat up in bed and swung her feet to the floor. Slowly, she stood up and walked toward him, holding his gaze the same way she had a few minutes ago. In this final moment, too, there should be no walls between them.

Her limbs felt heavy, weighted down as if she was walking through cold molasses. In slow motion she made her way to him. She bowed her head, vaguely registering that her tears were landing on his foot.

"I deserve your retribution. I lied to you. Led you into that trap. Your injuries, your brother's death, they're all my fault." *Ah, Carina. I tried. I did my best to break the chains our father put upon us. I'm so sorry, little sister…*

Why didn't Dutch kill her and be done with it? She looked up at him. His gaze was turbulent. Violent. The pistol wavered, turning in his hand. Away from her. More toward himself.

Growing impatient, she burst out, "Just do it! Go ahead and shoot me. Or if you need the satisfaction of blood for blood, slit my throat and watch me bleed. Gut me or strangle me, but one way or another, please get it over with!"

He took a staggering step back from her. And another. "What are you talking about?" he demanded hoarsely. "I told you. I'm the one who betrayed the team."

She watched in dismay as he grabbed his clothes, flung them on and headed for the door.

"Where are you going?" she asked, startled.

"I've got to get out of here, or I'm going to do something stupid."

Like kill her. Or maybe in his current frame of mind, stupid meant…she gulped as the door slammed shut behind him.

No. He couldn't be contemplating suicide.

Sudden silence echoed around her as panic erupted in her breast. She was so alone.

She leaped for the door. Tore it open and shouted his name.

Nothing. The bitter, crystalline cold of the night was silent. Undisturbed. Ice picks of cold stabbed her naked flesh painfully, and she backed inside and closed the door. Shivering violently, she shrugged on clothes and huddled in front of the fire to warm up. She'd go after Dutch right now, except if he didn't want to be found, there wasn't a chance in heck she'd be able to find him.

Too agitated to sit still, she jumped up and paced the cabin, which at least warmed her up. The walls closed in on her as she waited, pressing in until she wanted to scream.

Then an idea hit her like a thunderclap. There *was* something she could do. Something to strike a blow back at her father and maybe give him pause before he murdered Carina.

Fumbling in her haste, she found Dutch's laptop computer, put it on the table and turned it on. She ransacked the machine, desperately seeking the information she needed. She had to find the account number of Charlie Squad's overseas checking account—*now*.

Thanks to her father's paranoia, she was no amateur when it came to computer security. Once she found Dutch's private files, it boiled down to getting past his password. That took a while, but eventually she found his operating system's back door. And then it was a simple matter of opening the file labeled CSBankAccount.

The exact number she needed flashed up on the screen. Hallelujah.

Crossing her fingers that it would work in this weather and in this valley location, she signed on to the Internet using the computer's wireless capability. Thankfully, her Internet server popped up without incident.

She accessed her father's secret bank account in Hong Kong, the one she'd found a couple of days ago. While it loaded, she rooted around in her purse until she found a scrap of paper in the bottom. It was a list of her father's banking passwords that she'd brought with her when she ran away.

She typed in the password when the computer prompted her. A screen loaded with ponderous slowness. Finally, it blinked open. She sagged in relief. She was into the account. She typed frantically and hit the enter button. A second strike of the enter button to confirm that she did, indeed, want to transfer the entire contents of the account, and it was done.

In another hour, when the banks opened in Hong Kong, every last cent in this secret checking account would be transferred to Charlie Squad's Swiss bank account.

It was her last ace in the hole. If this didn't give her father pause, Carina was dead.

Exhausted, she shut down the computer. She'd done her best to buy her sister a normal life. Only time would tell if she'd succeeded or not.

She looked at her watch. Dutch had been gone for almost two hours. Panic hovered very close to the surface, but she pushed it down as best she could. She didn't have the luxury of freaking out.

The night grew deep and cold around her, and she hauled in more wood to put on the fire. How was Dutch standing the cold for this long? Or maybe he wasn't standing the cold at all—

She broke off that thought. It wasn't in his nature to run away from his problems. He would never take the coward's way out.

Midnight came and went, and her apprehension blossomed into full-blown terror. But not for herself. For him. It was far too cold and isolated outside for a man alone to survive for long, particularly without proper clothing or equipment. Visions of him lying in the snow, injured and half-frozen, tortured her.

She couldn't find him, but there were others who could. She pulled out her cell phone and punched in the long phone number to Charlie Squad headquarters. Static filled her ear. It beeped to indicate no connection had been made. Damn! Hers wasn't a fancy satellite model like Dutch's. She needed to be clear of the surrounding mountains for her phone to work.

She had no idea how to contact Charlie Squad over the Internet. They surely had an e-mail address, and just as surely, she wouldn't find it in any search engine on the Internet.

She had no choice. She'd have to hike high enough up out of the valley for her cell phone to function. She bundled up in layer after layer of warm clothes, tucked the cell phone inside her sweater to keep the battery warm, and headed for the door.

The night was still and black and the stars glittered like shards of carved crystal in the frigid air. Her breath hung in thick clouds, and within seconds, her teeth ached from the cold. An insidious chill penetrated her clothing. She needed to get moving if she wasn't going to freeze to death.

The snow lay in a deep blanket, deceptively flat, hiding dips and drifts that made her stumble every few steps. She headed up the driveway toward higher ground. It was slow going, and snow slid inside her collar and the cuffs of her gloves, miserably cold against her skin. But fear for Dutch kept her plodding forward. She had to call for help and find him before something terrible happened to him.

How long she struggled through the nearly impassable snow, she had no idea. But her hands and feet went numb, and her face was half frozen. It couldn't be much farther to the main road. Once she reached it, she'd hike toward the summit of the nearest mountain until the phone worked.

The trees on either side of the narrow driveway towered

dark and menacing around her. Every whisper of wind made her jump, every creak of a tree limb made her whip her head in its direction. She was so bloody tired of being afraid.

An icy wind brushed over her skin, chilling her bones until they felt brittle enough to break. She had to keep going. Reach her destination and get help for Dutch.

She passed under a particularly thick stand of pines, into shadows so black that even the snow disappeared before her. A dark shape moved beside her. She lurched away from it, but the deep snow hampered her, clutching her feet and legs so she couldn't run. She floundered away from the apparition, flailing as an arm wrapped around her neck. Human muscles jerked her backward against a hard, living body.

They'd found her. Her father's men had caught up with her. Darn it, she had too much to live for to go quietly into the night! Her sister still needed her, and she had to save Dutch. They couldn't kill her. She wouldn't let them! She fought like a wildcat.

But the man at her back was too big. Too strong. Inexorably, he subdued her. She subsided for the moment, but vowed silently to fight again at the first opportunity.

"What the hell are you doing out here? Running away?" a voice snarled in her ear.

Dutch. She sagged in relief, limp in his arms. "Thank God, it's you," she gasped.

"You didn't answer my question. Where are you going?"

"I was heading for higher ground so I could call Charlie Squad."

The arm around her neck lurched. "Why do you want to call them?" he asked suspiciously.

"I was worried about you. I thought you were hurt or lost out here. I was hoping they would come and help find you."

"I don't ever get lost," he retorted disdainfully.

"Yeah, but my father's men could've found us and attacked you."

He didn't reply to that one. Instead, he turned her loose. "Let's get you back inside. It's too cold for you to be out here."

"But it's not too cold for you?" she retorted.

"I'm used to living exposed to the elements. You're not."

She followed him silently as he led the way back toward the cabin. The downhill trip through the trail she'd just broken went much faster. In no time, they were back at the cozy little cabin.

While Dutch went outside to haul in more firewood, she quickly stripped off her wet clothes and changed into dry attire. Why she should be shy about him seeing her body after he'd already had his hands and mouth on every inch of it, she had no idea. But when he began stripping out of his wet clothing, she felt compelled to turn her back. A terrible chasm had opened between them. Ironic that making love, the ultimate intimacy, should have driven them apart.

Dutch piled more wood on the fire. Then he looked over at where she perched on the side of the bed. "Why?"

She didn't need to ask what he was referring to.

"I told you. My father made me do it," she answered simply. "He said he'd kill Carina if I didn't set you guys up, and I believed him. There's no excuse for what I did. I wasn't strong enough to say no to him and make him do his own dirty work. And your brother died because of it. I'm guilty of every terrible thing you're thinking. Please don't blame yourself. I set you up."

He stared at her expressionlessly, absorbing her confession without comment. She wished he'd say something, rage at her or shake her, anything but this stony silence.

She moved to sit beside him by the fire. He wouldn't look at her. She knelt down in front of him, injecting herself into his line of sight. "I'm so sorry," she choked out.

Still no response from him. Just that cold, closed stare. There was nothing else left for her to say. Nothing that would assuage his guilt. Nothing that would change his mind about her. She'd blown it. She'd ruined the best thing that had ever happened to her. But then, they'd been doomed from the very start. She'd fought fate and lost.

She pushed slowly to her feet, feeling much older than her years. She stumbled across the room, blinded by tears that burned her eyes like acid. And then something vibrated against her chest. She froze. It vibrated again. Her cell phone. How was it working now? Had the battery been too cold before?

She fumbled in her sweater for the gadget. As she pulled it out, she glimpsed the incoming phone number displayed on its face. And gaped in shock. Something inside her snapped at the sight of her father's cell-phone number.

She turned on the phone and said sharply, "What do *you* want?"

Dutch leaped across the room and strode toward her, but it was her father's words that galvanized her attention.

"What the hell have you done with my cash, you conniving little bitch?"

Man, that was fast. She answered evenly, "Why do you ask?"

She flinched as her father spewed a string of vicious curses at her. "Don't play games with me," he snarled. "Where did you put it?"

Her toes curled in fear. "It's safe," she answered, fighting to keep a quiver out of her voice.

"When my men catch up with you, they'll do whatever it takes to make you talk. You understand?"

She flinched. She'd heard his men torture information out of people before.

Her father sounded as if he was trying to temper his snarling rage to cajole her, but the result was a disturbing vocal discord. "Tell me where the money is, and I'll let Carina live."

Bingo. She opened her mouth to accept the offer, but Dutch ripped the phone out of her hands and jammed it to his ear.

His voice was colder and deadlier than Julia had ever heard it before, including even earlier tonight. "Listen here, you slimy piece of filth. Your thugs can't lay a hand on Julia, and neither can your stooges in the FBI because I've got her. I've got you by the *cajones,* and I'm going to tear them off and shove them down your throat until you choke. Quit hassling and threatening your own flesh and blood, you sick bastard. And take my advice. Put your affairs in order. Now. I'm coming for you. Real soon."

Dutch punched the off button and flung the phone down on the bed. He ran a distracted hand through his hair. "You all right?" he asked her tersely.

Heck no, she wasn't all right! She'd had her father right where she wanted him and Dutch had interfered. "Why did you do that?" she cried out. "He was ready to make a deal!"

"By threatening your life? I saw you go pale. Don't deny he threatened you and your sister."

"He did. But he was ready to make a trade with me for Carina!"

Dutch frowned. "What do you have of his that he'd be so willing to trade for?"

"It's not what I have. It's what you have."

His frown deepened. "Come again?"

"Earlier tonight I transferred the thirty million I took from my father into Charlie Squad's Swiss bank account."

Dutch jerked. And stared at her in shock. "How in the Sam Hill did you do that? And why?" he demanded. "As soon as he traces that transaction and checks out who owns our account, the bastard will know for sure that Charlie Squad's protecting you, not just me. Your sister's dead meat."

She answered quietly. "That money's only the tip of the iceberg. I found the other bank account I was looking for. It's in Hong Kong. I've had the account and password for years, but I didn't find the bank until yesterday. About five minutes ago, the entire remainder of my father's liquid assets were transferred to your account, too."

"And how much was that?"

"Six hundred million dollars."

Chapter 14

Dutch's jaw sagged. "Your old man is worth half a billion dollars?"

She nodded. "Let's just hope my sister's worth that much."

Dutch paced the tiny space restlessly. "Why in the hell did you move that money into our account?"

"I had to put it somewhere safe. Of all the enemies he's made over the years, Charlie Squad is the only one he fears. And, if you have his money, he can't kill you and take it back."

"What are you planning to do next?"

"Exchange my sister's freedom for his money."

"Then what?"

"Then I hide until he's put in jail for good, along with his flunkies, and Carina and I begin our lives over again."

Dutch stared at her speculatively. "You do realize that after this stunt with the cash, he's going to order his men to catch you at all costs."

She shrugged. "Your account is protected by the government. He can't get into it. Now he has to keep me alive until I can transfer the money back to him."

"As secret as we try to keep our financial information, he'll eventually find out where our money is kept. As soon as that happens, he can afford to kill you."

She met his gaze candidly. "I know."

For a moment, the tiniest instant, she saw a hint of concern in Dutch's eyes. But the wall of ice slammed back into place immediately.

"How soon do you expect my father's men to find us?" It was a given that they eventually would, of course.

Dutch scowled. "Not tonight, but within the next few days. They know we're in this general area, and there are only so many places we could be holed up. It's Charlie Squad policy to plan for the worst, so I'm going to assume at least a couple of your father's men will spot us soon. Now that the snowfall has let up, I'll dig out the driveway so when the roads are plowed we can skedaddle. I'll get on it first thing tomorrow."

She breathed a sigh of relief that tomorrow they'd get out of this death trap.

Dutch responded to her sigh, "Don't get your hopes up too fast. It may be a day or two before the roads are clear enough for us to leave."

"Will Charlie Squad come get us?"

Dutch shrugged. "There's nowhere nearby to land a helicopter. They won't be able to get in any faster than we can get out."

Julia's blood ran cold. So she and Dutch were on their own for another day or two. Alone against her father's goons who were already in the area. Any time now, they could come for her on snowmobiles or on foot. And she and Dutch were still stranded and snowed in. They were sitting ducks.

Every groan of the wind against the walls, every clatter of bare branches, made her jump. The idea of actually sleeping was a joke. The bed felt lonely without Dutch. She missed his reassuring warmth. But he stretched out in a chair with his feet propped up on the hearth, a mismatched pair of pistols in his lap.

Every time she tossed or turned, his masculine scent rose from the sheets, defying her to forget the power and the beauty of what had happened between them earlier. Before he pulled away from her. She didn't know how much more she could take of being so near Dutch, but so far away from him. The night stretched on and on.

Even though the coming day held a real risk of dying, she'd never been so grateful to see the faint light of dawn finally creep through the window.

Dutch spent most of the day digging out the driveway and splitting more wood to replenish the woodpile.

As the daylight began to fail, Dutch burst into the cabin on a rush of bitterly cold air and announced, "Guess what just drove by on the main road?"

She looked up at him hopefully.

He nodded. "A snowplow."

Thank God. She put out the fire while he changed into dry clothes. She blew out the flame in the lantern. The little cabin went dark and cold without its welcoming glow. She looked around the dim interior, unsure of whether she was going to miss this place horribly or she never wanted to see it again. Its sturdy walls held the best and worst moments in her life.

Dutch pulled out his wallet and flipped a small square of white onto the table.

"What's that?" she asked, breaking the impenetrable silence he'd surrounded himself with once more.

"My business card. The owners can contact Charlie Squad headquarters and get compensated for our use of their property."

She started to reply, but Dutch froze abruptly and waved her to silence. He glided over to the door as fast and silent as a snake. What was out there? Or rather, who? She prayed fervently it was something simple like an angry bear or a pack of ravenous wolves. After a minute or so, the tension drained out of Dutch's shoulders.

"What did you hear?" she ventured to ask.

"Snow crunching."

"You can hear snow crunching from inside a house?"

He shrugged casually. "You could, too, if you knew what to listen for."

But she didn't. Her life depended entirely upon his skills. And upon his precarious goodwill.

She asked, "If that noise is my father's men, why haven't they barged in here and killed us already?"

Dutch grinned, the sharklike expression of a predator. It had very little to do with humor. "Because they know better than to mess with me in a straight-up fight. I'd chew them up and spit them out. And they don't know how heavily armed I am. They can't risk me circling the wagons and hunkering down in here. Inside this log cabin, I'm practically impervious to a gun battle. I could pick them off at my leisure."

She blinked, startled, and took a fresh look around at the sturdy walls. A fortress, eh? "If this place is so safe, then why are we leaving?"

"Because the bad guys can always bring in bigger guns. We're safer on the move and out of shooting range of your father's men."

She flinched at the disgust in his voice when Dutch mentioned her father. Shame ripped through her to be related to a monster like Eduardo Ferrare.

Dutch muttered gruffly "I'll go start the car and let it warm up while you gather the last of our things."

She nodded around the lump in her throat. The easy comfort they'd shared between them was completely destroyed. Its loss ached like a sore tooth. She sighed and gathered up the laptop computer and her overnight bag.

Only a faint glow of white from the blanket of snow illuminated the darkness when she stepped outside. Dutch was just finishing digging out the car door enough to open it. He slid into the driver's side and left the door open—probably a safeguard against carbon monoxide buildup in the Jeep—as he turned the key. The engine roared to life.

But in the split second after the engine started, a bright flash enveloped the entire vehicle like a supernova. A microsecond of blinding light, and then the Jeep leaped up into the air as a second, tremendous explosion lifted it completely off the ground. The open door flew off, tumbling across the snow like a Chinese acrobat.

Flames engulfed the car as a wall of sound and heat slammed into her, throwing her bodily against the wall at her back. For a moment the blast pinned her to the logs. Then just as suddenly, it dropped her to the ground. She slumped in the snow for a second, dragging a painful breath of scorched air into her lungs.

And then she screamed.

She scrambled toward the burning hull, clawing and scrabbling through the waist-high snow, sobbing Dutch's name. She couldn't make out the shape of his skeleton in the intense blaze. But she was determined to pull him from the fire even if it cost her life to get him out.

She ran and fell, stood up and stumbled forward again. The explosion had melted a ring of snow around the vehicle, and it was already freezing into a bowl-shaped sheet of ice. And somewhere within it was the man she loved. Suffering. Dying.

A strange clarity came over her. The terrible heat of the fire burned away everything except the certain knowledge that she did not want to go on living without Dutch. On a sob, she rounded the corner to the driver's side of the vehicle. She lunged forward to throw herself into the flames. She would find him…. Something black and strong snaked around her waist. Yanked her back.

Her father's men. No! She would not go meekly back into his cruel clutches. "You bastards!" she screamed. "You've killed him!"

She fought with all the pent-up fury in her being, unleashing twenty years of terror and misery upon the head, shins and ribs of her captor, any part of the man she could punch, scratch, kick or hit.

"Julia!" a harsh voice barked in her ear. "Stop it!" The arms around her tightened mercilessly, an inexorable noose strangling the very life out of her. Just the way her father always did. Any show of independence or defiance was crushed.

She fought until the last of her strength gave out. Until the horror of her loss overcame her, drained her of any fight she had left. It was too much. The pain was too great. She'd never defeat her father. She just wasn't strong enough, ruthless enough, to beat him at his own game. And what was the point, anyway? Dutch was dead and Carina was her father's prisoner. She went limp in her captor's arms.

Cautiously, the vise of the arms around her loosened.

"I'm done," she said woodenly. "You win. My father wins. I can't do this anymore."

"Don't give up on me now," a deep voice retorted. "I'd hate to give the bastard the satisfaction."

She blinked. Turned around very slowly. And flung herself against the tall, blackened form holding her.

Dutch fell over backward in the snow and she landed on

top of him, heedless of the cold and snow showering down on her. Hot tears flowed, unchecked, down her cheeks. "Oh God, I thought you were dead," she sobbed.

He pushed her hair back from her face. "So did I for a minute, there."

"How?" she stuttered. "How are you…"

"Alive?" he finished for her. "I left the door open when I started the Jeep and the first blast blew me out of the car."

She looked up abruptly at the wall of snow over their heads. "Who?" she gasped. "Are they here? Now?"

"That's a damn good question," Dutch growled. "If they're not here already, they will be soon. In these mountains, the sound of that blast will carry for miles."

Julia looked over her shoulder at the column of light and smoke rising high into the night sky. It could probably be seen for miles, too. Her father hadn't gotten word to his men to back off until he got his money back. Was it just that the message hadn't been received yet or—Oh, God—had her last-ditch strategy failed.

Dutch growled, "We've got to get out of here now. Are you hurt?"

She shook her head in the negative. "I was still on the porch."

Dutch set her aside swiftly and rolled to his knees. "Stay low. Follow me," he murmured. He crawled away from the burning shell of the Jeep, tunneling a path through the snow. Bemused, she followed him down the hill, toward one side of the cabin. But the road was the other direction!

Nonetheless, she scrambled along behind him, her gloves soaked and the snow cold on her face and neck. Dutch angled slightly away from the cabin itself and headed into the woods behind the log structure.

They almost made it to the perimeter of the trees when a spray of snow shot up in front of her.

Dutch swore and dropped flat.

He didn't have to tell her to do the same. Someone was shooting at them. He motioned for her to crawl beside him. She inched forward on her belly, getting snow in her mouth and up her nose.

"I'm going to move away from you and lay down some suppression fire. Do you know what that is?"

She nodded immediately. Her father's men talked about such things all the time. Dutch was going to spray a bunch of bullets at the bad guys to force them to duck and stop shooting long enough for her to go somewhere. "Where do you want me to go?" she murmured.

He pointed farther down the hill. "Head for those trees. I'll catch up with you. Keep going the same direction we've been heading."

She nodded her understanding.

He nodded grimly at her and pushed forward into the snow, slithering away from her quickly.

When he popped up out of the snow and began firing back toward the cabin, she took off running in a half crouch as fast as she could through the snow toward the trees. She dived for the dark shadows of the woods, relieved when its black blanket wrapped around her. She was tempted to stop and wait for Dutch to join her, but he'd said to keep going.

And then, out of nowhere, a hand grabbed her elbow,

Dutch grunted, "One shooter. But he has no doubt called in the rest of the goon squad. We need to hurry."

They slipped and slid down the mountain, and then, without warning, Dutch swerved hard to the left. He didn't go far. Maybe a hundred feet. He stopped.

She listened carefully to the sounds around them, and heard nothing but a faint whistle of wind moving through the treetops far above. Dutch stepped around a bushy juniper and disappeared from sight. She followed him and stopped in her tracks when she rounded the tree. A wooden door lay in front of them, recessed into a vertical wall of rock. What in the world was this?

Dutch stepped up to it and bent down to work on the lock. It was pitch-black where he stood. Was it even possible to pick a lock in total darkness? But then Dutch stood up and his hand twisted as if he was releasing a padlock. The wide door opened inward with a gentle creak. She cringed as the noise split the silence around them.

Dutch waved her forward to join him. She stepped into the cavelike space. He shined his pocket light around the room, and relief flooded her as the narrow beam landed upon a pair of powerful snowmobiles. *Praise the Lord.*

Dutch was already moving, poking around behind the vehicles. Triumphantly, he held up a red plastic gas can and a ring of keys. He pressed a gun into her hand. "Watch the door. Shoot anything that moves."

She nodded, even though the idea of shooting anyone scared her out of her mind. Out of the corner of her eye, she saw him move to the nearest machine and begin trying keys in the ignition. About the fifth key slid in. He pulled it off the ring and went to work on the second snowmobile's ignition.

He commented quietly, "The tanks read full on both of these puppies. There's another couple gallons of gas in the can I found. Can you drive one yourself? We'll go faster if we each have our own."

She nodded gamely.

Dutch murmured, "The second we start the engines, we'll need to blast out of here fast. The noise will draw whoever wired the Jeep. I'll go first and you follow me. We'll head down the mountain, away from the road. Got it?"

She nodded. And started when his gloved hand came up

to touch her cheek for an instant. But it was enough. They were still in this together.

Dutch pushed the door wide open and came back inside, flinging his leg over a snowmobile. "Let's do it."

She straddled the other big machine and gripped the handlebars. At his nod, she turned the key and gunned the throttle. The machine roared to life between her knees. The sound inside the enclosed space was deafening.

Wasting no time, Dutch shot outside. She followed clumsily, still getting a feel for the throttle. Her eyes adjusted quickly to the dim light in the forest, and she followed his shadow doggedly as he wove in and out among the trees in front of her.

Her back itched like someone was watching her, tracking their descent. But given how thick the trees were around them and overhead, it was no doubt just her imagination. But that didn't stop panic from bubbling just beneath the surface of her mind.

Her fingers went numb in a matter of minutes, and her feet weren't far behind. Although she was dressed warmly, she wasn't dressed for the artificial windchill of shooting down a mountain like a bat out of hell. She lost the feeling in her cheeks first, then her whole face went numb. Needles of icy snow stung her skin, and an insidious lethargy stole into her limbs.

She dared not stop, though. Dutch would never hear her over the roar of his snowmobile, and she'd be all alone, lost somewhere in the wilds of the Rocky Mountains with a pack of killers behind her.

Their flight turned into an interminable nightmare of snow and shadow whooshing past her half-frozen body.

And somewhere during the endless ordeal on that frozen mountain, she realized something. She'd been right, back at the cabin. She would never beat her father at his own game. It just wasn't in her to play dirty enough to win. She'd been a fool to think she could save herself, and she was a fool to believe that Dutch alone could save her.

She had to cut her losses as best she could. Odds were she wouldn't walk out of this alive. But maybe Dutch and Carina could.

Besides his money, there was one other thing her father wanted. And she'd willingly hand it over to him in return for Dutch's and Carina's lives. Now she just had to figure out how to do it without Dutch stopping her.

Chapter 15

After about an hour, Dutch stopped long enough to siphon the remaining gas out of Julia's snowmobile. Speed no longer mattered. Now distance was the name of the game. They'd go farther if they saved the gas and traveled on one snowmobile. He poured the spare gas into his fuel tank and said a silent prayer that the machine would get them to the nearest human habitation.

He took his bearings and mentally pictured the map he'd studied at the log cabin the day before. As best he could tell, they'd fled mostly to the south. If he was correct, then a couple of little towns lay not far to the west of them now.

They climbed on the machine and set out. Julia's body pressed intimately against his, sending his thoughts careening off in a dozen different directions. Concentrate, buddy. Bad guys were running around out here somewhere, hunting them like animals. He had to stay sharp.

But it was damn hard to do with her breasts pressing against his back and her arms wrapped around him like that.

After about half an hour, he paused just inside a line of trees, eyeing the road before him. Did he dare travel it in search of fuel and a phone? What were the odds that whoever had narrowly missed killing them earlier would be patrolling the local side roads? His basic survival training warned him that a road was far too open. Far too dangerous to risk.

But they couldn't run around in the mountains indefinitely. Sooner or later, they'd have to come out of hiding. If they did it now, they stood some chance of running into Ferrare's goons. But if they waited, the bastards would have time to call in reinforcements. The longer he waited, the higher the odds were that they'd be caught. Even though it made him twitchy, he guided the snowmobile onto the snow-packed road.

The gas gauge on the machine was getting dangerously low when they finally rounded a curve and saw a building in front of them. Two gas pumps out front proclaimed it to be exactly what he was looking for. More relieved than he cared to admit, Dutch drove into the parking lot of what turned out to be an old-fashioned general store.

The proprietor pointed Dutch to a pay phone in the back corner by the rest rooms. While Julia slipped into the bathroom to run her hands under warm water and thaw out a bit, he dialed Charlie Squad headquarters. A command-post controller picked up the line.

"Dutch here. Is the old man available?"

"He said to patch you through to him no matter when you called. And boy, is he antsy to talk to you. Haven't seen the colonel this worked up in a while. Where are you?"

Until the mole was caught, he wasn't telling anybody but the colonel anything. He laughed lightly into the controller's ear. "Hell if I know where I am."

Dutch waited impatiently as his call was transferred to Colonel Folly's home. It was only a few seconds until his boss came on the line.

The colonel wasted no time on niceties. "Where in the hell have you been?" he growled.

"Would you mind throwing this on to your secure line, sir?"

The colonel complied in silence. A faint buzz came on the line, indicating that nobody else could listen in. The colonel announced grimly, "I'll delete the recording of this call when we're done so our mole can't get at it. Now, what's up, Dutch?"

"Eduardo Ferrare's thugs blew up our Jeep with me in it a couple of hours ago. Fortunately, I had the door open and got blown clear of the fireball."

The colonel uttered a sharp curse under his breath, a sure sign he was not a happy camper. "Did you see the perpetrators?" he asked tersely.

"Nope. But it had to be Ferrare's people, unless the locals around here have started blowing cars up for fun."

Folly retorted, "I need you to bring her in. Let's get her into custody and talking so we can find out everything there is to know about Eduardo."

Dutch sighed. "Don't think I can do that, sir."

The colonel's voice went dead flat. "And why not?"

Dutch flinched at the ominous chill in his boss's voice. He couldn't blame the guy. In their line of work, a disobeyed order usually led to someone dying.

Dutch explained carefully, "Julia's doing her best to help us already. But she's refusing to testify until we get the sister away from her old man. And I can't say as I blame her. In the meantime, Julia's moved six hundred million dollars of her father's money into Charlie Squad's Swiss bank account."

"Holy sh—" the colonel exclaimed.

"But she's not willing to cooperate much more than that until Carina's safe. Since we don't know who's working for Ferrare at the FBI or within our own organization, I think it would be safer for her to go to ground out here with me. Especially now that the bastard's demonstrated a willingness to kill her."

Folly sighed. "You've got no choice, man. She's wanted by the FBI. You have to bring her in and take your chances that the one or two bad agents in the whole bureau won't be the ones you hand her over to. The odds are stacked strongly in favor of her being just fine."

Dutch closed his eyes in frustration.

Colonel Folly continued, "Even if bringing her in is a risk, we have to take that chance. What she knows is too important to us."

Dutch's anger flared up. "Since when do we sacrifice innocents in the name of achieving military objectives?"

The colonel's next words fell heavily against his ear. "She's not an innocent, Dutch."

And therein lay the rub. She wasn't an innocent. She'd been in cahoots with her father, willingly or otherwise, for years. Even if her old man was holding her sister hostage to make her cooperate, Julia's hands were far from clean.

The colonel spoke into the heavy silence. "Have you forgotten she's the one who set us up and got Simon killed?"

It was a low blow, but he couldn't blame the colonel for taking it. "She wants to do the right thing."

The colonel's opinion of that was succinct. "Bull. Bring her in, Dutch. Now. That's an order."

"I'm sorry, sir. I don't think I can do that. I'm not willing to endanger her life like that."

"Come on, Dutch. Don't do this. We're talking about your

career, here. In six months, maybe a year, you could be in command of the squad. Don't throw away the last dozen years of distinguished service for a woman. We're talking court-martials here. A dishonorable discharge. Hell, jail time. She's not worth it."

Dutch sighed. "That's the problem. She is worth it."

The colonel let loose a rare string of curses having to do with conniving women turning gullible men's heads. Finally he composed himself and said, "Look. I've got to make this official."

Dutch heard the colonel say away from the receiver, "Annie, honey, I need you to pick up the other phone."

The click of a receiver indicated she'd come on the line.

"Hi, Annie."

"Hi, Dutch. How's it going?"

He laughed with scant humor. "You're about to find out it's not going so great."

Colonel Folly said formally, "Annie, as a duly appointed officer in the armed forces, I'd like you to witness the order I'm about to give."

"Ah. Okay," she said soberly.

Folly continued, "Dutch, I am ordering you, under my full authority granted by the Uniform Code of Military Justice, to bring in Julia Ferrare and turn yourself in immediately. Do you understand my order?"

Dutch answered heavily. "Yes, sir."

"Do you for any reason believe this to be an unlawful order?"

"No, sir."

"And do you understand the potential consequences of refusing to follow this order?"

"Yes, sir."

A pause. The colonel said grimly, "Don't do this, Dutch."

He replied equally grimly. "I have no choice. I'm sorry, sir."

"Me, too. And Dutch?"

"Yeah?"

"You be careful. Don't take on Eduardo Ferrare by yourself."

"I've got no choice on that one, either."

"Stay in touch. Your leave expires in a couple of days. I don't want to have add going AWOL to the list of charges you're going to face."

Dutch hung up the phone slowly. Stared at it for a long minute. Bloody hell. *He'd just flushed his entire goddamn career down the toilet.*

Julia peeked out of the bathroom cautiously a few moments later. Dutch's murmured voice had gone silent with the click of the phone receiver into its cradle. All clear. Thank goodness. She also needed to make a phone call. A private one. And her cell-phone battery was getting low. The little hallway in front of the bathrooms was empty. Dutch had disappeared. She sidled up to the pay phone and quickly dialed a familiar phone number. A woman answered in Spanish.

Julia replied in the same language. "Inez, it's Julia. Is my father home?"

The maid answered in fearful surprise. "No, Miss Julia, he isn't. But he left orders to forward your call to him if you contacted him."

"Tell his assistant to transfer me, will you?"

It was a measure of just how ticked off her father was that he came on the line almost instantly. "So, my wayward daughter decides to grace me with her attention, does she?" he purred menacingly in her ear.

Julia quailed at the sound. If she'd been standing in front of him in person, she'd have been in mortal fear for her life.

It was the same tone he used to order peoples' deaths. "We need to talk," she managed to force past her constricted throat.

"Do tell," he replied cagily.

"If you kill me, it could take you months or years to find your money, and even then you could have a very difficult time getting any of it back. I can hand it all to you in a matter of a few minutes."

"Indeed," he said silkily. "So where exactly is my money?"

"That's what I want to talk to you about. I've got something you want, and you've got something I want."

"Not over the phone," he whispered.

She winced. She'd been afraid he might say that. The man had been bugged, tailed and wiretapped so many times over the years that he never, ever, did serious business except in person.

"All right. We'll meet," she agreed reluctantly.

"Where? And when?" he demanded.

My, my. Daddy dearest sounded plenty eager to get his hands on all his millions. Maybe this plan might work after all. She thought fast. "Montana. I'll call you tomorrow with an exact location and time."

"Call my cell phone," he ordered tersely.

"All right," she mumbled. "I'll be in touch."

"You do that, baby girl. Oh, and your sister sends her greetings."

Julia gnashed her teeth at the reminder that he had Carina and wouldn't hesitate to hurt or kill her. She hung up the phone and glared at it. Baby girl, indeed. Once, just once, she'd like to best him. Make him really squirm. Now, if she could only embrace her anger long enough to hold at bay the panic careening in her gut at the thought of facing her father, maybe she wouldn't faint.

She turned and rushed from the phone, eager to get away from an instrument dirtied by the projection of her father's voice.

As her footsteps faded away, Dutch slipped out of the men's room. He stared bleakly at the phone. Son of a bitch. She was going to sell him out to her father to save her hide. *Again.*

Wasn't this day just getting better and better? First the car, then his career, and now his woman. What else could blow up in his face?

Grimly, he questioned the store owner and found out a man in town ran a taxi service out of his home. Dutch gave the guy a call and arranged for a pickup from the store and delivery to the nearest rental-car agency.

It was after midnight when Dutch closed Julia's car door and went around to jackknife himself into the midsize rental sedan. Not too many cars were built with men his size in mind. The steering wheel banged his knees, and he crouched in the seat, packed in like a sardine. Doggedly, he guided the vehicle to the nearest major highway and pointed it toward northern Montana. Far be it from him to cause Julia to miss her meeting with her father.

Damn her! What was she thinking? She knew her sister's life hung in the balance. Why would she mess around with trying to make deals with her father? Surely Julia knew better than to trust the bastard.

Dutch eased off the accelerator. It wasn't fear making his foot heavy. Rather it was fury. Frankly he didn't give a damn if anyone was following them tonight. He drove directly toward his parents' cabin high in the mountains of northwestern Montana.

Nonetheless, an ominous itch at the back of his neck warned him to get under cover soon. It was the kind of intuition he'd learned over the years not to ignore. Eduardo Ferrare was coming. He could feel it in the air.

An unmarked Learjet taxied to a hangar at a small, private airport just south of the Glacier Falls National Park in western Montana. The four men inside the plane got out quickly and loaded oversize bags of gear into the trunk of the two cars waiting for them in the dark.

Tom Folly ordered tersely, "Doc, you're with me. Tex, Howdy, you take the other car. We're all clear on how to get to the Dutcher place?"

His men nodded grimly. None of them were happy about the idea of running an op against one of their own. But Dutch had turned. Of all people! Folly thought. Levelheaded, rock-solid Dutch was the last man he'd ever guess would fall for a woman. Especially not for the conniving, dangerous kind of female who could get him killed.

Tom climbed behind the wheel of the car and headed up into the mountains. He half hoped he was wrong about where Dutch had gone to ground. But he doubted it. He'd do the same thing in the same situation. Dutch was heading for his home turf to circle the wagons and make a last stand.

They pulled into the driveway of a neat, rustic ranch house a couple of hours later. Jens Dutcher turned out to be a giant bear of a man, easily as tall and broad as his athletic son. And as unrevealing of his thoughts and emotions, too. Usually when Tom met the families of his men, there was at least a flicker of response at meeting the commander of the legendary Charlie Squad.

But all Jens Dutcher did was ask cautiously, "So, Colonel, what brings you way out here to our place? Everything all right with my boy?"

Tom answered hastily. "Dutch is fine. This visit is nothing like that." He continued carefully. He sensed it would not be wise to tick off Papa Bear. "But speaking of your son, has he contacted you in the last twenty-four hours?"

Jens replied noncommittally, "Why do you ask?"

As cagey as the younger Dutcher. "We have reason to believe a criminal by the name of Eduardo Ferrare is chasing him, and we're here to help Dutch." It wasn't exactly the truth, but it wasn't exactly a lie, either. They were here to help. To save Dutch from himself and the black widow who'd gotten her fangs into him.

Jens rocked back on his heels and stuck his huge hands into the pockets of his jacket. "Seems to me my boy'd ask for help if he thought he needed it."

Tom nodded with a calm he didn't feel. "We received some information today that indicates Ferrare is closer to Dutch and more dangerous than your son is aware of. Since he's not in constant contact with us, we haven't been able to get word to him yet."

Jens leveled a measuring look at him. Damn, this guy would make a great cardsharp with that expressionless poker face of his.

Tom added with quiet authority, "I launched every available member of the squad to Montana on less than one hour's notice because I think Eduardo Ferrare poses a serious threat to Dutch." He added lightly, "Hell, I'm not even supposed to be out in the field with my bum leg. But I felt the threat was grave enough to get up from behind my desk and come myself."

Dutcher nodded. "My son thinks very highly of you, Colonel."

"Do you know where he is?"

Jens shrugged. "Maybe. If he's in this area and he feels threatened, I'd expect he'd go to my hunting cabin. He knows every rock and tree on that whole mountain."

Julia followed Dutch inside the tidy chalet-style cabin, not so unlike the last one they'd stayed in. It had the same rustic charm, albeit with a few more amenities, like electricity and running water. And a phone. The way her cell phone was acting up in these mountains, she'd need the landline to set up the meeting with her father. Her insides quivered in terror at the prospect of seeing him again.

But she couldn't go on living like this. Running from place to place, desperately trying to stay one step ahead of thugs intent upon killing her. She couldn't ask it of Dutch, and she couldn't do it by herself. It was time to end this.

Dutch's voice interrupted her turbulent thoughts. "You can have the upstairs loft. I'll take the downstairs bedroom. It's safer that way."

Yeah, and he didn't have to confront his conflicted feelings for her that way, either. A neat dodge for Mr. Never-Deal-With-His-Emotions. She climbed the steps to the chalet's loft, and stopped in astonishment. The space was filled with memorabilia from Dutch's youth. Trophies, newspaper clippings, photos and a leather letterman jacket hung on a hook.

He called up to her about doing a perimeter check, and then the back door closed behind him. She took the opportunity to have a peek at the boy behind the man.

The outstanding athletic and academic achievements were pretty much as she'd expected. But one thing did strike her as odd. He laughed and smiled in almost all of the pictures lining the walls. And another young man showed up over and over again beside Dutch, often with Dutch's arm thrown over his shoulders in brotherly affection. It had to be Simon. Such a handsome young man. A lot like his older brother.

She swallowed back the tears that threatened. She was doing the right thing. She owed Dutch a debt she could never repay. The best option now was to sacrifice herself to save Carina and Dutch. It was the only course of action that could even begin to make up for what she'd already taken from him. She sighed and began the long wait until night-fall and her reckoning with destiny.

"Señor Ferrare, the helicopter and pilot you requested are standing by."

Eduardo turned to his flunky and growled, "Any sign of them yet?"

"No, sir. The soldier and your daughter disappeared after they took off on the snowmobiles."

"Keep looking. They can't have gone far without getting some help. Somebody out there knows where they are."

Dammit. This soldier Julia'd hooked up with was one of the slipperiest bastards he'd ever come up against. Lord knew his daughter wasn't smart enough to evade his grasp like this, over and over.

He'd crush them both like bugs when he got hold of them. Soon. Very soon. He'd stick them on pins and pull their wings and legs off, one by one, until he tired of listening to their pain. And then he'd kill them both.

When Dutch was sure that Julia was ensconced in his room, no doubt playing Peeping Tom with his past, he slipped outside. He tromped over to the detached garage that also acted as a toolshed and rummaged around in his dad's tool-box.

After checking to make sure Julia wasn't watching him out the upstairs window, he eased over to the side of the house and opened a gray utility box mounted on the wall. He cut a pair of wires, and quickly spliced in secondary wires that led to a walkie-talkie he'd found in the garage that would act as a receiver.

It wasn't the prettiest phone tap he'd ever done, but he also didn't have the usual tools to accomplish such a task. Besides, it didn't have to be a sneaky job. It wasn't as if Julia was going to come outside to check the lines in twenty-below-zero weather, assuming she even knew what to look for. He stowed the walkie-talkie inside the phone box for use later tonight. When Julia called her old man to set up the rendezvous, he'd be able to listen in and hear what she had in store.

He made his way back inside, his heart heavy. God, he hated distrusting her like this. But what choice did he have? She'd betrayed him once. And she sure as hell acted as if she was in the middle of doing it again.

As he knocked the snow off his boots, a little voice in his head told him that she didn't know him ten years ago, so her betrayal hadn't been an attack on him personally. She'd done what she must to stay alive and protect her sister. Honestly, if he and Simon had been in that situation, he'd probably have done the same thing to keep the kid alive and well.

But that didn't make it right, his logical brain argued.

Yeah, but it did make her actions understandable. And maybe even forgivable.

Never, his hard, military side declared.

But what would it cost him if he couldn't forgive her for doing what she was blackmailed into all those years ago? She'd been barely more than a girl, for crying out loud.

Frustrated, he stepped into the chalet's cozy warmth. He'd better catch a nap if he could. He had a nasty feeling that tonight was going to turn into a fiasco of the first water.

Tex reported through Tom's earpiece. "He's gone inside, sir."

"Did you see what he was doing around the side of the house?" Tom asked.

"Yeah. Looked like he was setting up a wiretap."

"On his own telephone?"

"Yes, sir."

Folly frowned. What the… "Can you get over to the phone line and set up a second tap? If he thinks something's going to come across that line that's important enough for him to hear, then I want to hear it, too."

"Done," was Tex's short reply.

"Make it neat," Tom ordered. "We don't want to tip him off in any way."

"You got it, Colonel."

Julia picked at the leftovers of the hearty stew Dutch had cooked for supper. It was delicious, but she had no appetite whatsoever. How did condemned prisoners manage to eat only hours before they died? She was too busy fighting the urge to throw up.

"You feeling all right?" Dutch asked.

"Uh, yes. Fine," she replied hastily. "I'm just getting tired of all this running around and hiding. I'm worried about your safety and Carina's, and I want it all to be over."

"It will be soon," he said bluntly.

He sounded so confident when he said that. As if he knew something she didn't. Suddenly suspicious, she asked, "You wouldn't go and do something really dangerous to bring this thing to a head, would you?"

He looked at her blandly. "Now, why would you ask me something like that? Have I done anything stupid so far?"

"No," she answered. "It's just that— Oh, I don't know. I guess I'm just being paranoid."

He reached out with a big, warm hand and covered hers where it rested on the table. "You're authorized to be tense. Just keep your wits about you and stick to me like glue, and you'll be fine."

But that was the problem. She *had* to face the dragon

alone. And she was woefully unprepared to do battle with him. She had no doubt her father was going to chew her up and spit her out. And there wasn't a darn thing she could do about it. She just had to close her eyes tight and fling herself upon her sword. She could do this. No problem. No problem at all.

Not.

Chapter 16

Dutch tarried in the living room with Julia after supper until she was so nervous she could hardly sit still. He wanted there to be no doubt that, the second he gave her a chance, she'd bolt straight to the phone and call her old man. She went into the kitchen on a pretext, and he followed her casually, watching her get herself a glass of water and gulp it down.

"Hot chocolate?" he asked her mildly.

"Uh, no thank you," she replied nervously.

Oh yeah. She was eyeing the phone as if she couldn't wait to get her hands on it. Jittery as a racehorse. Perfect. Time to let her off the hook.

He reached for his coat on the hook by the back door. "I'm gonna run a perimeter check and make sure we're still alone. Will you be okay in here by yourself for a while? I'll be keeping an eye on the place from a distance, so you'll be safe the whole time."

She nodded instantly. *The woman could not lie to save her life.* He slipped outside into the dark and made a production of moving away from the house toward the woods, but as soon as he was out of sight of the kitchen window, he circled back to the phone box. He picked up the radio he'd left there and pressed the icy plastic to his ear.

Julia waited until Dutch's big shadow faded into the night, and then she headed for the phone. She dialed her father's cell-phone number quickly.

It rang only once before Eduardo's voice growled, "What?"

She took a deep breath. Here went nothing. "It's me, Daddy."

Tom Folly jolted at the voice on the other end of Julia Ferrare's phone call. He'd know that gravelly, commanding voice anywhere. She was in direct contact with her father? Dutch was in a whole lot more trouble than they'd realized!

He listened carefully as she described a rest stop and scenic overlook on Route 2, a couple miles north of Martin City. He and the squad had passed the spot on their way up here to the high-mountain passes of the northern Rockies.

Son of a— She was arranging a secret rendezvous with her old man! It could mean only one thing. She was in cahoots with the bastard again. Her line to Dutch about wanting to save her sister and testify against her father could only be a lie.

Tom looked down at his watch. She'd set the meeting time for a little under three hours from now. Not much time to get into place. He gave a hand signal to the other men and the four of them faded back silently into the darkness of the woods. Once they cleared the sight line of the house, they sprinted for the cars. He gave them a quick brief on what he'd heard, and every jaw went stiff at the mention of Eduardo Ferrare.

"Let's move out," he ordered tersely. He'd been waiting for this night for ten long years. It was high time for a whole lot of payback.

Eduardo hung up the phone and gave his men a smile dripping with malice. "The little bitch thinks I'm going to make a deal with her. That I'm going to let her walk away from this thing alive." He snorted. "With what she knows, she could put me in jail for the rest of my life and then some."

He turned to the hired pilot. "Is everything arranged like I told you?"

"Yes, sir," the mercenary replied smartly. "I'll be flying myself."

"Perfect," Eduardo purred. The guy ought to be doing the mission himself with the kind of money he was paying the man's company.

He announced to all the men in the room, "Let's go catch us a little bird and stop her from singing."

Dutch went back into the house noisily. Julia had already retreated upstairs to the loft. Excellent. He walked around in the bedroom downstairs, ostensibly getting ready for bed. He ran water and flushed the toilet, opened and closed a couple of drawers, and made sure to walk on the floorboard that squeaked. He turned out the lights and crawled into bed as noisily as he could, all but jumping up and down on the springs.

Then, in stealthy silence, he plumped the pillows into the shape of a human body and stuffed them under the covers. He pulled the comforter high up over where his head would be and eased away from the bed. Carefully, he slipped out of the room. He double-checked that the rental car's keys were hanging prominently on a hook by the back door where Julia couldn't fail to see them. Then he slipped outside, stepping only in footprints he'd made earlier. He made his way quickly and quietly to the garage and eased open the well-oiled doors. He pushed out the dirt bike stored inside.

The motorcycle was way too noisy to start up here, so he pushed it down the driveway and away from the house. He gave himself a good half mile of distance before he dared step on the kick-starter and let the engine roar to life.

The machine wasn't made for snow, but he'd been riding motocross for fun since he was a kid, and he knew his way around a bike and bad traction.

He tore down the mountain, the throttle wide open. He didn't have much time to get to the meeting place, scope it out, and get into place before the two Ferrares arrived.

"Dutch is approaching the security perimeter. Want us to pick him up?" Doc asked.

"No," Tom answered on a hunch. "Let him through. Eduardo will expect him to be lurking around somewhere, so let's give Ferrare what he's expecting. Any sign of Julia or Eduardo?"

Howdy's quiet voice. "Not yet, sir. They're not due for another half hour.

"What's Dutch up to?" Tom asked.

"Setting up a couple of explosives on remote detonators. He's centering around that big gazebo on the far side of the clearing."

Tom looked that way. Good call on Dutch's part. That's where he'd guess the meeting was going to take place, too. It was far enough away from the parking lot to ensure privacy, but close enough to it to make for a fast getaway.

"Each of you take a quadrant around the gazebo. Howdy to the west, I'll take the south, Tex, you slide around to the north side, and Doc, you cover the east. Let's back off a couple hundred feet and give this thing plenty of room to develop. And, gentlemen, don't let Dutch spot you. Remember, he's every bit as good as any of us."

Tom sidled backward on his belly, easing beyond the far end of the parking lot. The thigh wound that ended his field career protested, but he gritted his teeth and ignored the pain. Dutch was his fellow officer. More than a friend, even. He owed this to his old comrade-in-arms.

Julia sneaked down the stairs in her socks, one careful step at a time. A quick peek into Dutch's room through the partially open door. He was asleep on his side, facing away from the door. Perfect.

She eased into the kitchen and sighed in relief at the faint glint of metal by the door. The car keys were hanging on the same hook Dutch had put them on when they arrived. She lifted the keys, taking extreme care not to rattle them.

She stepped into her boots, cracked open the back door and slipped outside. She put the car into neutral and released the parking brake. Thankfully, the vehicle began to roll slowly down the driveway. She let it get a good long ways from the house before she reached for the ignition.

Her heart pounded. An image of the Jeep going up in a ball of fire filled her mind's eye. The good news was her father would no doubt call off his goons until after tonight's meeting. He wanted his money before he waxed her. Tomorrow, all bets were off, though. The car started, and she was still alive.

Her watch said it was twelve-fifteen. She was cutting it a little close, but she should be able to make the rest stop by the 1:00 a.m. meeting time she'd set. The last thing she needed was to make her father even madder by being late.

Dutch set the last charge and headed for cover. He'd chosen a spot in the rocks high above the rest stop. There were outcroppings interspersed with heavy snowfalls up here. It wasn't the best cover in the world, but the granite boulders would stop a bullet, and he was close enough to the action for the crude parabolic mike he'd built in high school to pick up the conversation. He adjusted the white camo parka around his shoulders and hunkered down with his bag of assorted gadgets and weapons to wait. His watch said 12:45 a.m.

He went through his usual routine of calming his breathing and slowing his pulse to help him focus. But tonight it didn't work worth a damn. Figured. The one moment in his entire career when he really need to be calm, and he was as nervous as a virgin in a whorehouse.

A pair of headlights came into view on the highway. His senses went into high gear as the headlights slowed down, pulled off at the exit and slowed down in front of the rest rooms. A middle-aged man sporting a hefty beer gut climbed out of the car and went into the men's room. Dutch silently urged the guy to hurry and get the hell out of here. It was 12:55 when the guy finally moseyed to his car and drove away.

Literally moments later, another car slowed down on the highway, maybe a half mile away. And this time Dutch recognized the sedan he'd rented earlier that day. His adrenal gland emptied itself into his bloodstream with a jolt so powerful he could hardly hold his position. Julia had arrived.

The parking lot was deserted as she pulled her car into a space. She turned off the ignition and sat there in indecision.

Should she get out and go find a spot for the meeting, or should she stay here and let her father call the shots?

If he stayed true to form, he'd want her to climb into his plush, heated limo. And then she'd be at his mercy. No way. Tonight it was her turn to be in charge. She got out of the car before she could change her mind or chicken out. She walked out across the expanse of snow behind the rest rooms.

A covered gazebo a hundred feet away caught her eye. It held a small picnic table, and a lone light bulb overhead illuminated a ten- or twelve-foot radius around it. Plus, it was free of snow.

She headed for the table. After walking a complete circle around it, she took the bench facing the parking lot. For some reason, it felt like the position of power. The wood was cold beneath her thighs, but not nearly as cold as her heart. The slow rage that had been building in her heart ever since that fateful night ten years ago finally bubbled over. Enough was enough. She wasn't going to be her father's puppet any longer.

She jumped as a strange sound intruded upon the night. It got louder and louder, but no car approached on the deserted highway. And then a light abruptly shone down from above. A helicopter.

Leave it to her father to make a spectacular entrance, bound to intimidate his opponent.

The aircraft made a slow three-hundred-sixty-degree circle around the rest stop before settling slowly to the ground in the parking lot. Her father's broad-shouldered silhouette stepped out of the chopper, flanked by a pair of burly men.

This was it.

Chapter 17

Tom frowned as Howdy reported in a bare whisper, "I've got movement out the back side of the helicopter. Four men. Fanning out quietly. They look to be surrounding the meet. Armed, blacked out, night-vision gear, but no IR equipment or radios."

That was good news. Infrared equipment was a trick to hide from. And if the men didn't have radios, that meant they couldn't act in a coordinated attack. Like his men could. Tom replied tersely, "Keep an eye on them. Report their movement. Don't let them get too close to Dutch. It's him they'll be looking for."

"Roger," Howdy replied with icy, competent calm.

Tex commented, "I doubt they'll go up that cliff."

Dutch had himself parked up there like a damn billy goat. So Tom turned his attention back to the helicopter. He'd order his guys to booby-trap the thing right now, except for the possibility that Dutch and Julia might end up on it with Eduardo. And despite his doubts about Julia's sincerity or Dutch's transgressions, he wasn't prepared to order their deaths just yet. It was the hardest part of command. Deciding who lived or died.

The biggest threat the helicopter posed was that Ferrare could make a getaway they couldn't follow. Charlie Squad had come in prepared for a ground pursuit, and the slippery bastard had outmaneuvered them by choosing an aerial escape route.

"Doc, get on the horn and radio the state police. Ask them to get a helicopter into this area ASAP."

"I'm on it," came his medic's quiet reply.

"The hostiles are hunkering down," Tex reported. "One behind that stand of holly bushes about fifty feet beyond the gazebo. One about a hundred feet to the left and down the hill from Dutch. One behind the rest rooms." A pause while he located the last man with his extraordinary eyesight. "The fourth guy is attempting to sneak—very noisily, I might add—about halfway between my position and Doc's."

Howdy's voice. "They're setting up telescopic rifles."

Tom breathed a sigh of relief. If they weren't on radios and weren't within easy earshot of Eduardo Ferrare, then they couldn't receive a verbal command to kill Julia or Dutch. Which meant most likely that their instructions were only to see to it that Ferrare got away from this meeting in one piece. The two thugs who were sticking to Eduardo like mold on bread would be the executioners if it came to killing Julia or Dutch. Both men were huge. It would take several well-placed slugs to drop either one of them. Those two could be problematic if it came to a shooting match.

"Get a microphone on Ferrare and his daughter. It looks like they're getting ready to talk," he ordered. "And stay sharp. This could turn ugly real fast."

* * *

Julia watched her father walk toward her, his two body-guards scoping out the area, their heads swiveling constantly.

Eduardo wore a long, beige cashmere coat, a maroon wool scarf wrapped high around his neck and ears, and a pair of black leather gloves. His nose was red, and he sniffed loudly. He was not a fan of cold weather. He looked significantly thicker than usual through the torso. Wearing body armor, was he? Well. That spelled out what the rules of engagement for this little tête-à-tête were going to be, then.

He sat down in front of her at the table and stared at her in stony silence. She didn't rise to the bait and start babbling like an idiot. She met his glare with a cool look of her own and held her silence, as well.

Finally, he broke the stalemate. "You're enjoying dragging me out here to this godforsaken tundra in the middle of the fucking night, aren't you?"

She answered grimly, "I'm not enjoying anything about this meeting."

His gaze narrowed. Reassessing. Take that, Daddy. Mousy little Julia's not rolling over and jumping through your hoops tonight. She'd changed over the last couple of weeks. She'd grown a spine, with Dutch's help.

Eduardo's tone of voice changed. Grew harsh. "You said you want to make a deal. What sort of deal?"

"A trade. You let Carina go and promise not to harm the man who's been helping me, and in return, I'll agree not to testify against you to the U.S. authorities."

An immediate snort of derision from her father. But then, she'd expected that. He was too shrewd not to bargain for more than her initial offer. He countered, "How about this for a deal? You tell me where my money is, and I let you live."

She let out her own snort of derision. And saw surprise flicker through his steely gaze.

"I do believe, Father, I'm the one in a position to call the shots here. Frankly, your money should be the least of your worries right about now."

He slammed his hands down on the picnic table and half rose from his bench. He growled, "You think six hundred million dollars isn't important?" He ended in a shout, "I want it back, and I want it now!"

She shook her head and tsked chidingly. "Temper, temper, Father."

His face went beet red. She was playing a dangerous game, baiting the bull like this. But her instinct told her to keep him off balance. Do the unexpected.

He subsided back onto the bench, but a vein continued to throb rapidly in his temple. "What did you do with my money?" he snarled between clenched teeth.

"Obviously, I moved it," she replied lightly, "since it's not in your accounts."

"Where to?" her father choked out.

The man looked in danger of having a stroke.

"Let Carina go and swear you'll leave my friend alone."

"Never," her father said.

"Well, then, I guess we have nothing to talk about." She made to stand up.

"Sit down," her father barked.

She raised an eyebrow at him and took her time about it, but she did sit down again.

"You've had your say, you spoiled little brat. And now it's my turn. My men have guns aimed at you and have orders to kill you when I say the word. You start talking right now and tell me where my goddamn money is, or you'll never walk out of here alive. In addition, I swear *this* to you. I'll kill your sister and I'll hunt your boyfriend to the farthest corner of this planet and see him dead, too."

Fear twisted and coiled like a nest of vipers in her stomach. But this was the crucial moment. She either caved in now and never again had a moment's peace, or she made her stand. Once and for all.

She released a long, slow breath. "I'm sorry. No deal."

Her father leaned across the table and grabbed her hand. He yanked her forward until the edge of the table dug into her midsection. His face loomed a scant foot from hers. Close enough to see the rage boiling in his gaze and a speck of saliva flecking the corner of his mouth. He looked too apoplectic to speak. She felt the explosion building inside him.

She spoke succinctly. "If you ever want to see your money again, you'll let Carina go and swear never to harm my friend."

"What about you, my traitorous flesh and blood?"

She shrugged. "You can do whatever you want to me. But let them go."

Calculation whirred through his eyes. "Somebody put you up to this. Your boyfriend."

"No," she answered firmly. "I'm acting on my own."

"I don't know why, but for some strange reason, I believe you. Here's my counteroffer. I'll let you and your sister live, but you hand my money and the big, blond bastard over to me. Your sister for your lover," Eduardo growled. "Take it or leave it."

Dutch leaned forward, listening hard to the conversation. His gut yelled at him to reveal himself, to cut into the conversation and tell Eduardo to go to hell, then blow the guy's head off. He was positively itching to rescue Julia. He could hear in her voice that she was so scared she could hardly breathe, but there she was, going nose to nose with the bastard without flinching.

Dutch froze as Eduardo issued his ultimatum. And there it was. The sixty-four-thousand-dollar question. Carina or him. Sister or lover. Which would Julia choose?

Obviously, she had to choose her sister. Carina was the innocent here. Dutch knew what he'd walked into and it had been purely his choice to see this through. He couldn't blame Julia one bit for the choice she was about to make. Besides, Eduardo was already trying to hunt down and kill Charlie Squad. This new threat from Ferrare wouldn't change the status quo one bit. It was a win-win situation for Julia. Her sister would live, and he'd carry on as he had before they met, locked in battle with Eduardo Ferrare.

Except she was taking a long time to answer. She shifted in her father's grasp and Dutch's attention snapped back to her. The wind changed direction, and Eduardo's voice grew muddled. Dutch adjusted the parabolic mike slightly and her words carried clearly to him once more. "…you know who my boyfriend is, Father?"

"Of course I do, you ignorant little slut. You're sleeping with James Dutcher. From Charlie Squad. Does it give you a cheap thrill to sell your body to the American soldiers you set up?"

Even from up here on this hill, Dutch felt the pain Eduardo's insult caused Julia. But she rolled with the blow, absorbing it stoically and climbing back to her emotional feet. Pride in her resilience surged through him.

"You know, Father," she said slowly, "I let you blackmail me into betraying Charlie Squad ten years ago. The way I see it, I owe Charlie Squad an enormous debt. And now I owe you one, too, in a strange sort of way. You see, tonight you've given me a chance to finally pay back my debt to those brave men."

"What are you jabbering about?" Eduardo demanded sharply.

She straightened deliberately, pulling free of her father's grasp. What the hell was she doing? Dutch sensed what was coming as she opened her mouth. *No, Julia! Don't do it! Take the deal!* he shouted silently.

Her voice was utterly calm as she pronounced each word. "Father, you can take your deal and shove it. I will never betray Charlie Squad again. At any price."

Dutch's heart actually missed a beat. *She wasn't going to betray him again.* She would choose death for herself and her sister rather than turn on him. Did it mean… Hell, how could it mean anything else? She loved him!

"You'd let your sister *die* for a bunch of commandos?" her father roared.

Julia lifted first one leg over the picnic bench and then the other. She looked down at him for a moment and then said clearly, "If you kill your own daughter, her blood will be on your hands, not mine. I know my sister, and she'd rather die than let you go on harming and killing innocent people. As much as I love her, and as long as you've used that against me, it ends now. It's over, Father. Carina and I are done being the tools of your evil. And you can kiss all your millions goodbye."

Oh, Lord. She'd done it now. Dutch jumped up and took off running down the mountainside without bothering to wait and see what was coming next. Eduardo was going to blow a gasket. As Dutch slid down the steep, icy bank, he saw Eduardo's head turn in slow motion. The man said something to his two henchmen, and the big men reached slowly under their coats for the weapons concealed there.

Dutch yanked up his own semiautomatic rifle and opened fire at the thugs. In surreal clarity, he saw the pair of goons jump at the sound of gunfire and dive for the ground.

He noted vaguely that Julia never flinched as the gunfire erupted around her. She just walked away, one foot in front of the other, her back straight and her head high.

"Julia! Get down!" Dutch bellowed as he reached flat ground and took off sprinting toward her.

Eduardo stood up then, reaching under his own coat. No. Oh no. *The bastard was going to shoot his own daughter.* Dutch put on a burst of speed he didn't know he had in him and dived for Julia as Eduardo's silver-plated revolver came up into firing position. Dutch's feet left the ground, and he stretched out at full length in midair in a desperate attempt to catch the lead projectiles meant for the woman he loved.

They impacted him in a quick barrage, four shots one right after another in his chest. Their impact knocked him to the ground. He felt no pain. The gazebo light spun overhead for a moment, and Eduardo's face came into view above him. Leering in rage.

Ferrare spoke, his voice dragging out slow and distorted, deeper than it ought to be. "You stupid son of a bitch. You made a whore of my daughter to get to me and now you'll pay."

The silver pistol glinted as it came up to point at his head. And then something dark and fast rocketed into Dutch's line of sight from the right, plowing into Eduardo's bulky form like a football lineman.

"Nooo!" Julia screamed as she knocked down her father.

The collision rolled the two of them over and over on the ground. No! Bad! She'd get herself killed. She didn't know how to wrestle an armed man! Dutch somehow got a message to his body to push itself upright. He felt completely detached from his limbs, and it took extreme concentration to move forward. Left foot. Right foot. Julia was in trouble.

* * *

Tom watched in intense concentration. If he called the squad's assault too soon, they'd be exposed to hostile gunfire from those four concealed gunmen. Too late, and Dutch and Julia could die. Thank God Dutch had his vest on. He'd be bleeding like a stuck pig right now if he hadn't been wearing the bulletproof garment.

Tom drew breath to call the attack, when Howdy's voice came across the headset tersely. "Movement. Ferrare's backup thugs are closing in."

Outstanding. The gunmen were about to give his team their backs. Tom closed his mouth and watched the four mercenaries run at a half crouch toward the confrontation in the gazebo, rifles held at the ready in front of them. They acted confident. Sure that they were in charge. The corner of Tom's mouth curled up sardonically. Clearly, they didn't know Charlie Squad was on the field.

One of the commandos shouted in a British accent. "Freeze! We've got you covered, Dutcher."

Dutch rolled and climbed to his feet slowly, dragging his right leg. Tom nodded knowingly. Dutch's standard fake-injury move. Dutch wasn't anywhere near as hurt as he was pretending. Tom recognized the act from a dozen previous missions.

Another few seconds to let this farce play out. And then it would be time for the endgame.

Julia lay in a tangled heap with her father, unsure of what to do next. If she stayed on top of him, maybe his men wouldn't kill her. But then she looked up. Into a beautiful pair of sapphire-blue eyes. Dutch was alive! The man had more lives than a cat. She'd seen the bullets slam into him. How was he still standing?

He offered a hand down to her. Dazed, she reached for it and let him help her to her feet. He squeezed her hand tightly and displayed easy strength as he pulled her up. But then he limped away from her and her heart went into her throat at the sight of him wounded. Her gaze went frantically to his torso, looking for mortal wounds.

No blood. How was that possible? She frowned. She'd been certain several bullets had hit him in the upper body. How was it his leg was hurt, then? Maybe a ricochet. And then she had no more time to think as four armed men dressed in black burst into the light.

"You should've taken the deal, baby," Dutch murmured wryly as he raised his hands over his head.

"Shut up!" one of the British commandos yelled. One of Eduardo's personal bodyguards helped Julia's father to his feet and brushed at his cashmere coat until Eduardo snapped at him to quit fussing.

Her father sneered at her. "Did you honestly think I wouldn't expect G.I. Joe to come with you tonight?"

She glanced over at Dutch. How had he found out about this meeting, anyway? She'd been so careful...

Her father was talking again. Giving sharp orders. "Tie them up and get them into the helicopter. Then take me someplace where I can dispose of their bodies. After I hurt them a lot."

One of the commandos stepped forward and prodded her in the back with the barrel of his rifle. Dutch slapped the metal away and took a fist in the kidney for his trouble. He doubled over beside her with a moan of pain.

She bent down beside him, grabbing his arm to help him back up. "Don't get yourself hurt on my account," she murmured frantically. "I'm dead, anyway. Get yourself out of this alive. Please. Do it for me."

"Sorry. No can do," he murmured back.

"Shut up, you two," Eduardo barked. "Get some rope on them and gag them, for God's sake. I don't need to listen to them whining at each other."

She saw a flash of anger in Dutch's icy, calculating, blue gaze, and then it was masked instantly. Thank God he had such iron self-control and wouldn't rise to Eduardo's bait. Not that it was going to do them a bit of good now.

She stumbled alongside Dutch toward the helicopter, and tears began to run down her cheeks. She would have loved to grow old with him. Fill a home with laughter and children. His children. To have given him all the love in her heart. Drawn him out from behind his walls for good. But none of that was going to happen now. He was going to die because she'd led him into this trap. Again. She'd done it unwittingly this time, but the result was the same. Anguish speared through her.

"I'm so sorry," she half sobbed to Dutch. "This is all my fault. You're going to die because of me."

Eduardo glared over his shoulder at her. "If you don't shut up, I'm gonna make both of your deaths even slower and more painful. Got it?"

She glared back at her father and dashed at the cold tear tracks on her cheeks.

And then a loud sound behind them made her jump half out of her skin.

"Freeze!" someone shouted through a bullhorn. "Everyone drop your weapons!"

Another sound, a ripple that sounded like dozens of safeties being released on weapons. The black-clad mercenaries around them froze.

"Do it!" the amplified voice barked. "We have orders to shoot to kill."

The four mercenaries bent over slowly and began to lower their weapons.

"Don't you dare!" her father screamed. "You work for me! You take orders from me!"

One of the men retorted, "You ain't payin' me enough to sacrifice my hide for you, mister. I'm out of this fight."

One by one the four mercenaries laid down their weapons. But Eduardo was having none of this peaceful-surrender stuff. He whipped around, yanking his pistol out from under his jacket. Julia watched in horror as his gaze met hers, only a few feet in front of her. The pistol pointed at her for an instant, and then it shifted. To her right. Toward Dutch. The bastard was going to inflict maximum pain on her before he went down, and he had realized that killing her wasn't the way to do it. Killing Dutch was.

She opened her mouth to scream, then she leaped.

Dutch yelled as Julia jumped in front of him. *To take a bullet for him.* "No!"

He caught her in his arms as she fell. Wet warmth flowed over his hands and onto his lap. Oh God. She was hit!

"Doc! Medic!" he bellowed, oblivious to the shooting going on all around. Brass bullet casings rained around him, and dimly heard explosions rocked the ground, but none of it was real. Just Julia's limp body in his arms, her life's blood flowing out of her from entrance and exit wounds right over her heart.

He pressed both hands frantically over her wounds, willing the flow of hot blood to stop. But it was futile. Like trying to stem the flow of a mighty river with his bare hands. God, no. Not now! Not when they'd nearly made it. Not when he finally believed her. When he could finally let go and love her.

Feet pounded past him and weapons fired nearby. Members of Charlie Squad in hot pursuit of Eduardo and his bodyguards as they hightailed it to the helicopter. And then a heavy *thwock* noise. A rush of bitterly cold wind as the craft leaped into the air. And through it all, his one true love lay bleeding, dying in his arms.

Finally, Doc came. Pushed aside his hands. Slashed away fabric with a knife. Frantically applied pressure bandages.

Tom Folly's voice over his shoulder. "How's she looking?"

Doc's voice was clipped, choppy, as he worked. "Entrance wound in the chest cavity. Exit wound in the upper back. Bleeding just above her heart. Pulse erratic and thready. Rapid loss of blood. Left lung collapsed. Going into shock."

"What do you need?" the colonel bit out.

"Blood. Chopper. A trauma center ASAP."

"Roger," the colonel replied sharply. "Get on the horn, Howdy."

"Already calling, sir."

Dutch pushed her hair away from her pale forehead. "Hang on, baby. You've got to fight, honey. Don't you die on me. I can't lose you," he begged her.

"Uh, Colonel, we've got a little problem," Howdy said behind Dutch.

"Talk," the colonel ordered.

"The police have one chopper close enough to respond right now. They can chase down Eduardo Ferrare or they can come here and pick up Julia. But they can't do both."

Dutch looked up at his boss. A plea for Julia's life stuck in his throat. Instead, his eyes filmed over with moisture. Must be some sweat or something burning his eyes like that. He understood Colonel Folly's duty. An international criminal who'd killed hundreds, if not thousands, of innocent people was getting away. Julia would have to make do with Doc's best efforts.

Colonel Folly looked at Julia, then at him, his gaze hard.

"Please, sir," Dutch finally managed to whisper. "She's my life."

The colonel looked up at Howdy. "Tell the police to get their chopper here as fast as they can. We've got an innocent down."

"They'll be here in fifteen minutes, sir," Howdy reported.

"Make it ten," the colonel reported. "Tell the pilot to fire-wall that bird."

Dutch sagged over Julia's inert form and hot tears splashed down upon her porcelain pale cheeks.

Chapter 18

"Get my kit out of the car," Doc ordered.

As if on cue, Tex raced up out of the dark and shoved a black, nylon pack into the medic's outstretched hand. "Thought you might need this," Tex panted.

As Doc rummaged in the sack, pulling out surgical instruments and alcohol, he ordered, "Lay her on her back, but keep her head and shoulders elevated on your legs, Dutch. She'll drown in her own blood if we lay her out flat."

"What're you going to do?" Dutch asked, eyeing the scalpel and clamps.

"She's losing too much blood. She'll never last until that chopper gets here. I've got to get the bleeding clamped off. I need you to hang on to her. Thing is," the medic continued, "she's too shocky for me to use what anesthesia I've got. I'm gonna have to cut on her without painkillers. Can you hold her down or do you want one of the other guys to do it?"

"I'll do it," Dutch said instantly. He cradled her head in his lap and wrapped his arms around her shoulders. "I've got you, Julia. You're safe now." He nodded and Doc leaned forward.

"This is gonna be messy, Dutch. Don't look if you're gonna faint on me."

"Just do it," Dutch bit out.

Doc swabbed Betadine on the wound just above Julia's heart, and she lurched in his arms. It was the first sign of life she'd shown, other than her faint breathing. "Hang on, baby," Dutch murmured in her ear, feeling her pain as if it were his own. "I'm here with you."

A rip of sterile packaging, and then Doc was slicing on her ragged, torn skin, digging with his fingers into her flesh. A stab with a clamp.

"Got one end of the artery," Doc grunted. "Can't find the other one."

"You've *got* to save her," Dutch gritted out.

The medic nodded as he fished around in the slippery pool of blood and flesh that was her wound.

"Come on, come on," Dutch urged. Seconds counted with bleeding like this.

"Got it!" Doc crowed. A quick flick of his wrist, and the second clamp was closed. "Get me the blood-pressure cuff."

Folly passed the sleeve and a stethoscope to Doc, who wrapped the cuff around her arm and pumped it up tight.

Dutch bit out, "Aorta?"

Doc shook his head in the negative. "No, it wasn't a major artery."

Thank God. Dutch held his breath as Doc pumped up the cuff and listened intently. Dutch urged her, "Come on, baby. Fight. You still owe me a houseful of kids."

The medic announced, "Vitals are way low. And she's lost a ton of blood."

"Give her some of mine," Dutch suggested. "A direct transfer."

Doc frowned. "We don't know if she's HIV negative or if your blood types match."

Dutch growled, "I'm O positive. I match any blood type. Take it, dammit!"

Doc nodded in decision and pulled out surgical tubing and needles. "Give me your arm."

It only took a matter of seconds for Doc to hook up the arm-to-arm blood transfer. And then a stream of life giving fluid flowed from his body into hers.

Doc timed the exchange. "That's about a pint. Should hold her until the chopper gets here." He reached for the needles.

Dutch put his hand over Doc's. "Leave it a little longer. I'm not taking any chances."

"It won't do anyone any good to have you bleed out, too," Doc argued.

"I can spare some more. Let her have it."

Doc opened his mouth to argue, but the colonel's hand landed on the medic's shoulder. "Let him do it," the colonel said quietly.

Doc subsided. He took her blood pressure again. "A little better."

The medic was just removing the needle from his arm when Dutch heard a faint noise in the distance. The chopper. *Please God, let Julia hang on just a few more minutes.*

While Doc watched over Julia's wound dressings, the other men lifted her carefully and rushed her over to the helicopter that swooped down into the parking lot. Doc climbed in beside her, but there wasn't enough room for Dutch to go along.

The medic looked up at Doc. "I'll take care of her for you. I promise."

Dutch nodded, his throat too tight for words.

One of the pilots gave Colonel Folly quick driving instructions to the hospital they'd be going to, and then the craft lifted off and disappeared into the night.

Dutch watched until he couldn't see its lights anymore. His heart—hell, his life— winged away into the blackness with it.

He turned to head for his motorcycle. And staggered.

"Easy there, big guy," Colonel Folly chuckled as he wedged a shoulder under Dutch's armpit. "That second pint of blood must have come out of your head."

Tex commented as he caught him under the other shoulder, "Nah, it's all thick skull in there. No room for blood."

Dutch drew breath to tell Tex where to stick it, but was arrested by a stabbing pain in the ribs. He let out an involuntary grunt of pain.

Colonel Folly ordered quietly, "Bring the car around, will you, Howdy?"

The sniper melted into the night, running fast and silent. How Dutch got into the back seat of the car, he wasn't quite sure. The last thing he remembered was his forehead landing against the cold glass of the window as he passed out.

Julia woke up slowly, swimming through thick layers of fog toward consciousness. Her throat hurt. And there was something in it. A tube of some kind. A steady sucking sound came from off to her left. A machine. The light was really bright. It hurt her eyes and she squinted against it.

"How are you feeling, Julia?" a male voice said from her right.

She turned her head in that direction, but stopped short when the movement sent pain shooting through her chest. She remembered that voice from somewhere. Barking orders at people that had to do with saving her life.

"Who..." she tried to croak, but failed, instead making a rasping noise in her throat.

"Who am I?" the voice asked. "You can call me Doc. I'm a friend of Dutch's."

She tried to pronounce the word "Where..." but only her lips moved. No sound came out of her throat.

"Where's Dutch?" Doc finished for her. "Recuperating nicely and very impatient to see you. When you're a little more conscious, I'll go tell him you're awake."

She tried to say, "See..." but it was hopeless.

"You want to see him? I figured you would. He wants to see you, too. That tube will come out of your throat soon so you two can talk."

She subsided against the mattress. Thank God this Doc guy was psychic. But what did his comment mean? *Dutch wanted to see her, too.* To rail at her for nearly getting him killed again? For leading Charlie Squad into yet another shoot-out with her father? She truly hadn't intended for it to work out that way.

A cool hand smoothed her hair back from her forehead. "Rest now," a female voice murmured. "You'll need your strength to get through the next few days."

No kidding. How was she ever going to survive losing Dutch again? Tears slipped out of the corners of her eyes as she squeezed them shut in misery.

Stay in bed? Forget it! Not until he knew Julia was going to be all right. When the nurses argued with him, threatening to restrain and sedate him if he didn't calm down, Dutch raised such a ruckus that the staff finally fetched Colonel Folly and Doc to his bedside in a last-ditch effort to keep him in the damn thing.

"Doc, tell them I'm fine. Tell them I can walk."

The medic laughed at him. "Dude, you've got six broken ribs and your right lung is only just reinflated. You're going to have to cool your jets for a while. In bed."

"How is she?" Dutch asked raggedly.

"She's going to be fine. The bullet that nicked the artery also grazed her heart, but the surgeons found no life-threatening damage to it. She's going to be in some serious pain for a couple of weeks, but I swear to you, she's going to live."

Dutch subsided against the pillows. "I want to see her as soon as she wakes up."

Doc nodded. "She regained consciousness briefly after she came out of surgery, but they knocked her out with painkillers right after that. She'll be out for a good twenty-four hours."

They were the longest twenty-four hours of Dutch's life. He kept remembering her standing up to her father and refusing to betray him or the squad again. Remembering her willingness to sacrifice her sister's life for him. Remembering that awful moment when she threw her body in front of him, sacrificing herself to save him.

Sleep eluded him, even when he reluctantly agreed to swallow the little pills the nurses insisted he take. How could he sleep when the woman he loved was fighting for her life?

The next evening, Colonel Folly walked into his room. Not exactly the person he'd choose to see just now, but at least the visit would keep him from climbing the walls in his frustration at being separated from Julia.

The colonel closed the door. "We need to have a little talk," he said quietly.

Dutch swallowed. Time to pay the piper for disobeying orders.

"Turns out you were right about her," Colonel Folly said. "We had a microphone on the entire conversation with her old man. And she didn't sell us out."

Dutch nodded cautiously.

"That being the case, a person could make an argument that you did the right thing in disobeying my order to arrest her and bring her in. I'm prepared to lose the cassette in my desk drawer of that particular phone conversation."

Hope flickered in Dutch's chest.

"However, I'm putting your promotion to major on hold for six months. And—" the colonel leaned forward and nailed him with a razor sharp glare "—if you *ever* disobey another order I give you, I'll personally hang you from the highest tree I can find. You got that, mister?"

"Yes, sir."

A brief silence fell between them. Dutch took a deep breath. Time for the confession that had kept him up all night along with his fear for Julia.

"Colonel?"

Folly leaned a hip against the foot of the bed. "What's on your mind, Jim?"

Youch. First names, not field handles. The colonel had picked up on the fact that this was going to be a *serious* conversation. Sometimes having a perceptive boss sucked.

He spoke carefully. "After my brother died, I did some pretty heavy drinking."

Folly's mouth twitched. "I know. I paid a couple of the bills for bars you busted up."

He had? Son of a gun. Dutch pressed on doggedly. "I blacked out eventually. Lost a good chunk of my memory."

Folly nodded again like this was no surprise.

"I've never told anyone, but I lost my memory of the night that Simon died, too. Until I met Julia again and spent this time with her, I had no recollection of what happened during the days leading up to the ambush or of the ambush itself."

Folly's eyebrows shot up, but the colonel made no comment.

Dutch pressed on. "I had a blackout the first time I saw Julia in Colorado. Since then, I've been having nightmares and I've remembered pretty much all of what went on in Gavarone ten years ago."

A heavy sigh from the colonel. "Nasty piece of business. Too bad it couldn't just stay buried in your brain."

"Yeah, well, another nasty piece of business was buried in there, too. One I'm obligated to tell you about."

The colonel actually sat down on the foot of the bed now. He crossed his arms and fixed a penetrating gaze on Dutch, who did his damnedest not to squirm under the intense scrutiny.

"Lay it on me," the colonel said quietly.

"I think I knew that Julia was setting us up. She dropped little hints here and there that I picked up on. But I was too…attracted to her…to admit to myself that she was a plant. I'm responsible for leading the squad into that ambush. I should've seen it coming. I *did* see it coming. But I let you all down."

Folly didn't move a muscle. Just continued to stare at him intently. For a very long time.

Finally Folly said slowly, "We were all half in love with Julia. She suckered us all. Hell, I'm the one who led the team into that disaster. I'm the one who split everyone up in firing positions all around the compound. I'm the one who put Simon into a forward position, even though he was brand new to the squad. It's just as much my fault that he died as it is yours."

"That's not true—" Dutch protested hotly.

Folly raised a hand and cut him off. "We were young. Inexperienced. The squad had just been formed and none of us knew what the hell we were doing. This gorgeous babe came along and warped all of our brains. She was a great actress and she fooled us all."

"But—" Dutch interjected.

"But nothing," Folly retorted. "We succeed as a team and we fail as a team. We all failed Simon that night, Dutch. So maybe you did have an idea in the back of your mind that Julia was a plant. I should have seen it, too. So should all the guys. Besides, even if we had known it was a setup, we very well might have gone in, anyway. I shouldn't have put responsibility for the whole interaction with the informant on your shoulders. We should have called for more backup firepower." He threw up his hands. "We did a dozen things wrong that night, all of which contributed to Simon's death. You're not the only one whose hands are dirty. We all carry your brother's memory around on our consciences. Why else would nobody on the squad ever talk about that night, even now?"

Dutch stared. "I thought it was out of respect for my feelings."

Folly snorted. "Since when are the guys in Charlie Squad that sensitive?"

Dutch grinned. The man had a point.

"Thanks for coming clean with me, Dutch. That kind of trust between us is what makes the squad work. But quit beating yourself up over Simon's death. Or at least include the rest of us when you decide to have a guilt session so we can all wallow in it together."

Dutch stared at the colonel. That was it? No court-martial? No walking papers from the squad?

Folly continued, "You'll need to have a standard psych evaluation when you get back home to clear the blackout thing, but based on what you've told me, you had a damn good reason for blacking out. I can't imagine it'll pose any problem to you going back out into the field."

Dutch blinked. His eyesight blurred for a second. What was it with all these sappy moments broadsiding him like this recently? Julia'd made him go soft, dammit.

The colonel nodded crisply, thankfully either ignoring or not noticing Dutch's reaction. "So. Now that we've got that cleared up, you wanna go see your lady?"

Dutch surged up in the bed.

The colonel put a restraining hand on his shoulder. "Hold on, cowboy. They're making me take you down to ICU in a wheelchair. Seems none of the nurses want to get anywhere near you. Have you been a problem patient, Captain?"

Dutch grinned up at his boss.

He managed to get out of bed and into the wheelchair without flashing his bare ass at the colonel, but was surprised at how winded he was by the brief exertion. Ferrare's bullets had really done a number on his chest through his bulletproof vest. He had four melon-size purple bruises to show for it.

The colonel wheeled him down several long, quiet corridors. And then they turned into the intensive care unit.

Doc got up from a chair outside a door. The medic grinned. "Good to see you up and about, man."

Dutch replied seriously. "Thanks for saving her, Joe."

"Anytime, my friend. Anytime."

And then the colonel pushed him into a roomful of machines and monitors. In the middle of it all lay Julia. God, she was pale. So small and fragile-looking in the midst of all those tubes and gadgets.

The colonel parked him by her side and slipped from the room, closing the door behind him.

"Hey, gorgeous," Dutch murmured.

Her eyes fluttered open. It took a moment for her to focus, but then she saw him and her whole face lit up. "Thank God you're alive," she said on an exhalation of relief.

"I almost lost you," he said gruffly. "What were you thinking, trying to save me like that?"

Her lips curved up in a faint smile. "The way I hear it, you're the one who ended up saving me. Like you always do."

He shrugged. He'd be just as happy if he could forget those frantic moments when he thought he was going to lose her. Maybe he could arrange another memory block somehow. "Doc did most of the work."

She replied gently, "Yes, but it was your voice I heard, giving me a reason to fight to live."

"You heard that stuff, huh?" he mumbled.

"Some of it. Enough of it," she replied softly.

Had she heard the part about how he couldn't live without her? "Julia," he started. And stopped, at a loss for words.

Julia held her breath, even though doing so caused her intense pain. *Please God, let him not be about to end their relationship.* She waited as he continued to struggle for words.

Finally, she reached out, dragging an armful of tubes with her, and touched his cheek. "What's on your mind? You know you can be honest with me."

He sighed. Started again. "Julia. I've said some pretty harsh things to you. Believed some pretty harsh things of you. And I was wrong."

She blinked in surprise.

"I owe you an apology. And I owe you a thank-you for diving in front of me to take that bullet."

"You must really think I'm a numbskull for jumping in front of a guy wearing a bulletproof vest."

A smile twitched at the corners of his mouth. "Doc told you about that, huh?"

"Yeah. I guess I looked incredibly stupid, didn't I?"

"What I saw was an incredibly brave woman willing to sacrifice her life to save mine."

She looked away, abashed by his praise. An awkward silence formed between them.

Dutch cleared his throat. "Actually, I came to negotiate a surrender."

She closed her eyes. Of course. Charlie Squad still wanted her to testify against her father. Now more than ever, since he'd slipped through their grasp yet again. "I'll testify against my father under one condition. You have to get my sister away from him safely."

Dutch blinked in surprise. "Boss!" he called out.

Colonel Folly opened the door and looked in, along with Doc. "Yes?"

"Julia says she'll testify against Eduardo as soon as we get her sister away from him."

"Outstanding." Colonel Folly turned to Doc. "Are you up for a trip to Gavarone?"

"Yes, sir," Doc replied crisply. "I'll get on it right away."

Folly nodded and told his medic, "I'm not going to tell any of our support people what you're up to until we find Ferrare's mole, so you'll be operating on your own until I can slide some more guys from the team down there without anyone finding out. Will you be all right on your own for a couple of weeks?"

The medic nodded confidently.

The colonel turned back to Dutch and Julia. "Don't you two have anything more important to talk about than testimony in some dumb old federal investigation?"

Julia grinned at the Colonel's comical waggle of his eyebrows before he left the room, dragging Doc along with him.

She turned her gaze back to Dutch, whose ears were turning pink, if she wasn't mistaken. She bit back a smile.

"Actually, that wasn't the surrender I was talking about," he said reluctantly.

She drew in a quick breath that she instantly regretted. As the stabbing pain in her chest subsided slowly, Dutch stood up out of his wheelchair.

"Some pair we make, all beat up like this," she remarked lightly.

"Yeah," he said gruffly. "Some pair. Why break up a good thing?"

She frowned. She was missing the point. "What do you mean? What does this have to do with my surrender?"

"Actually, I was thinking in terms of *my* surrender. Of surrendering my heart into your care for, oh, forever."

She lurched, heedless of the shooting pain in her chest. "Are you serious?"

He grimaced as he leaned down over her, his lovely blue eyes gazing deep into hers. "That's not exactly the sort of thing I'd joke about, sweetheart."

"Oh, yes. I accept those terms of surrender!" she cried out softly.

She reached up for him and he reached down for her, but both of them stopped partway and gasped in pain. They both laughed—gingerly. She didn't care if it felt as if her chest was going to split in two.

She put her hands on his face and looked deep into the beautiful blue ocean of his gaze. "I love you, Jim Dutcher. Forever."

He leaned forward and kissed her gently on the lips to seal the deal.

And her surrender to him was complete.

* * * * *

Look for more of Cindy Dees's
CHARLIE SQUAD
stories coming in 2006!
Only from Silhouette
Intimate Moments.
And don't miss Cindy's next
book, TARGET.
Available May 2005
from Silhouette Bombshell.

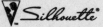

#1357 SWEPT AWAY—Karen Templeton
The Men of Mayes County

Oklahoma farmer Sam Franzier and Carly Stewart weren't likely to get along: he was a single father of six, and she wasn't one for children. But when the two unexpectedly became neighbors, Carly found herself charmed by his kids and falling for this handsome family man. Problem was, love simply wasn't in Sam's plans—or was it?

#1358 RECONCILABLE DIFFERENCES—Ana Leigh
Bishop's Heroes

When Tricia Manning and Dave Cassidy were accused of murdering her husband, they did all they could to clear their names. Working closely, the passion from their past began to flare. But Dave wasn't willing to risk his heart and Tricia was afraid to trust another man. Could a twist of fate reconcile their differences?

#1359 MIDNIGHT HERO—Diana Duncan
Forever in a Day

As time ticked down to an explosive detonation, SWAT team agent Conall O'Rourke and bookstore manager Bailey Chambers worked to save innocent hostages and themselves. The siege occurred just hours after Bailey had broken Con's heart, and he was determined to get her back. This ordeal would either cement their bond or end their love—and possibly their lives.

#1360 COLE DEMPSEY'S BACK IN TOWN—
Suzanne McMinn

Now a successful lawyer, Cole Dempsey was back in town and there would be hell to pay. Years ago his father had been accused of a crime he didn't commit and Cole was out to clear his name—even if it meant involving long-lost love Bryn Louvel. Cole and Bryn were determined to fight the demons of the past while emerging secrets threatened their future.

#1361 BLUE JEANS AND A BADGE—Nina Bruhns

Bounty hunter Luce Montgomery and chief of police Philip O'Donnaugh were on the prowl for a fugitive. As the stakes rose, so did their mutual attraction. Philip was desperate to break through the wall between them but Luce was still reeling from revelations about her past that even blue jeans and a badge might not cure....

#1362 TO LOVE, HONOR AND DEFEND—Beth Cornelison

Someone was after attorney Libby Hopkins and she would do anything for extra protection. So when firefighter Cal Walters proposed a marriage of convenience to help him win custody of his daughter, she agreed. Close quarters caused old feelings to resurface but Libby had always put her career first. Could Cal show Libby how to honor, defend *and* love?

SIMCNM0305